Cast of Characters

Fergus Gandon. An artist. He's as talented as he is difficult. Is someone deliberately feeding him arsenic?

Hester Fennelly. His sister. She's a sensible woman with a gift for gardening who takes Fergus into her home while he recovers.

Paul Fennelly. Hester's even more sensible husband. Like most men, he never gives a thought to whether or not he likes another man, in this case Fergus.

Barbara Fennelly. The Fennellys' pretty and idealistic daughter. She recently has taken a great interest in art. It will pass. Ultimately, she's a sensible girl.

Nell Gandon. Fergus' hot-tempered wife. Without even trying, she's attractive enough to have caught the eye, some say, of her landlord.

Lord Kilskour. The landlord. Fergus and Nell live on the grounds of his country estate. Kilskour has a dark secret he'll go to any lengths to hide.

Mosney. An ex-convict, he acts as the Gandons' general factotum.

Paddy Purtill. A former student of Fergus', he blames the older artist for stalling his career. He and Barbara share a secret.

Arnold Silke. An art dealer. He has great faith in Fergus' ability.

Fringley Pole. An art collector. He's interested only in Old Masters and once outbid Barbara for a painting at auction.

Claud Colville. The Fennelly's physician. He notifies the police.

Brian Caraway. A former student of Colville's, admired for his athletic prowess, he is Fergus' doctor and first treats the poisoning. The young doctor knows little about art but sees something in a painting he likes.

The Irish Guard. Chief District Superintendent Healy, Superintendent Lancey, Inspector Devlin, Detective Inspector Grace, Detective Officer Lemon, and Sergeant Nolan. No dumb coppers here.

Books by Sheila Pim

Crime Fiction

Common or Garden Crime (1945)
Creeping Venom (1946)
A Brush with Death (1950)
A Hive of Suspects (1952)

Novels of Irish life

The Flowering Shamrock (1949)
Other People's Business (1957)
The Sheltered Garden (1965)

Nonfiction

Getting Better (1943)
Bringing the Garden Indoors (1949)
The Wood and the Trees (1966, 1984)

A Brush with Death
by Sheila Pim

The Rue Morgue Press
Boulder, Colorado

About Sheila Pim

SHEILA PIM took to crime, as she put it in the dedication to her second mystery, *Creeping Venom*, for her father's sake. Frank Pim loved his thrillers but was unable to get as many as he would like in neutral Ireland during World War II. Her first effort, *Common or Garden Crime*, was set in 1943 and published in 1945, followed a year later by *Creeping Venom*. *A Brush with Death* appeared in 1950 and *A Hive of Suspects* was released in England in 1952 and the following year in the United States, the only book of hers to appear in the U.S. in her lifetime. Two other books, *Other People's Business* (1957) and *The Sheltered Garden* (1964) had some mystery elements but were primarily novels of Irish life, prompting some reviewers to describe her as the Irish Angela Thirkell. Gardening was a key element in all of her books.

She was born in Dublin on September 21, 1909, of a Quaker father and an English mother. Her twin brother Andrew survived only two weeks. She had a second brother, Tom, two years her senior, who was born developmentally disabled and would need constant supervision for most of his life. Sheila bore the brunt of his care, as well as the maintenance of her father's home, after her mother died in 1940. Prior to this, she was educated at the French School in Bray, County Wicklow, and "finished" at La Casita in Lausanne, Switzerland, where she perfected her French. In 1928, she went to Girton College, Cambridge, where she took a Tripos in French and Italian and passed some of the happiest days of her life. Shortly before finals, her mother took ill and Sheila returned to Ireland to look after her and to provide some diversion for brother Tom.

Although she was forced to abandon any thought of formal training in botany, she became an enthusiastic amateur and contributed many essays to the Irish magazine, *My Garden*. Several of these were collected and published in 1949 in a slender volume entitled *Bringing the Garden Indoors* (a selection from which can be found on page opposite the opening chapter). Her major work in this field, however, was the biography of another gifted horticultural amateur, Augustine Henry, an Irish doctor who was one of the foremost plant collectors of his age. *The Wood and the Trees* was published in 1966 and revised and reissued in 1988.

After her father's death in 1958 and Tom's in 1964, Sheila threw herself into her activities at the Historical Society of the Religious Order of Friends, researching and conserving archival embroideries and portraits. At about this same time, she began an involvement with the Irish Travellers which she would continue for the rest of her life. Ostracized by much of Irish society, the Travellers are a nomadic people native to Ireland who follow a gypsy-like life and speak their own language, Shelta, which is closer to English than to Irish. Travellers are sometimes known as Tinkers—now considered a derogatory term—partly because many of them worked as tinsmiths, as well as itinerant farm laborers and door-to-door salesmen. Pim took many Traveller children into her home and eventually adopted an entire family which had been abandoned to the care of their travelling grandfather.

In Sheila Pim's last years, her growing deafness forced her to move into a sheltered housing complex where she still managed to grow a few herbs by her door. She fell ill and died on December 16, 1995, at the age of 86. For more information on Pim and her books see Tom and Enid Schantz' lengthy introduction to *Common or Garden Crime* (Rue Morgue Press, 2001).

Gardening Tips from Sheila Pim's
Bringing the Garden Indoors

Close-Ups

I have been struck by some advice given on the wireless by Mr. Wilfrid Blunt, to look at flowers through a magnifying glass, but not a microscope. One should look, he means, with the eyes of an artist who tries to draw flowers, not a botanist who dissects them. Botany is a good thing in its sphere, but one may discriminate between that kind of intellectual and scientific way of taking pleasure in flowers, and the more spontaneous delight of discovering for oneself such details as the spotted shoots on pear trees, or the twisted leaves of certain narcissi, or the green horseshoe on every snowdrop. There was once a kind of snowdrop with a yellow spot, but I am told it is now lost.

It was a botanist who long ago showed me how a periwinkle flower has in the middle of it a most tiny miniature sweeping brush, but this you can find only by pulling the flower to pieces.

CHAPTER 1

DUBLIN is a great place for fine art auctions; the kind of auction, I mean, where you have oil paintings and wine coolers and candlesticks and mustache cups and coasters and old china toilet sets, but not golf clubs or motor mowers. The contents of the old "big houses" in which, as may be gathered from many novels and plays about Ireland, everybody except the peasantry at one time used to live, are now being turned out and transferred, by way of the sale rooms, to the modern labor-saving villas in garden suburbs in which the whole population will be housed in a few years' time.

The crowd admitted to the Dawson Hall "by catalogue only" one chill February afternoon was the usual blend of professionals and amateurs: dealers, serious collectors, and casual bargain hunters. Some were smart and some shabby. Their outward appearance could not be taken as any indication of the state of their bank accounts, and it was no surprise to the auctioneer if some of the most down-at-heel customers made the highest bids.

Among the smarter women were an evident mother and daughter, sitting side by side, sharing a catalogue which had admitted the two of them, which showed they were not people to be carelessly extravagant, although their clothes were nice.

The daughter was pretty. She had soft fair hair, gray eyes, neat wrists and ankles, and a complexion only rivaled in that room by a china shepherdess who had been auctioned earlier on and was now clasped in the arms of a clergyman. If, as seemed probable, her mother had once been like her and she was destined to resemble her mother in the future, the girl had no great cause for regret in that, for the older lady also was prepossessing in appearance. But the older lady had worries plainly written in her expression, and while the daughter eagerly followed the bidding, the mother's attention wandered and every now and then she seemed to recollect herself with an effort.

The auctioneer worked through a batch of miscellaneous old pictures between the china and silver and the furniture. The order in which lots are taken at these auctions never has much connection with textbook classifications.

7

The rough idea seems to be to work up through a series of moderately attractive items to certain objects of outstanding importance, at which prices are sure to reach a climax, and then follow with duller stuff while the bidders are recovering their nerve.

Two Large Oil Paintings with Cattle, Sheep, Fowl, and Villagers in Extensive Landscape went for barely the value of their frames. A picture of Boors Drinking fetched a better price, and a Figure Subject went up to forty pounds. A small Circular Painting of Camp with Tents called "Judith with Head of Holofernes" unexpectedly bounded into three figures.

Next came a Flower Painting with Still Life, Dutch School. This was an enchanting picture. A stone vase overflowed with a medley of delightful old-fashioned flowers: old garden favorites and treasures of the eighteenth century nurseryman. This part was a song of everlasting summer, but either the painter had a melancholy streak, or had been told by his friends that art ought to have a message, or felt that a hard grayish surface was wanted as a contrast to the flowers and foliage, for at the base of the vase he had put in a human skull. Most likely he cared more about craftsmanship than sermonizing, for this extra did nothing to spoil the happy atmosphere. One felt that it was just a skull that its owner no longer required and that had often done duty as a studio prop.

The pretty girl sat up, her eye on the auctioneer. The auctioneer said a word of special recommendation of this interesting lot and started the bidding. The price went briskly up and paused at thirty pounds. The pretty girl drew in her breath, but before she could move the bidding had run on to thirty-five. The girl signaled thirty-six. Thirty-seven, thirty-eight, thirty-nine. There were two other bidders at the back, and one whom she could see, a man in a bowler hat and dark overcoat with a striped scarf wound twice round his neck. His chin was sunk in the folds of the scarf, and he peered at the auctioneer through glasses perched on a high-bridged nose. He had chilblains on the hand holding the catalogue.

The pretty girl's mother was again sunk in brooding. It was only when her daughter waved her catalogue for the second time that she woke up to what was happening.

"Don't do that!" she said. "They'll think you're bidding."

"I am bidding," said the girl and did it again, bringing the price up to forty-four.

"But you don't want a painting."

"Yes I do, it's lovely."

"But you haven't got the money."

"Yes I have." (Forty-six, forty-seven.) "I'm buying it instead of a fur coat, with my birthday money."

"Stop, Barbara! Are you mad ?"

"Shh, Mummy! Do stop arguing."

Forty-nine, fifty. At fifty there came a pause. The bidders at the back had dropped out, and now it was between Barbara and the man in the scarf. He bid fifty-one. The auctioneer looked inquiringly over his head at the two ladies, and several other people also looked round. The mother placed a hand very firmly on her daughter's arm. The auctioneer noted the signs of an expostulation and caught the mother's eye. He knocked the picture down to the man in the green scarf.

The pretty girl gave a soft, piteous moan. Her mother said, looking at her with an expression both anxious and severe:

"I've a good mind to take you straight home."

"I don't mind. There's nothing I want to stay for."

The daughter sat back drooping.

Her mother consulted her catalogue, on which there was a tick against a Sheraton table, lot 346.

"Oh well," she said, " they can't be long getting to the furniture now."

The auctioneer disposed of a series of portraits, somebody's distinguished ancestors, whose sole interest for anybody now was that some of them had sat to well-known painters. Then he came to the furniture, and in due course to lot 346. By that time the elder lady was brooding again, and her daughter had to nudge her. Once aroused she bid determinedly and secured the table, though not exactly at a bargain price. She paid her deposit to the clerk, giving her name as Mrs. Paul Fennelly, with an address in Rathgar. Then the two ladies made their way out of the hall.

As they walked from the auction hall to the Automobile Club where they had left their car, Barbara Fennelly's lovely face wore a look of reproach which her mother could not ignore, however much else she might have on her mind. Mrs. Fennelly sometimes asked herself anxiously if Barbara was spoiled. She did not think so, really, but the child was going through a difficult phase. Anyhow, to walk up Dawson Street in broad daylight beside a daughter wearing an expression like that was—on top of everything else—more than one ought to be asked to bear. As they stopped at the curbside to wait for a gap in the traffic she rounded on Barbara and said:

"You may thank me for saving you from yourself. Imagine squandering all your birthday money like that! You know you'll never have a twenty-first again."

"No, I know I shan't," replied Barbara in a sweet, sad voice, her gray eyes fixed pensively on some inner vision. "I may never again in all my life fall in love with something beautiful when I can afford to buy it. You see, Mummy, I don't feel a fur coat is essential to happiness. There are other things more worth having."

"You can't wrap up very warmly in an oil painting," her mother pointed out. Because the great thing about a fur coat is that it does for evening as well as day, and she was always anxious about Barbara going out in evening dress. But there was more in fur than its practical value in one's wardrobe. A fur coat is a symbol of a girl's being grown up.

"I can wrap up warmly in anything," said Barbara, thinking not so much of the oil painting as of the two winter coats she already possessed. "To tell you the truth, Mummy, fur coats just happen to strike me as rather vulgar."

Before Mrs. Fennelly could reply the traffic paused for them, and Barbara hurried her across. In the calm of the Mansion House yard among the parked cars, they took up the thread of the conversation.

"I mean," said Barbara, "it's vulgar to make comfort one's first consideration. There are things that matter more. Music, poetry, art, truth, beauty—"

"That's all very well," said Mrs. Fennelly, "but one must have common sense."

She spoke all the more impatiently that she felt all this was partly her fault. This high-mindedness of Barbara's was due to the careful way in which she had been brought up. On a day when she had less to worry her, Mrs. Fennelly might have admired this attitude in her daughter. There was something touching about it, and not many people have daughters who are pretty and idealistic too. And if Barbara had bought the picture, the chances were her father would have found some excuse for giving her the fur coat too. But it happened that today Mrs. Fennelly was on the lookout for dangerous tendencies, and she had a horrible feeling this unpractical strain in Barbara might be hereditary.

"You can't want to spend fifty pounds on a picture at your age," she said. "It's unnatural."

"But Mummy, you know how interested I am in art. I've read it all up and I've collected books and prints for years. It means ever so much more to me than it does to you and Daddy. Sometimes I think I must be much more like Uncle Fergus."

At the name of her only brother Mrs. Fennelly started. She shook her head decisively.

"Oh no, Barbara," she said. "You are not in the least like Fergus, not the slightest bit. At least, I hope not."

The club attendant, who had been patiently hovering, put them into their car, and going home through the rush hour, Mrs. Fennelly begged Barbara to concentrate on driving.

CHAPTER 2

THOUGH Barbara did not know it, Mrs. Fennelly had heard from her brother Fergus that morning, the first letter she had had from him for years. She had been clutching it in her handbag all through the auction, because she had not cared to leave it lying about at home. The time now drew near when she would have to discuss it with her husband. At breakfast, when the post arrived, Paul

Fennelly had been hurrying to catch his bus to the office, and there was no opportunity of broaching a serious matter. So although the letter urgently demanded an answer she had been obliged to take the day to think it over, and this was what had been filling her thoughts all through the afternoon.

Fergus wrote:

Dear Hester,

How would you like to have me to stay for a bit? I have got to go somewhere away from here. I have been getting ill off and on all winter for no obvious reason, and now the doctor says he thinks I have had a series of small doses of arsenic, which looks rather as if there was somebody here trying to do me in. I don't know who. Anyhow, he thinks I had better have a complete change of surroundings, and so do I. I can't afford a hotel or nursing home for long, and there is nobody else I can trust, so I hope you can take me in. Let me know by return.

Your affectionate brother,

Fergus.

The idea of one's only brother, or even of someone not related to one at all, being gradually poisoned by a series of small doses of arsenic administered by an unknown hand, is shocking to the average mind.

Hester Fennelly's first thought was that her brother had developed persecution mania. There had never been any insanity in their family, but it would be just like Fergus to start it and there was Barbara boasting of taking after him! But he said he had a doctor's diagnosis to go on. Besides, although she could not remember ever having had any letters from lunatics, she fancied that the style would be more incoherent and rambling. This letter sounded just like Fergus' normal self. Some people might have indulged in more preliminaries before inviting themselves to stay with a sister whom they had not seen for something like ten years, but not Fergus. He never made any bones about asking for what he wanted.

The idea of having him to stay weighed on Mrs. Fennelly almost more than the idea of his being the victim of an unknown poisoner. She was not heartless and had always been natural in her affections. She could remember a time when she had adored her brother, and she was still fond of him, but through the years his figure had become shadowy. For his sake she laboriously wrote a letter every Christmas to his wife, Nell, whom she hardly knew, but—Christmas being a busy time—it was never a very long letter, and as it always crossed the one which Nell laboriously wrote to her, they were never much the wiser as to having any questions answered. Still, they had at least succeeded in keeping up. Fergus did his share by sending Christmas cards made by himself, for he was a painter by profession and his name, Fergus Gandon, was now quite well known. At the cross-grained stage of Christmas, about the morning of Boxing Day, there would generally be an argument between Barbara and her father over Fergus' Christmas card; Barbara would profess to admire it, and her father would challenge her to explain what it was all about. For Fergus' work was of the unintelligible kind, and while it impressed his niece it annoyed his brother-in-law. Paul Fennelly held that art which had been called "advanced" for so many years ought to have got somewhere by now.

Hester Fennelly knew that Barbara felt a mild sense of grievance against her parents for not cultivating the Gandons. When one loves art and has a distinguished painter for one's uncle, it is hard never to see anything of him. Yet there were reasons for this.

No sensible woman, though she loved them both, could have expected Paul Fennelly and Fergus Gandon to mix. Hester, as a girl, had rushed into Paul's arms as a haven from the artistic temperament. For her father had been a painter too, and her mother had forsaken her own rich dull family in order to marry him, and so long as the house was crowded with intellectual people and humming with creative work, they had not cared if socks got used for dish-cloths, or cats kittened in the unmade beds. Hester's escape had been in the opposite direction, to a nice house in the suburbs where there was a cloth for every purpose and a housemaid trained to use them. She had made mistakes at first, but she had taken pains with herself and become metamorphosed by degrees into the perfect businessman's wife. For twenty years she had respected convention and eschewed originality. Yet she was still nervous of slipping, and Fergus could spoil everything.

Fergus and Paul, being men, had probably never even asked themselves whether they liked each other or not. They were each inclined to make fun of the other behind his back, but whenever they met, which was mostly at family gatherings like both their weddings, they had included each other in a general atmosphere of cordiality. No more ought to be demanded of in-laws, and as the families lived nearly a hundred miles apart it was easier for them to remain united.

Hester's and Fergus' parents were now both dead. They had not left any money, but Fergus had been tided over early difficulties by a rich cousin on his mother's side who was his godmother and granted him a small allowance for the sake of his career. Then a friend of Nell Gandon's, who was a landed gentleman, had offered them a small house on his property, rent free, if they would act as caretakers for his own larger mansion when he was away. It was in a dull part of the country, but it was healthy for the children and quiet for Fergus' work. The Gandons had been isolated down there through the war years of gasoline shortage and transport cuts, and their Dublin relations could hardly have seen much of them even if they had felt inclined.

Hester's last contact with them had been when Nell's first baby was born. There had been two others since, and as Hester faithfully sent them all Christmas presents appropriate to their ages, she knew the eldest little girl was nearly ten. Ten years is a long break. She wondered what Nell was like now. She had been attractive rather than pretty; vivacious and well-dressed. She was Irish but had lived a lot in England and acquired self-possession. She had an English voice. Hester had found her difficult to get to know, but saw the attraction for Fergus.

Nell was younger than Fergus and quite another generation from Hester, for Fergus was Hester's younger brother by five years. From this sprang a habit of taking care of him, which had an opportunity to reassert itself in this emergency.

When tea was over and Barbara safely elsewhere, Hester handed Paul her brother's letter, with a look that prepared him for bad news. She could see that he did not expect to be much affected by bad news about the Gandons, but as he read, his expression changed from polite concern to surprise and then disapproval. Paul never liked anything irregular.

At last he said, "Extraordinary business!"

"Yes, isn't it dreadful for them, poor things," said Hester. "One can hardly imagine their feelings under the circumstances."

"Queer chap, your brother," said Paul.

"I don't think it's fair to say that, Paul. It's not his fault."

"No, on the face of it I suppose not," said Paul, obviously holding Fergus to blame none the less.

"I can't believe anyone is really trying to murder him," said Hester. "Most likely it's Nell's cooking upsetting him."

"Does Nell do the cooking?"

"Either her or that man they have, Mosney. There isn't anyone else as far as I know. And I'm sure in their kitchen anything might get into anything."

"One knows so little about them," said Paul frowning. "We don't know who is down there about the house, or who they have in the way of neighbors."

"As far as I know there's only Mosney in the house," said Hester. "They had nobody at all before he came. All the country girls down there are 'flighted.'* Mosney just saved Nell's life when the house and children were getting to be more than she could cope with. As for neighbors, I don't believe there's a soul, except Lord Kilskour when he's there."

Lord Kilskour was the owner of Kilskour Castle and the Gandons' benefactor and landlord.

"What's he like, do you know?" asked Paul.

"Oh, rather dull. He has a theory about the future of agriculture and goes round giving lectures. He's in England most of the time; he has another big place over there."

"Oh well, he sounds all right," said Paul. "Fergus doesn't seem to have any ideas himself about who's at the bottom of it. You'd think if there was anyone likely to want to murder him, he'd know. But perhaps he'd rather not say."

* Gone to work in Dublin or England.

Fergus always dramatizes a situation," said Hester. "Nothing that happened to Fergus was ever an accident, but it often turned out to be in the end after all."

"It's to be hoped this is," said Paul, "but it might not be, all the same."

Hester could see he did not like the look of it. He did not want to criticize her relations, but he thought they might draw the line at getting mixed up in murder cases. And if they could not help it, the decent thing to do was to go and be murdered in a nursing home.

Irene, the houseparlormaid, came to take away the tea things, and her master and mistress had to look as if there was nothing the matter. She lifted the tray off the top of a low revolving bookcase and replaced a vase of irises which had been moved off the bookcase to the mantelpiece. Watching Irene's soundless movements, Hester thought how little Fergus would be used to this standard of service, and how she must warn him to pronounce the girl's name "Ireen," because they had discovered she thought "Ireenie" was familiar.

They were sitting in Paul's study, the room they all preferred when they were by themselves. It was devoted, in a tidy businesslike way, to hobbies. It was the room where they kept most of their books, on metal shelves which, though more utilitarian than elegant, toned with the plain brown curtains, the brown leather chairs, and the matting on the floor. Gardening catalogues were kept beside Paul's chair under the wireless. A desk in the square bay window was occupied by six bowls of bulbs, still only in leaf, and some late pears, put there to ripen. The whole room was scented with a single twig of Chimonanthus, flowering for the first time in their garden, and a symbol of triumph.

Gardening had grown on Paul and Hester with the years. Hester had never from the first felt worthy to be her husband's partner at bridge or golf, and Paul had never much cared for doing things without her. He had been sociable with his kind in his earlier years, but had now reached a worldly eminence where he need no longer concern himself about making contacts and was settling down to be his true self, domesticated, stay-at-home, and fond of home-grown fruit and vegetables.

Hester asked Irene to draw the curtains, for though the light still lasted it was a cheerless day, and the world looked bleak outside. Paul lit his pipe, an occupation he could always prolong for an indefinite time. When the maid had gone, he said. "I don't see much point in Fergus coming here at this time of year. It isn't as if he could be in the garden. Lot of work for you, too, looking after him. If he went to a nursing home, a tip-top one, I mean, and of course he'd let us help with the expenses, he'd be quite safe and much more comfortable."

Hester saw through this and could not let pass a slur on her well-run establishment. Heaven had given her two spare rooms with electric fires and hot and cold water laid on, and such blessings carry obligations. Never should it be said that Mrs. Fennelly was put out by visitors.

"He couldn't be more comfortable than here," she said, "and I'm quite used to nursing."

"But suppose he got worse?"

"Suppose," said Hester, "we refused to take him in and he went somewhere else and—and died?" Her voice quivered, which Paul hated.

"I'm sure it wouldn't come to that," he said, and he believed it. In his opinion Fergus Gandon was the kind of man who made endless trouble frightening people and upsetting their arrangements but never did anything decisive.

"Well then, we needn't be afraid of having him," said Hester. She had quite made up her mind to it by now. She was ready to accept having Fergus with the resignation of a Buddhist accepting his individual karma. Her only wish was to see Paul reconciled to the idea.

Paul had a more Occidental outlook and continued to argue. He reread the letter in case it contained a loophole he had overlooked.

"Nell and the children seem to be all right, anyway," he observed. "He'd surely say if they weren't. It's funny Nell didn't write to you. Isn't she usually the one?"

"Yes, Fergus must be ill," said Hester lightly.

"Nell would have given more details, I expect. We certainly haven't much to go on."

"It's funny Nell didn't say anything when she wrote at Christmas. Fergus seems to have been ill for some time."

"Perhaps Nell doesn't know."

Hester stared. Then she saw that Paul might be right. Fergus naturally would not want to alarm his wife. At least an ordinary husband would not, but it did not seem quite like Fergus to be so considerate. But there was another possibility better not mentioned, even to Paul. Suppose Fergus suspected Nell?

Paul was thinking along other lines. He said. "I wonder what that doctor fellow down there is like. It may be some old fool who doesn't know much. Do you know what? I think I'll have a talk with Claud."

Claud Colville was their own family doctor and a lifelong friend and adviser.

Hester approved of this but did not like the idea of more delay. Fergus was expecting to hear by return, and already a day had gone. She would have liked to send a telegram at once. Paul said that, if Fergus had been having ups and downs all winter, another twenty-four hours would hardly prove fatal, but then Fergus was not his brother. The simplest thing would have been for him to drop in at the doctor's the following afternoon on his way home from work, but to relieve his wife's mind, and since a human life might be at stake, he consented for once to turn out after dinner.

They sat all three in Dr. Claud Colville's Fitzwilliam square front drawing room crowded with *objets d'art.*

"Arsenic?" said Dr. Colville with a skeptical smile. "You might find that in anybody's tummy. If I took out Paul's this minute, the chances are there'd be some arsenic in it, especially as I know he's fond of lobsters."

"He doesn't often get them," said Paul, making a face at his wife.

"I always knew they were bad for him," said Hester. "Have they really got arsenic in them, Claud?"

"There's a very high percentage of arsenic in lobster meat," the doctor told her. "As much as forty parts per million. Don't know where they get it. Of course, the creatures' life processes aren't very active, and they absorb things quicker than they eliminate them."

"There now, Paul."

"Don't pander to my wife's prejudices," said Paul. "Forty parts per million isn't going to hurt anyone."

"Likewise with codfish," said Dr. Colville, disregarding interruptions. "Codfish eliminate things like arsenic through their livers. Has this chap been taking cod-liver oil?"

"He used to hate it," said Hester, "but of course he may have changed and got more sensible about things like tonics."

"It might be the worst thing for him," said Dr. Colville. "In my experience it often does upset people. I don't believe in forcing medicine on patients. People know what's good for them and what isn't."

"You can't depend on that," said Hester. " But he wouldn't be taking a tonic unless he was ill first. Or do you think arsenic might not be the original cause of his illness?"

"Oh, there are plenty of other ways he might have taken some. It gets into vegetables. I mean into, not on to. You can wash off the odd drop of arsenical weed killer, or what gets spilled over the ground when the apple trees are sprayed, but if the stuff's about in any quantity it gets right into the soil. Arsenic's an element, you know. There's exactly as much in the world as there always was because it doesn't get used up; it keeps going round and round. From the soil it gets absorbed into grass and vegetables. You eat the vegetables, or you eat cattle that have been eating the grass, and you absorb it into your system too. Not enough to hurt, luckily, as a rule. But I've read that in New York State, where their agriculture's run on big business lines and they do a lot of arsenate of lead spraying with high-powered pressure guns, the soil's so full of arsenic that everybody has it in their insides. It turns up regularly at autopsies, and they just take it for granted and treat it as irrelevant."

"Hold on a minute," said Paul, for the doctor showed signs of being thoroughly launched. "Do you mean, now, that my brother-in-law may have symptoms of arsenical poisoning and really be suffering from something else, or do you mean he may have been poisoned by accident?"

"Both."

"If it was any of those things you mention, other people would also be affected."

"We don't know if they haven't," said Hester.

"You might enquire," said Dr. Colville. "In Liverpool, about 1900, dozens of people were poisoned through drinking the local beer. It contained glucose which had got contaminated with arseniferous sulphuric acid."

"Fergus does drink beer," said Hester. "More than cod-liver oil."

"By the way," said Dr. Colville with an excited gleam in his eye, "I suppose they haven't got green wallpaper?"

The Fennellys had no idea.

The green coloring may contain arsenic," explained the doctor happily. "The starch paste sticking the paper to the wall ferments, and you get nascent hydrogen combining with the arsenic to form arseniureted hydrogen. People living in the room inhale it, and there you are! It sounds farfetched, but it's led to several fatalities."

The Fennellys were beginning to feel as if nobody's life was safe.

"But as far as we know his wife and children are all right," said Paul.

"It might affect one person more than another," said the doctor. "Allergies are commoner than murder, even in these wicked times. I always advise my students not to leap to melodramatic conclusions."

"Well, you have relieved our minds," said Paul, "though I shall not allow you to put me off lobsters. As for vegetables, we now grow all our own."

"Who's the doctor down there, do you know?" Dr. Colville enquired. Hester Fennelly thought she remembered hearing his name was Caraway.

"Caraway? Now I wonder would that by any chance be Brian Caraway? He was a student of mine about '39 or '40. The reason I remember him is he was—a simply—brilliant"—Claud Colville had a way of spreading out his words when he wanted to be impressive—"a—simply—brilliant"—he repeated, holding the Fennellys in suspense till he brought out the last word—"a brilliant center forward."

Paul and Hester both laughed. They had been afraid this Brian might have been a brilliant toxicologist. A center forward might not be infallible on arsenic.

"Of course if the chap does turn out to be suffering from arsenical poisoning," said Dr. Colville, "the fact ought to be reported to the Guards at the nearest barracks. Might help to prevent accidents, but I daresay that's been thought of."

The Fennellys did not know, but were not worrying. It was a weight off their minds to think that Fergus was most likely not being murdered after all. They sent him a telegram that night.

"One thing," said Paul, "if Fergus does come, the less said about this poison business the better. Don't let it get round to the maids, or Barbara either."

"Certainly not," said Hester. She added cheerfully, "Barbara will be pleased. She's always been interested in Fergus. She'll be trying to talk to him about art."

CHAPTER 3

MRS. FENNELLY drove in alone to meet her brother at the station. She would not let Barbara come because she wanted to take stock of him all by herself first, and especially to warn him not to talk about poison to all and sundry, for it was his way to hold forth on any subject that absorbed his interest, and his illness must certainly be his main preoccupation at present. Hester thought they might be able to get everything said about the poison on the way home, and Fergus could then settle down to more commonplace topics of conversation, of which there ought to be plenty after so many years.

Fergus' wife was not included in these calculations. He had said nothing about her coming too, nor had the Fennellys realized that he was too ill to travel alone. Hester was taken aback, therefore, when Nell got out of the train first. In spite of not having seen her for years and not expecting her, she recognized her sister-in-law at once. Nell was hatless and wearing a vivid red tweed coat and skirt. Except for being thinner and browner she looked very much the same as ever. She still wore her hair in a long bob like a girl.

Hester arranged her face in a smile and walked forward with outstretched hand, wondering all the while what she ought to say to Nell about Fergus' state of health; how much Nell had been told, how much she actually knew, and also how long she meant to stay. Could she be put into Fergus' double bed, or did the case call for separate rooms?

Nell said, "Oh there you are, that's good," shook hands perfunctorily, and turned to help Fergus down from the carriage.

The sight of Fergus was a shock. He was graying only at the temples, but his face was pale and drawn with illness, dead white above his black beard. His hand on Nell's red sleeve was thin and bloodless. His clothes hung loose, he looked shrunken and—so Hester thought—neglected. Nell said, as if interpreting Hester's expression:

"The journey's taken it out of him. He'll be all right after a night's rest."

"I get these bilious attacks," said Fergus, giving Hester her cue loudly. A small old woman standing near them with her luggage round her in baskets turned round sympathetically and began telling him what she suffered from cramps in the stomach and what she took for them. "Madam," said Fergus repressively, "you can't tell me anything I don't know about stomach trouble." The old woman was humbled; her recital petered out.

"Don't look so worried," said Nell to Hester. "I'm not staying the night. I can get a bed at the Purtills'; you remember Paddy? It's handy for the station and I've got to get the first train back tomorrow. Can't abandon the children to their own devices." Hester assured her it would be no trouble to put her up;

there was another bed, everything was aired, but Nell seemed set on the Purtills, whoever they might be (Hester did not remember Paddy), and in the circumstances there was no point in pressing her.

As they sorted out the luggage the sight of the Gandons' luggage brought back to Hester old times, old journeys. There was a brute of a dressing-case, very heavy, being fitted—as Hester knew—with little bottles; it had belonged to their mother. A shabby suitcase that had been to Pisa; a rucksack; Fergus' easel and paintbox; mackintoshes and rugs strapped together with mackintosh belts; books, magazines, and the remains of lunch in a paper bag. When what Fergus called *"la séparation des biens"* was completed, Nell took her mackintosh and the rucksack and a magazine, and a porter took the rest to the car.

Nell drew Hester aside.

"Write to me how Fergus is," she said in a soft, urgent voice. "If he doesn't seem to be picking up properly, get him to see some good man. He's had a bad go of this."

"I can see that," said Hester. "Yes, of course I'll write."

"The doctor thinks all he needs is a rest from his wife and children," said Nell, more loudly, and smiling brightly at Fergus.

All Fergus said was, "Hurry up and send on my paintbox."

"Isn't that it?" said Hester.

"He means his watercolor box," said Nell. " I forgot to pack it. Fergus has been making rather a thing of watercolor lately. He and Paddy Purtill have been trying new techniques."

"Haven't felt up to doing much in oils," said Fergus. He got into the car, and it struck Hester that he was already tired with standing. Nell got in after him to say good-bye, then picked up her rucksack and walked away to the bus. She would not accept a lift.

Hester did not get very much out of Fergus on the drive home. He leaned back with closed eyes, and his sister drove in silence and in considerable distress of mind. Having seen Fergus, she felt far more anxious than his letter had made her. It seemed as if they had allowed too much for exaggeration, she and Paul. Things were worse than they had expected.

When they were nearly home Hester had to speak. It was necessary to put in a word of warning.

"Fergus, Paul and I are the only ones who know what the doctor thinks may be wrong with you. You know what I mean. We must have a serious talk about it when you feel better, but meanwhile, do please be careful not to say anything in front of Barbara and the maids."

Fergus' eyes opened.

"We could talk French," he suggested. "I love practicing my French. Or does Barbara understand it?"

"She ought to," said Hester, "considering all we've spent on her education."

"Girls know too much nowadays," said Fergus, and closed his eyes again.

When they got home Hester sent him straight to bed.

They had the serious talk at tea time the following afternoon. Barbara was out, and Hester, Paul and Fergus sat in the three deep leather chairs round the study fire. Fergus was dressed, to the astonishment of the houseparlormaid, in a dark red woolen dressing gown, waisted, full skirted, and frogged across the front with red cord. It had come down to him from an uncle. He had excused himself from dressing on the ground that he had nothing else so smart.

In spite of Fergus having been sent to bed the moment he arrived and remaining there till half an hour ago, the impact of his personality had already been felt by each member of the household.

The bowls of snowdrops which Barbara had placed here and there about the spare bedroom to welcome the visitor—Barbara made doing the flowers her special business—were found in a row outside the door along with his boots. Irene was also instructed to remove the three watercolors by one of Paul's aunts which decorated the bedroom wall. Hester, if she had thought about it, would have known these were not what Fergus could be expected to like. She resignedly told Irene she could take them up to the attic.

"He asked me to put up these instead, ma'am," said Irene with a prim face. She held out some pages torn from The *New Yorker*. Hester put on her glasses to look at them, blinked a little, then happily recollected that Irene, for all her virtuous expression, sometimes had vulgar postcards sent to her by her young man.

"Certainly put them up if Mr. Gandon likes them," she said. "You can pin them to the wallpaper, but try not to make too much of a mark."

Irene's opposite number in the kitchen, Mrs. Mulhall the cook, had to wrestle with the question of what Mr. Gandon could and could not eat. Hester remembered a good many food fads of his from childhood, but since his illness the list of what he could not eat had been extended to cover nearly everything on an ordinary family menu. Fortunately it could be subdivided into what he would not touch however you cooked it, and what he might eat if it was presented to him in a novel and tempting form. Although it was Hester who had to do the thinking, the responsibility weighed on Mrs. Mulhall. She all but gave notice when Mr. Gandon sent away his dinner the first evening untasted, but thought of demanding a raise, as Hester could see in her eye, when he asked for a second helping of fish at lunch.

The invalid was certainly better after a night's rest. When Hester went to see him in the morning she found him filling in the *Irish Times* crossword puzzle, thus depriving Paul of his evening occupation. He looked at her as if really seeing her for the first time and greeted her with:

"You have got fat!"

It was not fair. Hester had put on flesh as many matrons do, and her at one time seductive curves now required, as the fashion papers say, to be controlled, but fat she was not; her step was brisk and her energy unimpaired. Some people were quite surprised to learn that she had a grown-up daughter. She considered Fergus was in no case to twit her with the ravages of time.

But it was not difficult to forgive trifles like this to one who looked so ill, and as Fergus sat fidgeting in his chair by the fire Hester cast solicitous glances at him and fetched him a rug and a footstool. His feet stuck out pathetically from the red folds of his dressing gown; his trouser ends were frayed.

They had Irene draw the curtains early again. Paul lit his pipe and Fergus a Turkish cigarette. It was Paul who had remembered this exotic preference of his and brought home a supply. Paul was so thoughtful at times. Hester, sitting nearest the lamp between her two men felt benevolent towards both of them, and reflected, while elegantly embroidering table mats, that for poor Fergus it must be a quite unaccustomed atmosphere of luxury and peace.

But when Hester and Paul did their best to persuade Fergus that he was not being poisoned, or that if he was being poisoned nobody could be doing it on purpose, they made no headway.

"Ask Caraway," said Fergus with a shrug. "He's got the jitters all right. He couldn't get rid of me fast enough. He doesn't want a murder case in his practice."

"But who is this chap, Caraway?" said Paul. "Just a country doctor. You ought to get a second opinion."

"Doctors!" said Hester scornfully. "If you'd seen as much of them as I have you would never allow yourself to be upset by anything they say."

"I wasn't upset," said Fergus. "I was delighted. If you'd been me these last few months, losing weight, getting pains, being sick, wasting away for no apparent reason, sweating and aching and collapsing and no one able to tell you why—you'd be thankful to have a diagnosis that makes sense at last."

"But surely there are other possibilities?"

"Do you think it would cheer me up to be told it was T.B.?"

"Of course not, but—"

"T.B. may be more fashionable and less shocking to the conventional mind," said Fergus, "but I prefer something less organic, thank you very much."

"But this doctor fellow, what's his name? Caraway," said Paul. "What's he got to go on? How did he arrive at his diagnosis?"

"Analysis of excreta," said Fergus laconically.

"Did he analyze anyone else's besides yours?"

"I was the one with the interesting symptoms."

"You don't know of other cases in the district? Nell and the children, weren't they ever affected the same way?"

"No, thank God! Not one of the kids has been sick in the last six months, not even at Christmas. It's a record."

Paul said, "What I'm driving at is, might it not be something in the nature of an allergy? You all eat the same things, but there's something that only disagrees with you."

"I should have thought most people were allergic to arsenic," said Fergus.

"Not necessarily. It's often ordered as a tonic, in infinitesimal doses."

"We've been told by our doctor," Hester explained, "that in some districts everyone has arsenic in their systems, because of the vegetables. Where they spray fruit trees with it on a big scale it gets into the ground."

"Couldn't happen to us," said Fergus. "All our vegetables come from the castle, and there's no spraying done there. It's against Kilskour's principles. You know he goes roaring up and down the land scolding farmers for polluting the ground with artificial manures."

"I have some of his pamphlets," said Paul. "I've been studying it from the point of view of the garden, finding out the best way to make our own composts here. He's against spraying too, is he? What are you to do if you've got aphis?"

"Ah," said Fergus, "and how many have? One in five, I expect. Do you suppose their best friends would tell them?"

"Never mind about that now," said Hester. "Fergus, do you ever have lobsters?"

"My good girl, how would the likes of us have lobsters? You can't get a bit of fish in the country even on Friday."

"Have you been taking cod-liver oil?"

"Never in my life."

"Oh dear. Well, have any of your rooms down there got green wallpaper?"

"Green wallpaper?" repeated Fergus, bewildered. "Look, what is this? Some kind of psychotherapy? Are you trying to tap thought-associations buried in my subconscious?"

"She's only trying to find out how you could have got arsenic into your system by accident," explained Paul. "Colville, our doctor, suggested those things as possibilities." But nothing of what had been said in the interview the Fennellys had found so reassuring now seemed to have any application to the case of Fergus.

"Caraway would have been on to anything like that," said Fergus. "He's been reading the thing up. He's thought of all that about the others taking arsenic too and not being upset by it. His answer to that is, get everybody's hair analyzed. I had to do a rape of the lock stunt on Nell and the children, without their knowing, and as for Mosney, I pinched an old shaving brush he had in the scullery. It was time he got himself a new one ; you never saw such a disgusting object."

"In the scullery?" said Hester, and shuddered.

"I still have to hear from Caraway about the hair," said Fergus. "He doesn't do things like that himself; he has to send them up to Dublin and it takes weeks, sometimes, to get a report. But I haven't much doubt what it'll be, myself."

It seemed to the Fennellys there was still a loophole, even if it was no use arguing with Fergus. They asked him instead to tell them more details about his illness and how it all began.

"I got ill in the summer," said Fergus. "The first time I thought nothing of it. I just took it for a hangover. We'd had Paddy Purtill down to stay, and some nights we'd sat up rather late celebrating. Then I seemed to be getting more than my money's worth of hangovers. Paddy'd gone back, and I don't drink much when there's nobody to lead me astray. I blamed Nell's cooking and the weather, and then I thought it must be overwork. I'd been doing a fair amount of work: a mural on a wall down there and a set of illustrations for Silke. You know Arnold Silke, Hester. He's going into publishing as a sideline to dealing. Fine art books. This one's to be on new watercolor techniques; he knew I was rather bitten by the subject. Paddy came down again in October and we tried a lot of experiments, but I was feeling rotten by that time, hardly up to painting at all if Paddy hadn't been there to keep me at it. Just before he left I downright collapsed. It was he and Nell made me have the doctor. That was October and I've been going up and down ever since, but more down than up on the whole. Caraway was puzzling his brains out over it. I can't tell you the relief when he put his finger on the explanation at last."

"Oh Fergus, do you mean to say you've been ill ever since last summer?" cried Hester, grieved that she had not been told. "But what happened? Did you have sudden attacks? Was it that food seemed to upset you?"

"No," said Fergus. "I couldn't make out what upset me. Attacks seemed to come on before meals as much as after. When Caraway started getting things analyzed naturally I snitched samples of food for him, but so far no luck in that direction."

"But, my dear chap," said Paul, " is there anybody you know who'd be in the least likely to try to poison you?"

"Of course there are, dozens," said Fergus. "Three or four anyway," he said, as they stared at him horrified. He sat beaming at them, and spinning the tassel of his dressing-gown cord round and round in circles. "There's Nell, for one," he said.

Hester started.

"Let's face it," said Fergus calmly. "Nell and I are ten years married. After ten years a wife's feelings towards her husband are likely to be, at best, ambivalent."

"Oh nonsense!" said Hester.

"I'm only viewing human nature with detachment. You must often have wanted to murder Paul."

"No I haven't."

"No? But you and Paul never loved with passion. The happiest marriages after all are founded on affection and habit. Passion so soon burns out."

"You don't know anything about it," said Hester crossly. A skein of embroidery silk fell off her lap. Paul picked it up for her. Fergus laughed.

"The fact remains," he said, "that at least fifty percent of murder cases on record have been wife killing husband, or vice versa. Divorce is so much more expensive, and such a slow process."

"But you and Nell, Fergus—have you—are you—surely things haven't come to that?"

Nell and Fergus had kissed each other good-bye affectionately at the station. But Nell had not wanted to come for the night.

"No, no," said Fergus. "Don't let your imaginations run away with you. Nell and I are ostensibly still devoted. All I mean is, it doesn't suit Nell being buried in the heart of the country. It's all right for me, I've got my work, but a girl like Nell, you couldn't wonder if she got a bit lonely. Honestly you couldn't blame her if she took up with the first fellow that came along."

"Do you mean this Purtill man?" asked Hester shrewdly.

"Paddy? Why Paddy? What do you know about him?" asked Fergus sharply. Then he shook his head. "Oh no, not Paddy. Damn it, I was with them the whole time. Besides, there was somebody else in the offing when Paddy was with us, and if we are looking for a corespondent—I don't say we need, but just for an example—the man for the part is Kilskour."

Paul raised his eyebrows. "Your landlord?"

"Him. He used to take Nell out for drives while Paddy and I were busy painting."

"I didn't think Lord Kilskour was that sort of man," said Hester.

"He's not abnormal as far as I know," said Fergus.

Hester frowned. She had only met Lord Kilskour once, at her brother's wedding, but she had a clear recollection of him, refreshed by seeing his photograph from time to time in the papers. He had an earnest expression and an aristocratic bearing. His brows beetled above a high-bridged nose, and he wore an intimidating mustache, but had gentle doggy eyes. Her ideas of normality differed from her brother's. Lord Kilskour was not unattractive, but she would not have expected him to have love affairs. He was too serious-minded.

Paul said in his sensible way:

"All this is sheer conjecture, isn't it? You've no real grounds for complaint?"

Fergus said cheerfully: "None whatever."

"Then stop libeling your wife and tell us who are your other suspects."

"Paddy Purtill."

"But you said just now—" said Hester.

"I know I did. I suspect Paddy on quite other grounds. He was there, you know, when I was taken ill, both times."

"Just who is this man?" said Hester. "Nell said I should remember him, but I don't. And yet the name sounds familiar."

"Have you not heard of Paddy Purtill? The coming president of the Royal Hibernian Academy? You wouldn't remember him from meeting him; he's since your time. But I should have thought his stuff would be quite in your line. Pupil of mine, once in the dim past."

"I may have seen his work," said Hester reflectively. "I think I have, in the RHA. Doesn't he do portraits? Honest, straightforward work, but not very exciting. Good drawing, though. Are you proud of him as a pupil?"

"I am not," said Fergus with vehemence. "I told him so not long ago. He's taking the best line for himself, of course. Sissy pictures of pinup girls; sunshiny landscapes. Just what the stockbroker likes to buy. Saving your presence, Paul! Paddy's just prostituting his gifts nowadays, sheer waste of my time when I thought I could teach him to paint."

"But why do you think this Purtill might want to poison you?" asked Paul.

"Jealousy," said Fergus.

"But not of your wife?"

"Nix. Of my work. Or revenge because I was rude to him. I can be very rude when I like," said Fergus proudly. "I was only criticizing him for his own good."

"In fact, you had a row. Is this chap at all queer in himself? You know what I mean—neurotic?"

"Well, no," said Fergus. "I can't say I've ever noticed it. If you ask me, Paddy's more the kind of chap to knock you down with his fists than to slip anything in your drink. All the same, he had the chance if he liked. Paddy had the run of the house as long as he was with us. Kilskour, for instance, might come into the parlor but never the kitchen."

As far as Hester could recall Mr. Purtill's work it was the essence of sanity. Its faults, she would have said, came from lack of temperament, not from excess of it. There was an absence of verve, of excitement; a weakness of emotional response. But this might mean nothing more than that painting provided an insufficient outlet.

"But talking of the kitchen," she said suddenly, "what about that man you have—Mosney? Haven't you suspected him?"

Fergus raised his hand, palm outward.

"Not a word against Mosney. Mosney's our bulwark."

"So he may be, but how much do you really know about him? You haven't had him very long, have you? Where did he come from?"

"Out of the everywhere," said Fergus. "Nell found him under a gooseberry bush. Yes, literally. He turned up one day asking for work in the garden and Nell found him a job, and he found several more for himself. So the end of it was he stayed on and became one of the family, and now we can't think how we ever managed to exist without him."

"Did he give you references?" asked Hester.

"Not at all. His last employer was dead and all his papers had been pinched when he slept in a night shelter. You and Paul, of course, may have heard that one before, but my wife still clings to a belief in human nature."

"But good gracious," said Hester, "he might be a homicidal maniac escaped from an asylum."

"Now that's sheer class prejudice," said Fergus. "There's no more reason to suspect Mosney of being a homicidal maniac than Paddy Purtill, a chap who'd sell his soul for money, or a decadent aristo like Kilskour. And we should miss Mosney much worse if he went."

"Mosney cooks for you, doesn't he?" said Paul. "And I think you said Lord Kilskour, at any rate, never went into the kitchen."

"Nothing to stop Kilskour slipping in when nobody's looking," said Fergus. "Or if it was him, he might have been working in collaboration with Nell. Or worked it through her, somehow, without her really knowing. He might give her his sugar ration to put in my tea or something."

The Fennellys had already noticed that Fergus put two teaspoonfuls of sugar in every cup. Nell would be open to borrow other people's rations.

"It's all very vague," complained Paul with a sigh, or it might have been a yawn. "None of this gets us much farther. But assuming, for the sake of argument, that you are being poisoned, the matter will soon be taken out of our hands by the police."

At this Fergus sat up.

"Not on any account," he said. " Not while I can prevent it. Our *Garda Siochana* are a fine body of men, but I don't want them putting their big feet into my affairs."

"But you must tell them, Fergus," said Hester, dropping her work. "It's the only thing to do, if things turn out to be really serious."

"Isn't the doctor bound to report it?" said Paul.

"Oh, him," said Fergus. "He did suggest something of the sort, but I choked him off. I can sit on Caraway's head all right."

"Don't be silly, Fergus. It's too dangerous. If there really is some madman—it would have to be a madman, surely—who is trying to take your life, you'll need all the protection and help you can get."

"And a fat lot I'd get from the Civic Guards, my sweet conventional sister. I can just see the great gobdaws tramp, tramp, tramping off along false trails. They'd have to frame somebody or other in order to justify their existence, and who'd be the first person they'd pitch on? Nell, of course. I'm not prepared to expose my wife to the machinery of the law, thank you very much. I don't share your bourgeois confidence in official justice."

"I think you underrate the Civic Guards," said Paul.

"I do not. I know what they'd be like. They'd drive us all mad with their questions. They'd frighten the children and arrest Nell, and they'd turn my studio upside down."

Hester knew that the last argument was unanswerable.

"What do you propose, then?" said Paul.

"Get better," said Fergus. "That's why I'm here. Get better, get a line on the fellow, and get even with him myself. No police. Keep the party clean."

The dressing-gown tassel which he had been spinning vigorously as he talked drooped from his hand. Talking had tired him. He lay back and closed his eyes. Hester shot a warning glance at Paul and said gently, "We'll wait a bit and see how things turn out. The first thing is to get you better, and you're safe here with us."

"Quite safe here with you," murmured Fergus, opening his eyes to smile at her in a way that stirred all her protective instincts.

Paul picked up the *Irish Times* with the crossword puzzle, but Fergus had finished it.

CHAPTER 4

A WEEK after his arrival Fergus Gandon was distinctly better; the Fennellys, on the other hand, were beginning to feel the strain. The maids were complaining: Mrs. Mulhall had never met anyone so particular about his food, and Irene's routine was upset by never knowing what time of day Mr. Gandon would get up. Barbara's flower arrangements were despised, and the Chimonanthus, pride of the Fennellys' gardening hearts, had to be thrown out because the scent oppressed the invalid. Barbara had no difficulty in getting her uncle to talk about art, but he upset all her ideas and called everything she admired either *"pompier" or* "chi-chi," terms which were new to her vocabulary. Paul was angelically polite and patient with the invalid, but Hester feared that some day soon, when Fergus was again found to have filled up the *Irish Times* crossword puzzle with the wrong words, something in Paul might snap.

Hester's worst worry, however, was that Fergus always seemed on the brink of forgetting her request for discretion. He left the large volumes of the *Encyclopedia Britannica* lying open at Toxicology and Forensic Medicine. He asked Barbara to bring him books on poison from the library. The idea of arsenic always seemed to be in the air.

"Is this your shopping list, ma'am?" asked Irene one morning. "I got it on the floor under the bath." Her face wore the buttoned-up expression of curiosity being suppressed.

Hester glanced at the piece of paper and saw that the list was not in her writing but Fergus's, a large bold hand easily read without glasses. It ran: "Fireworks, flypapers, artificial flowers, Scheele's green, insecticide, weed killer." "It's only some notes of Mr. Gandon's," she said, folding it. She hoped that no one who had not been reading up the subject would guess what all these commercial products had in common. They all contain arsenic, and offer a means of getting it into one's possession.

But what worried Hester even more than the fear of ideas getting into Irene's head was the idea of Mr. Paddy Purtill coming to tea. It seemed to her to be asking for trouble.

Fergus invited him. Mr. Purtill who knew, of course, from Nell where Fergus was staying, rang up one morning to enquire for him. Fergus, on being informed, leapt out of bed with an alacrity unexpected in a victim of poisoning hearing from one whom he has suspected of plotting to bring about his end.

"Hello, Paddy!" they heard him say. "How's yourself and how's the work?

Me, is it? Oh, I'm fine; at least I mean, lousy. I'm suffocating in respectability. Do come round and cheer me up. Hey, Paddy! Could you bring me round a watercolor box? Nell left mine behind, and I can't do any work."

He came back rubbing his hands and looking much better all of a sudden. Hester did not think he need have cast a slur on her hospitality.

She could not take him to task about Mr. Purtill because Barbara was present. Barbara was pleased at the prospect of meeting another artist. She knew Mr. Purtill's work. She had seen it hung in Royal Hibernian Academy exhibitions year after year as long as she could remember, which was at least four years back. She thought of him as one of the old guard, and was astonished to learn that he had been her uncle's pupil and was still quite young, but it did not make her any less interested in him.

Paul was some comfort. Hester discussed the situation with him that evening, out in the cold in the garden, the only place downstairs where they could get away from Fergus. At this time of year the Fennellys always spent a few minutes every evening peering into the earth to see what was coming up, and scattering little heaps of bran and slug killer round tender shoots. Paul said Fergus would never have invited Purtill if he had really been thinking of him as a Hidden Hand. Paul still thought Fergus' story was pure self-dramatization. What was there in it, after all, but a scare raised by an inexperienced country doctor ? Even if Fergus had taken arsenic it must have been by accident. If there had been the least doubt in Paul's mind he would have insisted on calling in the police.

Fergus then invited two more guests, though not suspects this time. One was his dealer, Arnold Silke, the other was a complete stranger.

Arnold Silke was the present head of Silkes' Galleries, a firm who had done business in the old days with Hester's and Fergus' father. It was the humane class of establishment where cash is subordinated to culture. The public were at all times cordially invited to view the collections, which were both of old and contemporary pictures. You could relieve your sense of obligation by buying pencils or paints in the art materials department or, of course, pictures, if you could afford them. You hardly ever saw anyone buying a picture, yet Silkes' flourished. These are the mysteries of the art world.

Old Mr. Gandon's business with old Mr. Silke had towards the end been to borrow money off him against unsalable canvases, while grumbling to his children about the grasping way of dealers who trafficked in the work of simple unmercenary-minded artists. At his death Paul had paid off the outstanding debt. Hester hoped history would not repeat itself. She was relieved to hear from Fergus that his work was selling steadily, and he could look his dealer in the eye.

The third guest, whose name was Mr. Fringley Pole, was a client of Silkes'. He was regrettably uninterested in contemporary art, but desired to inspect the collection of Old Masters at Kilskour Castle, and Arnold Silke had undertaken to procure him an introduction.

"Always pleased to do any friend of Arnold's a favor," said Fergus with a spacious gesture. " 'Bring him along,' I said, 'and I'll give him a note to my wife and tell him how to get there.' He'll be a little treat for Nell."

"I never knew there were pictures at Kilskour," said Hester.

"Dozens, dear," said Fergus. "Far more than anybody wants. Between you and me Kilskour wouldn't be sorry to part with some of them. No dealers, you know, but if this chap felt like making an offer, well—I could arrange it."

"On commission?" said Hester.

"Naturally."

Barbara had naturally tried to enlist her uncle's sympathy over the way she had not been allowed to buy a picture on which her heart was set. He at least, she thought, would agree that money was better spent on art than on personal adornment. Fergus told her not to be a fool.

"Never spend money on things you know nothing about," was his advice.

"But I knew it gave me pleasure," said Barbara.

"Ten to one it was a fake," said Fergus.

"Oh no, I'm sure it wasn't," said Barbara. Then she said, "Even if it was a fake, it was a lovely picture."

"So is a bank note for fifty pounds lovely, until you know it's forged."

Barbara did not think that was the same thing, but argument got her nowhere. She could not believe Fergus was sincere, and decided that he had been got at by her mother.

When Mr. Arnold Silke and his client entered the drawing room on the afternoon of the tea party, both Hester and Barbara immediately recognized in Mr. Fringley Pole the man who had secured the flower piece. He had unwound himself out of his striped scarf and left it with his overcoat and hat in the hall, but there was no mistaking his thin beaky nose, on which his rimless glasses sat slightly crooked. His chilblains must have broken, for his fingers were ringed with sticking plaster, and he shook hands only with the tips of them. He evidently could not place the two ladies; they had been sitting behind him, and also looked different in their indoor clothes; Hester was plumped in a quilted bridge coat for warmth, and Barbara was sheathed in a wool jersey frock which had drawn from Fergus the epithet "snakehips." Barbara at once revealed to him where they had met, and Hester was afraid she might find herself landed with the picture after all, but Mr. Fringley Pole had no intention of selling it, though he said it would fetch a hundred pounds in London. Barbara hoped her mother had heard.

Hester had heard, but was busy trying to prevent Arnold Silke upsetting Fergus by telling him how ill he looked. Silke was a small, neat, dark man with a sympathetic manner. He kept polishing a little magnifying glass, which he kept in his breast pocket, as if he would have liked to examine Fergus through it.

"My dear chap, you have got pulled down. It's easy to see how ill you've been. But now, is there really a perceptible improvement? You need not beat about the bush with me."

Hester said quickly that Fergus was much better and was thinking of starting some work.

"Good, good," said Mr. Silke. "Creative work is a strain, and painting can be tiring, especially oils, but still it would help to take his mind off himself. A little study in watercolor, perhaps. Some of these new tricks he has been trying. Have you seen any of his recent work, Mrs. Fennelly?"

Hester had not. She only knew that Fergus wandered round the house purloining objects which appealed to his artistic instinct. Ignoring the nice bits of china and furniture that his sister picked up at auctions, he grouped together such things as Mrs. Mulhall's wire egg whisk, an electric light bulb unscrewed from the landing light, an unripe pear from the late ones Paul was cherishing in the study, the head square that went with Barbara's country tweeds, and two lemons that were wanted to flavor a pudding. To Fergus it was all just still life, but it caused inconvenience when things were missed. The maids had complained again.

All this time Hester had a nervous eye on the door for the arrival of Mr. Paddy Purtill. Paul arrived first, a little in advance of his usual time, and she had tea sent up, and began to hope that her most sinister guest might not be coming, when there was rather a loud knock at the door, which caused a silence to fall, and Irene ushered the last visitor in.

Immediately they saw that he had not been warned it would be a party. It was obvious from his shabby clothes and look of reproach at Fergus. Fergus greeted him heartily

"Come in, Paddy, come in. Meet the family. We're too many men for once, but at any rate I've got one pretty girl for you." He thrust him at Barbara, who was annoyed to find herself blushing. "Doesn't she color up nicely?" remarked Fergus. "She's dying to meet you."

"One of these days, Fergus, someone will murder you," said Mr. Purtill.

Hester instinctively glanced at Fergus. Brother and sister were both struck by the same thought, but it simply would not do to catch Fergus' eye; he gave her a most obvious wink. Fergus was hopeless.

Mr. Purtill in the flesh did not seem at all the sinister figure of Hester's imagination. His appearance was most reassuringly normal in every way : a robust, tow-haired young man with no frills about him, clean-shaven, wearing a thick pullover over a gray shirt and slacks. His features were rugged, and one felt no doubt that he could use his fists, but it was hard to imagine that he had any touch of the Borgia about him. He had good manners but not much conversation. After recovering from his embarrassing introduction to Barbara he took no particular notice of her. Now Barbara was apt to make an impression on young men, and moreover was all prepared to be impressed by this one. Hester fancied he might be the kind of artist who likes women to be monumental, and it was probably all to the good.

The rugged Mr. Purtill and the debonair Mr. Silke, who knew each other in the way of business, exchanged amicable greetings and edged away from each other. Barbara, inspired by complicated feelings of pique blended with pity for the dullest person present, took up the task of conversation with that chilly middle-aged art lover, Mr. Fringley Pole. She said to him:

"My uncle thinks that a great many of the old pictures sold at auctions are really fakes."

Mr. Fringley Pole smiled.

"One must learn, of course, to exercise one's own judgment."

"Catalogue attributions are not to be taken seriously, you know, Miss Fennelly," said Arnold Silke. "The auctioneers guarantee nothing; they simply insert the description provided by the seller. And I expect you've noticed that every sale includes at least one Rembrandt."

"And two Reynolds and a Poussin," said Fergus.

"Some fakes must be very plausible," said Paul Fennelly. "The works of Mr. Van Meegeren, for instance, seem to have deceived all the experts."

"Van Meegeren wasn't the only one," said Fergus. "Anybody can take in an expert."

Mr. Fringley Pole said he thought there must be some psychological explanation for the occasional success of the most impudent impostures.

Paddy Purtill remarked in a deep voice that one way to be quite certain you were getting the genuine thing was to buy direct from the artist.

"Ah, but contemporary work is such a gamble," said Mr. Fringley Pole. "Reputations fluctuate so much before they are definitely made. When I buy a picture that has stood the test of time I can feel some confidence that it will hold its price. I am content to leave the moderns to the dealers and to the millionaires."

"He's right there, Paddy," said Fergus. " The likes of you and me can't expect to command the market in our lifetimes. I've got to wait till people get educated up to me, and you've got to die before the dealers can safely pass off your stuff as Constables or Wilson Steers."

If anyone thought this remark was intended as a compliment to Mr. Purtill's achievements they would have been disabused of the idea by the expression of intense annoyance that passed over his open countenance. Hester suspected there was some reference in what Fergus has said that had been deliberately aimed to get under the young man's skin. Fortunately he had no retort ready, and now Mr. Arnold Silke, a practiced conversationalist, was suavely taking charge.

"Everyone," he said, "abuses the unfortunate dealer. Let me put in a word in defense of my profession. Believe me, dealers are nothing like so grasping as private collectors. My father once had an old client in very reduced circumstances who had a pretty little picture by some eighteenth-century French painter. He offered her three hundred pounds for it, and he risked losing on it;

three hundred was the outside possible estimate of the picture's value, but it was a piece of disguised charity. Well, the old lady maintained it was a Watteau, treated my father as a robber, and died of semi-starvation with the picture still unsold. In the sale of her effects he picked it up for a mere fifty pounds. He sold it later for a hundred."

"Well, he reaped his reward," said Paul dryly.

"So people do still get bargains at sales," said Barbara.

"Oh certainly," said Mr. Silke. "Even Rembrandts are not always rubbish. Indeed people sometimes underrate the value of their own possessions, out of an anxiety to avoid wishful thinking. As a pendant to the other story: I knew an old lady who had a number of interesting pictures left her by a brother along with his house. I asked her to let us sell the lot for her, but she couldn't believe they would fetch enough to pay for re-papering the rooms to cover the marks they would leave on the walls. She died a few months back and her executors have been selling the pictures off at about half what we could have got for them. I remember one, a charming flower piece, unsigned, but I'm convinced it was a Van Huysum."

"Why, it might be the one you bought," said Barbara to Mr. Fringley Pole.

Fergus said, "I should think there's plenty of good stuff still hanging in country houses where nobody ever looks at the pictures or thinks about anything but huntin', fishin' and shootin'."

"Like the Boswell manuscript that turned up in a croquet box," said Barbara.

"I hear you're thinking of going down to Kilskour?" said Paul to Mr. Fringley Pole. "Are you in hopes of making discoveries?"

"No, no," said Mr. Fringley Pole with a deprecating smile. "I just happen to be specially interested in the minor Dutch masters, and I hear the collection is well worth a journey."

"Just the usual old stuff," said Fergus. "Hung up there by some ancestor who came over with William of Orange and never dusted since."

It may have been a trick of the light on Mr. Fringley Pole's glasses, but it seemed as if his eyes glittered.

Paddy Purtill, who had been the last to come, was the first to leave, slipping away as soon as he decently could, as if tea parties were not much in his line. He confessed to Paul, who saw him out, that he had been shocked by Fergus' looks.

"What's supposed to be wrong with him?" he asked.

Paul said guardedly that the doctor thought it might be some form of poisoning.

"Bad business," said young Mr. Purtill with a shake of his head. Then he mounted a bicycle and rode away.

Arnold Silke had hardly exchanged a word with Mr. Purtill as far as Hester knew, but he turned to Fergus as soon as the young man had gone and remarked that it had been delightful to meet him there like that.

"I was afraid you had quarreled for good and all," he said.

"Ah poor Paddy, I had to make it up with him," said Fergus. "Nell was upset about it, you know. Mind you, I haven't retracted a word I said. He knows my opinion, and he knows I'm right too, though he won't admit it. He's playing up to the demand, and he's ruining himself as an artist."

"Can one blame him?" murmured Mr. Silke, examining a piece of china through his magnifying glass.

"You needn't encourage him, anyway," said Fergus. "You may regret it one of these days."

"I? What can I do?" said Mr. Silke. "You know the position I'm in." He sighed. He put away the magnifying glass, seeming to recollect himself, and glancing apologetically at Hester.

"Has Mr. Purtill got a family to support?" asked Barbara.

Fergus gave her a quizzical look. "He's not married, if that's what you mean. He has a mother and sister, but he doesn't support them. The sister types and the mother lets rooms for the night."

"I think they feel that he could do more for them," said Arnold Silke. "They don't appreciate his work at all. It's not the best atmosphere in which to develop great gifts."

"No, his work's going all to pot," said Fergus, "and it's a pity when he knows better. After all, he was my pupil."

Mr. Fringley Pole, who took no interest in the moderns, was looking bored. Shortly afterwards Mr. Silke took him away. The dealer took an affectionate leave of Fergus, and at parting urged on him again the therapeutic value of a little experiment in watercolor.

CHAPTER 5

NOTHING much happened for two or three days after the tea party, and then: disaster.

There came a clear bright February day with a good light for painting, but it began ominously with a letter from Dr. Caraway by the morning post. This concerned the results of microanalysis of samples of hair from the members of the Gandon household. The sample from Fergus' beard showed that arsenic had been ingested at irregular intervals over a period of weeks. No trace of arsenic was found in any of the other samples. Dr. Caraway considered that this strengthened the hypothesis of crime against accident, and that there was now sufficient evidence on which to appeal to the Civic Guards. He thought it might even be his duty to do so and pressed Fergus to reconsider his objections.

Fergus passed Hester the letter remarking, "I told you so," but appeared more interested in unpacking a parcel which came by the same post from Nell.

It contained his own paintbox at last, with a pair of socks and a pound of butter. In ordinary circumstances the butter would have been welcome, for Fergus was heavy on the ration. But Hester's reaction to the doctor's letter was that he ought not to eat anything coming from Kilskour, not even from Nell. She took it away and hid it, and Fergus most unreasonably sulked.

He shut himself up in his bedroom to paint a complicated composition he had evolved out of the racks for making ice cubes in the metal trays of the refrigerator—lemons, grapefruit, and a gadget belonging to the vacuum cleaner.

Irene wanted the gadget when she was doing the rooms and boldly went to ask for it. Fergus roared at her to get out, and threw a sponge at her which hit her in the eye. It had paint on it. Irene came down with yellow streaks on her indignant face, and gave Hester notice.

Hester tried to explain what artists were like when jarred out of the creative dream, but she could not blame the girl for being annoyed. Irene was too frightened of Fergus to take up his lunch (they had found it saved trouble to bring him his meals on a tray wherever he was working; it was useless to expect him to come down). Hester took up coffee and sandwiches to him herself. Fergus was painting with intense concentration, for one cannot mess about with watercolor; it is hit or miss. She knew he hoped she would go away on tiptoe, respecting his work. She said coldly:

"Irene has just given me notice because you threw things at her."

"Damnation!" said Fergus. "Look what you made me do!" He snatched his brush back from the paper, licked the paint off it and thrust it back nervously into the box. Hester knew it was no good. She left his tray on a chair by the bedroom door and went down to have lunch with Barbara and discuss the prospects of getting another houseparlormaid. Irene had been a good, conscientious girl, not easy to replace.

They were having coffee when the first sounds from upstairs reached them. Doors violently opened and shut; hurried, unsteady footsteps; Fergus being very sick in the bathroom with the door open. He had had another attack.

The whole household of four women hurried to his help. Hester gave rapid orders for hot bottles and hot tea, for the bed to be got ready at once. She stayed by the patient, but told Barbara to telephone urgently for Dr. Colville.

"Tell him it's arsenic," she said.

Barbara stared at her.

Dr. Colville was starting his afternoon consultations. He deserted a waiting room full of patients and came at once. He and Hester organized the battle for Fergus' life. Barbara telephoned messages and ran errands. She put through a call to the doctor at Kilskour and asked him to break the news to Nell. It was the most direct means they had of communicating with her, and Dr. Colville thought she should be sent for.

Dr. Caraway at Kilskour sounded young and sympathetic. He could not have been more kind. After a shocked pause he became immediately helpful. He would not only break the news to Nell; he would drive her up to town himself. It was the only thing if she was to get there that evening. They were not to worry about him; eighty miles there and back was nothing.

For the first two hours Hester was tied to the patient's side. She held the patient's head, helped the doctor administer antidotes in teaspoonfuls, cleaned up messes, provided spare linen, and had no time to think.

Then two professional nurses came to her relief. She found herself all of a sudden with nothing to do at all. She sat down by the study fire, cold all through with nervous exhaustion, dully wishing herself back to the morning, to the time before anything had happened. Fergus' enemy had found him out in her house, in the midst of their happy security, and in spite of their watchful care. She found herself staring round the room at all its familiar contents—the ripening pears, Paul's gardening books, her own embroidery, and Fergus' Turkish cigarettes, which could faintly be smelt in the air. It seemed fantastic that they should all look just as usual, as if they expected people to take an interest in them again and go on as before.

Fergus might die before the day was out. But if he lived they had only won that round; the threat hung over him, and over them all.

She roused herself out of her meditations. The doctor had warned her that certain specimens must be kept for analysis, and she wished to find somewhere to lock up the unpleasant messes she had left in the bathroom till experts could take them in charge.

She found that the wretched tidy-minded Irene, who had to be doing something, had thrown everything down the drain. She had also cleared away and washed up the remains of Fergus' lunch.

Hester's nerves were unstrung. Though it was too late to be any use she berated Irene as she had never berated a maid before. Irene imagined that she had been helpful ; she knew nothing about any question of poison and could not understand what all the fuss was about. She had half intended to withdraw her notice, feeling that Mr. Gandon had been sufficiently punished by heaven. This unjust scolding quite changed her mind about that. She went off to pack her bag.

Hester told Dr. Colville what had happened. He said there was no use crying over spilled milk, but that it was unfortunate, to say the least.

They went into the study. Hester sat on the edge of the seat of an armchair, and Dr. Colville balanced on the arm of one, his foot waggling with impatience to be off, for his afternoon engagements had all been shelved and a dozen things and people awaited his attention. But he looked down at Hester professionally through his horn-rimmed glasses and told her she must take care of her own health and that it would not help the patient for her to go wearing herself out. Hester nodded wearily. The door closed with a dull thud behind the departing houseparlormaid.

Dr. Colville said: "You do realize this is a matter for the police?"

"Yes," said Hester. "Will you tell them?"

"Yes, I'll report it. The only thing is, I'd like a word with his own doctor first."

"He'll be here before long," said Hester. There had been a telephone message to say that Dr. Caraway and Nell had started.

"Then I think it could wait till he arrives. It would be better, I think, for me not to have the appearance of going behind his own doctor's back. But would you phone me as soon as he comes?" He glanced at his watch. "I must go," he said. "The nurses can carry on all right. Don't lose hope. It was a lucky thing we knew what poison we had to deal with. Oh, one thing more! Be a bit careful what you eat, the rest of you. Better lock up what you've got in the house and get in fresh stuff to be on the safe side."

Hester had thought of that, and had sent Barbara to the shops.

Dr. Colville said he would be out in ten minutes if Hester telephoned and repeated his advice about not wearing herself out. Then he bustled away, a good doctor but a somewhat fussy man, punctilious about etiquette towards fellow practitioners and not fond of being mixed up in a police case. He tried not to show his distaste, but Hester understood.

The door of the study was flung suddenly back and in came Mrs. Mulhall, the cook, in a dirty apron and exuding the smell of onions. Hester supposed she had come to give notice too, and waited stoically, for she had reached the grim mood in which one almost welcomes an aggravation of one's difficulties. But instead, it seemed that Mrs. Mulhall had come to swear fealty, and especially to exhibit herself in a noble light compared with Irene, whom she had never liked. The fact was, Mrs. Mulhall welcomed any break in the monotony of everyday life, such as is provided by a funeral. She was looking forward to Mr. Gandon's, and it would have been her idea of a pleasant afternoon to sit by Mrs. Fennelly on the drawing room sofa, wiping away her tears.

Hester thought that even if Mrs. Mulhall was prepared to be magnanimous about illness in the house, she would hardly overlook such a *gaffe* on the part of her employers as getting mixed up in a murder case, especially a poison case, which might cast reflections on the cooking. She might as well be told now; there would be no room for any more concealment when detectives arrived on the doorstep. She put the whole situation plainly before her, and Mrs. Mulhall listened in ghoulish fascination; it was the biggest thing that had ever happened to her; life was coming near the films. Giving notice had never been further from her thoughts; she would not miss the detectives for worlds.

The afternoon transformed Mrs. Mulhall from a domestic of six months' precarious standing into a faithful old retainer of the kind one can never get rid of. Adversity singles out those whom we can truly trust, but also causes us to incur obligations we are saddled with for life.

After telling Mrs. Mulhall, Hester braced herself for the worse task of explaining everything to Barbara, who had just come in from the shops. The child was already shaken by Fergus' sudden collapse; it was cruel to open her eyes to further horrors. Till then she had had no idea of the unknown enemy in the background, the deliberate intention at work. Hester spared her all she could and said nothing of suspicion resting on anyone in particular, especially not on anyone known to them. She said, "Your uncle has many queer acquaintances, like anyone who has knocked about a lot." She also emphasized that no one was in danger but Fergus. The strangest feature of the case was that that each time the poisoner had been able to single him out.

Barbara was terrified. Yet she was sustained by a feeling that she now knew what life was like. Her mother had found her a help in a crisis (Hester stressed this in order to encourage her). This was a testing time, and Barbara would be strong. She had inner resources denied to her mother—the strength to be found in books and works of art. To distract her mind she would go up and look at her favorite reproductions. But first she would make her mother a cup of tea.

Hester swallowed it to please her. Then they both went away and cried in separate rooms.

Paul came in late. It was he who had tracked down and successfully engaged the two nurses, and his own business day had consequently been prolonged. But Paul was a man who generally contrived to be looked after, and he had had tea made for him by his typist. When he got home he went straight out to the garden before the light faded, and Hester found him spreading newspaper over a box of geranium cuttings. He was surprised she had not noticed that the weather had grown colder and it looked like frost.

Paul was not worrying about Fergus. Was not everything possible being done? Paul did not believe in worrying, but he was not unfeeling. When they went in to the fire and there was the paper lying by his chair with the crossword puzzle for once completely blank, he put it away from him without a glance.

Hester stood by the fire, trying to get warm.

Paul asked for the letter that had come from Dr. Caraway that morning, and which he had only read through hastily before he left for town. Hester had locked it in the desk drawer with the housekeeping money, so it was close to hand. Paul said, holding up the analyst's report:

"We shall want this to show the police."

Hester shivered.

"What will they do, Paul?"

"Oh just ask a few questions, nothing to be afraid of. It's a very good thing to be getting experts on the job at last."

"We haven't any choice, have we?" said Hester. "I wish I knew why Fergus was so much against it."

"You don't think it was just a spirit of independence?"

"No, I don't. I think he has something to hide."

"Well, you know," said Paul, "that had occurred to me too. But it need not necessarily be anything discreditable. Fergus has knocked about a lot and probably knows large numbers of shady characters. He may be sheltering some old pal from the law. He would."

Hester sighed. "Maybe. But it's just as likely he's been up to something himself. Fergus never had any particular scruples. What I dread, Paul, is that you may get dragged into some scandal on Fergus' account. I've always dreaded it."

Indeed, Paul's good name was something of an obsession with Hester. Having grown up herself amid the shifts of a family to which banks and tradesmen were increasingly reluctant to give credit, she was almost exaggeratedly proud of her husband's high standing in the business world. It seemed to her as if Paul's good name was a precious, fragile possession which a mere breath of scandal would shatter, and which was in great peril from the irresponsible actions of her own relations. Paul was less easily alarmed.

"Yes," he said, "it does look as if the silly ass had got mixed up in something. If only we knew what, we'd probably know everything, and the police could go straight to the address of the fellow who's out to poison him."

"No, because Fergus doesn't know."

"I bet he does," said Paul. "He must have an inkling. Stands to reason a man would know who was likely to be murdering him."

"I don't think he has, Paul. Unless—"

"Unless?" said Paul, as Hester stopped and stood frowning into the fire. She crossed her arms on the mantelpiece and leaned her forehead on them as if her head was bursting.

"Unless," she said, "Fergus really means it about Nell. It's so hard to tell. At the time I didn't think he was serious, but you know what he said. If the police were called in, Nell would be the one they'd suspect. Whatever she might have done, he couldn't face seeing her arrested. One can understand that."

Paul sat up. "The butter!" he exclaimed.

"Not Nell's butter. I hid that."

Paul relaxed. "Good thing you did, that's one thing off. Not that I seriously suspected Nell for one moment."

"Didn't you? I did. It seems so clear that she was the only person with an opportunity to do anything. Except Mosney, of course. I don't see how one could help suspecting her."

"I don't know Nell very well," said Paul, "but I must say I always thought her a good sort with no nonsense about her."

"She's a very attractive woman, and a type that makes an impression on men."

"Oh come now, she doesn't lay herself out to be attractive. She's generally rather untidy, as I remember her."

Hester gave him a pitying look.

"It seems as if she has been flirting dangerously, by Fergus' account. It doesn't follow, of course, that she has no conscience."

"Fergus is the most frightful liar," said Paul. Recollecting Fergus' position at death's door he qualified his statement. "I don't mean he deliberately tells lies, I only mean what Fergus says isn't evidence."

"He isn't completely irresponsible," said Hester. "Well, not completely. I do think he may have had some provocation."

"To my mind," said Paul, moving to less controversial ground, "by far the most likely explanation is that your brother has fallen foul of some queer fish he picked up on his travels. Very likely someone who's already known to the police. They keep track of aliens and they'll be able to put their hands on him."

Fergus Gandon's friends abroad were not only foreigners but artists, not only artists but foreigners. In Paul's view anything might be expected of them.

"This last bad go Fergus is having may be a lesson to him," said Paul, looking on the bright side. "He'll have to make a clean breast of things. He must see we can't have that kind of thing happening in this house."

"You needn't talk as if it was poor Fergus' fault, Paul. We ought to have prevented it. But how could we? Can you think of anything at all that we could have done? We seem so helpless—"

Hester, who had been about to try her husband's patience with a fit of hysterics, took fresh hold of herself. A car was drawing up at the door.

"That must be Nell," she said. The Fennellys prepared their faces for meeting a sister-in-law in ambiguous circumstances.

CHAPTER 6

NELL GANDON stumbled in out of the dark wearing a man's overcoat which quite swallowed her up and made her look particularly forlorn. She looked cold and dazed and had been crying. She stared wildly round and demanded to be taken to Fergus.

Hester hesitated involuntarily. She murmured something about asking the nurses first. Nell leapt to the conclusion that Fergus was dead. She collapsed sobbing. Hester remorsefully put her arms round her, but the effort of supporting another in the flood tide of emotion made her realize suddenly that she was deathly tired herself.

The hall seemed crowded to suffocation. Barbara had crept down from her room to support her parents, and Mrs. Mulhall had dropped her dinner preparations and bustled out from the kitchen to see the wife of the murdered man. One of Fergus' two nurses had come quietly out of his room and was peering discreetly down through the banisters, trying to catch somebody's eye. The space seemed filled to capacity when it somehow enlarged itself to include an outsize young man, who wore two pullovers under a zip-fastening golf jacket that declined to zip across the width of his chest. Obviously Dr. Caraway, and the chiv-

alrous owner of the coat encasing Nell. Obviously too, a descendant or a reincar-
nation of the ancient Danes, such as keep cropping up in Ireland. He was looking
at his watch and remarked that eighty miles in just over the hour and a half was
not bad going in a ten-year-old Ford-ten.

"There's a fog on the bog roads too," he said. "Lord Kilskour wouldn't
have done it much quicker in the Hillman on a night like this."

"Oh, but are we really in time?" sobbed Nell. "Don't keep things from
me. Don't think I can't bear to know."

"Nurse?" said Hester helplessly. The nurse came downstairs in a rustle of
starched linen, and took charge of Nell.

"Don't worry now, Mrs. Gandon. Worry never helped anybody. Your
husband's fairly comfortable—"

"Comfortable! I don't believe it."

"Fairly comfortable," repeated the nurse placidly, "and we've given him
something to make him sleep. When he wakes up he'll be able to talk to you a
little."

"I want to go to him."

"Suppose you have a nice cup of tea first, Mrs. Gandon. You must be tired
after coming such a long way in the cold."

Mrs. Mulhall, who had been prepared for this, darted into the kitchen and
returned with tea in Hester's largest teapot which was silver and slightly tar-
nished from lying out of use. She dumped the tray down, causing the milk to
slop over and a jet of hot tea to shoot from the spout as from a flame thrower
over the polished surface of one of Hester's cherished pieces—a Sheraton
table that stood by the drawing-room door.

"There now," said the nurse, pouring out. "There's nothing like a nice cup
of tea."

Nell Gandon took the cup and sipped at it as if mesmerized. The nurse
began a whispered conversation with Dr. Caraway. Hester surreptitiously moved
over to her precious table and mopped it with her handkerchief, as it seemed
callous to send for a cloth.

"I'll just have a look at him," said Dr. Caraway.

"I'm coming with you," said Nell, putting down her cup with a clatter.
"Do get out of the way, woman," she said to the nurse, who only smiled brightly
and said to Hester that she was quite used to patients' next-of-kin being upset.
To label Nell "next-of-kin" struck Hester as dreadfully funereal.

Paul was telephoning to Dr. Colville, to let him know his fellow practitioner had arrived.

"Please, ma'am, how many will there be for dinner?" asked Mrs. Mulhall.
Hester didn't know. Mrs. Mulhall then asked if it was too soon to put on the
fish. Hester thought it was. All through her more desperate anxieties ran an
undercurrent of such problems.

Dr. Caraway came downstairs again alone. The Fennellys pulled themselves together and invited him into the study. He sat down heavily in Paul's

armchair, and they thought his expression looked reassuring, but it might have been only his native geniality. He was the kind of doctor who does his patients good by looking the picture of health himself, but who does not really know what it feels like to be them.

Paul offered him whiskey, but he said he never drank when driving. Barbara brought in tea from the hall and went to look for further nourishment for this large young man who had come eighty miles. There seemed a great deal of him to nourish.

"You know," said Dr. Caraway confidentially, "there are points of awkwardness about this case. Er, did he tell you all the ins and outs of it?"

"He told us somebody was trying to poison him with small, repeated doses of arsenic. May I ask if that's your idea too?"

"Well, it's hard to see what else to think," said Dr. Caraway. "He told you about the analyst's report on all their hair? And this last attack seems to clinch it. It's not a very pleasant business for all of you."

"Nor for him," said Hester.

"Nor for his wife," said Dr. Caraway. "She's in an awful state about it. I expect you noticed. As a matter of fact it's come as rather a bolt from the blue to her. We'd kept it from her up to now, about the arsenic you know, and foul play being suspected. Least said, soonest mended. But she made me tell her the whole story on the drive up. It was the only thing to do, wasn't it?" He appealed to the Fennellys ingenuously. "It seemed best to pave the way a bit. You see, I thought we might arrive to find the police actually on the spot."

Hester looked at Paul. "So she knows," she said. "How did she take it?"

"Couldn't believe it," said Dr. Caraway. "I'm not sure how far she's taken it in, even yet. Naturally it's an idea that takes a bit of getting used to."

"Yes, it does," said Hester.

"Er, about the police—" said Dr. Caraway with diffidence.

"We're all in agreement about that," said Paul. "The sooner we get them here the better. Dr. Colville, who should be here any minute, just wanted to have a talk with you before he reported the matter, so as to be able to put the whole thing before them at once."

"Good!" said Dr. Caraway. They could see he was not sorry to be able to share the responsibility.

Barbara came in with sandwiches. "They're egg and cress," she said. "Eggs must be safe and the cress was grown in my room on clean flannel. The bread only came this afternoon, after it happened. The butter's margarine, I'm afraid, but it's quite safe, just as it came from the shop."

Dr. Caraway had not waited for this detailed guarantee. He nodded cheerfully with his mouth full. Presently he asked. "Have you no idea what did it?

"He'd just had lunch," said Hester. "I'd brought it up to him not twenty minutes before. Coffee and sandwiches. Ham, not egg and cress," she added.

"Twenty minutes? Too quick," said the doctor.

"I know." Hester's reading had included this. "But before that he hadn't, as far as we know, had anything since breakfast at nine, which would be rather a long time, wouldn't it?"

"It all depends. But it's a funny thing," said Dr. Caraway, "that we've never yet been able to track it down to anything he's eaten. Never a trace of arsenic in any foodstuffs I could get hold of to analyze. Of course, one difficulty was to get hold of all the doings. We couldn't always, without Mrs. Gandon knowing."

"From now on," said Paul, "we shall have the advantage of everything being in the open. We shall simply lay all the facts before the police and let them reach their own conclusions."

It sounded quite simple as Paul said it.

Dr. Colville arrived as Dr. Caraway was on his last sandwich. The Fennellys retired into the background, leaving the field to the doctors and nurses.

Dr. Colville was calmer by now. His day's work was done except for Fergus; there was only this one visit between him and his dinner. He summed up Dr. Caraway at a glance as a young man who would be no trouble. If one must be associated with a country practitioner on a murder case it is convenient to have him young, deferential, and imbued with professional solidarity. Neither of them would suggest that the case could have been reported earlier.

Dr. Colville's first action was to turn Nell out of Fergus' room. He spoke to her kindly, but his expression betrayed antipathy for women who broke down over sickbeds.

He and Dr. Caraway then had rather a long conference in the study, while Nell was with difficulty restrained from listening at the door. She could not be persuaded to go up to her own room, or into the drawing room to sit down, but took root in the hall and kept her brother- and sister-in-law standing there too. Mrs. Mulhall, who was getting more and more anxious to put the fish on, opened the kitchen door and shut it again every few minutes.

It was Paul who unwarily made the first reference to the police being called in and precipitated a scene.

"That's out of the question," said Nell. "Fergus wouldn't like that at all."

"On the contrary," said Hester, "it's settled. I'm afraid we just have to make up our minds to it."

"But if Fergus won't have it?"

"I'm afraid we can't wait for him to be asked."

"I tell you, he'd be furious. You don't know how anything like that would upset him, and above all he mustn't excite himself. I can't let you take the risk."

"It might be better if Fergus did not know just yet," said Hester. "I am sure that could be explained to them."

"Not know? Of course he'd know. How could anyone help knowing if the house was full of detectives? Besides, they'd want to cross-question him."

"Not till the doctors gave permission."

"We must take precautions against any further accidents," said Paul.

"Precautions, my God! You're going the right way about it if you want to kill him."

"I'm sorry, Nell," said Paul, "but the matter really is out of our hands. The doctors are obliged to report a case of this kind. It's the law."

"Can't the law wait till a person dies?"

"Don't, Nell!" cried Hester. "Don't speak of Fergus dying!"

"Weren't you all expecting him to?" said Nell. "Otherwise I don't suppose I should have been told anything, even yet. I'm only his next-of-kin, the last person to be consulted. What a time the doctors are in there! What can they be talking about? Brian! Dr. Caraway!" She rapped on the study door.

"Nell!" said Hester, scandalized. But the doctors were just coming out. Nell instantly appealed to the younger one for support, but it was Dr. Colville who answered

"I'm afraid the matter doesn't admit of argument any longer, Mrs. Gandon. We must look facts in the face. What Dr. Caraway has been telling me leaves no room for the slightest vestige of doubt that your husband has long been suffering from the cumulative effects of a series of slight doses of arsenic. I had already formed my own opinion of this culminating attack. We are not only bound to report the case; it is the wisest thing we can do in the patient's own interests and in your interests."

"But didn't Dr. Caraway tell you that my husband expressly told him it was against his wishes?"

"Now, why should your husband mind?" said Dr. Colville, looking penetratingly at this obstructive woman.

Nell seemed momentarily at a loss but rallied quickly.

"That isn't the point, Doctor. The point is that he would mind; did mind very strongly. My husband is given to strong prejudices. He hates to be crossed. You don't know my husband as I do." Her tone changed to pleading. "He's an artist highly strung—"

"The police shall not disturb him without our permission," said Dr. Colville. "Try not to worry so much, Mrs. Gandon. There is no use, you know, in wearing yourself out. That won't help the patient. Take care of your own health if you want to do the best thing for him."

"Stop, stop!" interrupted Nell. "Stop before you make me scream."

"Take some aspirin when you go to bed," said Dr. Colville putting on his coat. "One tablet or two, you know yourself what is your usual dose. Now, Caraway, if you're ready we'll be going."

"Where?" said Nell.

"To the Guard barracks."

Nell drew herself up. "Dr. Colville, if—if my husband dies, I shall hold you responsible."

"Madam, if your husband dies—which we are doing our best to prevent— the police will no doubt be able to fix the responsibility."

Everyone was against Nell: her in-laws exchanging long-suffering glances, her stalwart escort turning yes-man to the Dublin dictator. Dr. Caraway offered her some ill-advised consolation.

"The Guards are mostly very decent, Mrs. Gandon. I'm sure you'll find them considerate."

Nell gave him a withering look and turned away with compressed lips. Dr. Caraway picked up his overcoat from the floor, and the two doctors went out.

Mrs. Mulhall shut the kitchen door and put on the fish.

CHAPTER 7

THE following afternoon a number of persons met in conference on the Gandon case in Dublin Castle.

The Castle in Dublin is a compendious building, the equivalent, more or less, of Buckingham Palace, the Tower, Whitehall, and Scotland Yard all rolled into one. The former Chapel Royal and what are still the State Apartments stand out in the middle of a large courtyard circled round by other buildings, which are honeycombed with little offices for civil servants. From this court you proceed through an archway to the headquarters of the metropolitan division of the Civic Guard and the offices of the Detective Branch.

It is a little like entering a Cambridge college; there is the same atmosphere of a masculine sanctuary and the same incongruous glimpses of preparations for meals; also the same sensation of being surrounded by history which you ought to look up. One would like to be sure, for instance, exactly which tower was the scene of a famous escape by Red Hugh O'Donnell. Red Hugh would find the dice weighted against him now, what with a radio set in one little room off the inner court calling all cars and teleprinter machines installed in odd corners here and there tapping out messages to police stations all over the city. These items of equipment look out of place in their ancient setting, but they are much in use, the teleprinters especially. Little jobs like bicycle stealing, theft from cars, pilfering, pocket picking, bag snatching, housebreaking, damage to property, come in over the teleprinters from the various metropolitan stations at the rate of about a hundred a day. All the details of each have to be filled in on forms, circulated to various departments, and indexed under at least six separate headings in the criminal record office. The taxpayer is getting all this for his money, even if he never sees the Flying Squad called out.

Dublin cannot be called a very wicked city, as cities go. There is a dearth of ex-public school jewel thieves, beautiful foreign spies, international crooks, sinister Chinamen of the old school, mad inventors of death rays, and much that makes life interesting for the police of other countries. The human side of the work, apart from the perpetual filling up of forms, is mostly concerned with habitual criminals born and bred in the slums who go drifting in and out of jail all their lives without very much option, unemployables to whom no more respectable form of existence is open. Improvements in housing, education, the penal system and the probation system may reduce their numbers, but can hardly completely rid society of its inevitable substratum. Experience, for a detective, largely consists in getting to know the criminal classes and all their relations. Between the Civic Guards and the habitual criminals it is all very much in the family. Mere ordinary householders who get robbed are only of minor, incidental importance.

The complex machinery of the records is founded on the depressing fact that crime generally becomes a habit. So long as it is all in the family, you can solve any problem by turning up a card in the files to see who has committed just that sort of offense in that particular way before. But murder cannot be allowed to develop into habit. This makes murder mysteries peculiarly troublesome and much too much like work. They are also too apt to attract publicity, so that anything the detectives may do wrong is sure to be brought home to them. They may recover stolen bicycles by the thousand without ever a word said, but not to be able to state offhand who has been poisoning a celebrated artist in the comfortable suburban home of a respectable stockbroker, for no obvious motive and by some means that eludes observation, is to bring discredit on the Force.

No wonder there were gloomy faces round the inkstained table in the bare room warmed by one small electric fire, with light fading in uncurtained windows, but glaring down from an unshaded bulb. Through the windows could be seen the civil service calling it a day. For the Detective Branch the day was nominally an hour longer, but with a new case opening up and Detective Superintendent Lancey appointed O.C. Investigation, nobody need entertain any hope of getting off at six o'clock.

It made things still more unsatisfactory that the victim was not even dead. You cannot hold a post mortem until a man is dead, and a murder case ought to begin with a post mortem, following the customary routine. The only person present who was glad Fergus Gandon had not been completely finished off by his latest dose of poison was a keen young Guard only recently promoted to the Detective Branch, whose name was Mick Lemon. Mick was out for experience and had great hopes of assisting for the first time at a dying declaration.

They had reached the stage defined as follows on page 11 of the Manual of Criminal Investigation or General Murphy's Book (this is the young detective's bible): "When the primary stages of an investigation have been concluded and it appears that no immediate success is likely to be achieved, the facts of the case should be reviewed, the evidence analyzed, and further lines of enquiry determined. Personnel should then be allocated to each of these lines of enquiry."

It was the task of Detective Superintendent Lancey to allocate the personnel.

He was more in the position of secretary to a committee than of hound leading the pack. For years his work on crime had been confined to paper filing, indexing, and cross-referencing documents and knocking evidence into shape for presentation to a state solicitor. For years he had not been near the scene of a crime, and he seldom met any of the principals in a case.

Once upon a time a lady had called on Lancey in his lair and put him on the way to solving a mysterious affair of aconitine poisoning. To her he owed his promotion to the rank of superintendent.* In spite of this he did not encourage visits from ladies or any kind of outsiders. He was a hermit by nature. His superiors thought of him as a fine type of hard-working and conscientious officer and his juniors as a dry old stick.

Lancey was a long way from being the most important person at the conference. It was blessed by the presence of such VIPs as the divisional superintendent of metropolitan police in whose area the crime had been reported, and the district superintendent over the country district which comprehended Kilskour. Also the superintendent over the Technical Bureau of Information, which is where the backroom boys of the Civic Guard go to work in laboratories on material clues such as bullets, bloodstains, fingerprints and dust.

Under them, the men to do the actual detecting on the spot were a sergeant and detective inspector from the staff of the Guard barracks nearest the Fennellys' residence; a sergeant from Clogh, the nearest barracks to Kilskour; various experts from the technical bureau, and two staff men from the Branch. All of them had definite jobs to do, with Lancey to see there was no overlapping. Some might soon be out of the case, others would find it coming their way and the work piling up for them. Any of them might happen to make a brilliant contribution, but nobody was cast for the role of supersleuth.

Healy, the district superintendent from the country, and the longest promoted of the VIPs, automatically took the chair. He was the very opposite of Lancey: a sociable countryman, fond of sport, and a great man for knowing everything and everybody. He had met everybody at the conference before except Detective Officer Michael Lemon, the junior of the two Branch men and rawest recruit, and him he made a point of shaking hands with before the meeting and mentioning that he knew his aunt. He also gave them all a tip for the Grand National. Then he came briskly to business, remarking that the first thing to do was to discover the motive for the crime and then they would know who did it. Collecting proof would then be just routine.

Lancey said that unfortunately there was no motive really, as you might say, sticking out. It didn't seem as if it was money; everyone knew there was no money in art. If Gandon died nobody that he could see was going to be financially any better off. It might be working off a grudge; the man had certainly had his quarrels. The most likely thing on the whole was sex, in which case it would be Mrs. Gandon, but in spite of sex being one of the commonest kinds of motive he had a feeling this time that it was not so easy as that.

"Haven't the family any ideas themselves?" said Healy.

The two men from the local barracks who had gone back with the doctors to the house, the two Branch men who had been sent out later and had taken statements, and the metropolitan divisional superintendent who had rolled round majestically in the morning to show an interest, all said that nobody had accused anybody or dropped any hints or even bricks. The Fennellys had been exceptionally discreet and had taken refuge from the first under the wing of the family solicitor. It had not yet been possible to interview the victim himself.

Fergus Gandon had been taken to hospital and was in a private ward with a Civic Guard sitting outside the door.

"The first pointer," said Lancey, "is that Mrs. Gandon made a scene about calling in the police. We got that from the cook. Nobody else had said a word about it but they all confirmed it when asked. Dr. Colville said he thought it was just hysteria, but Dr. Caraway had a different idea about it. He said the objection to the police began with her husband and she was only standing up for him according to her lights. That's what she said herself, too. She just knew he wouldn't approve because of his prejudices. He's agin the police on principle. The police are the protectors of bourgeois morality, and he isn't a bourgeois, he's an artist."

Lancey was skimming through Nell Gandon's statement. Duplicated copies of everybody's statements lay before each member of the conference. "The Fennellys," he continued, "confirm that Gandon had mentioned his objections to them. She isn't just making it all up."

"He's been up to something illegal and she knows," the chairman summed up. "It may or may not have any bearing on the crime. She might have been counting on him being afraid to call us in. Any gossip about Mrs. Gandon and any other man?"

He looked at Sergeant Nolan from the barracks at Clogh, who had driven up with him that afternoon. Nolan had been telling him all he knew about the Gandons on the way. Nolan knew, without words actually spoken, that the district superintendent would not like to have any annoyance caused to a leading resident like Lord Kilskour unless there was solid ground for action.

Nolan was of two minds about the case. He had been stationed ten years at Clogh, a village where the incidence of crime was not more than would barely support a sergeant and three Guards. For the last nine years his wife had been wishing for a change and asking why he didn't get promotion. This case might be his big chance. On the other hand, it might be a big chance to make a fool of himself.

"There's been talk," he said cautiously. "She went driving a good bit with Lord Kilskour when he was over last. You know what it is in a small place. The people haven't got enough to talk about in those parts, with no war on. What gave it some color was that Lord Kilskour had a disagreement with Mr. Gandon and they were known not to be on speaking terms, but the cause of that was something else altogether. It was Mr. Gandon painted something on a wall which his lordship said was damage to property. Lord Kilskour threatened to have him in the courts, but nothing came of it. I shouldn't wonder if Mrs. Gandon talked his lordship round."

"Maybe she went too far," murmured somebody.

"What's Mrs. Gandon like?" asked the metropolitan divisional superintendent. Nell had not shown up when he called.

"Regular scarecrow, sir," said Nolan. "Goes about dressed in slacks and with her hair streeling. You couldn't accuse her of laying herself out."

This drew protests from four or five of the men who had seen Mrs. Gandon at the Fennellys. They had got an impression of a smartly dressed woman wearing bright red and lipstick to match. Silk stockings, too, or rather, according to the trained observation of Detective Officer Michael Lemon, nylons. The slacks had concealed from Sergeant Nolan the fact that she had a right pair of legs.

Healy nipped an animated discussion in the bud, saying that they had no time to waste on side issues. Sex was only one angle. Family quarrels were another, but on the face of it the Gandons' Dublin relations seemed to be above suspicion. The next thing was, what about the servants?

Sergeant Nolan cleared his throat. His manner conveyed both a desire to be impartial and an intimation that in his opinion they were now getting nearer the mark.

"That man they have called Mosney," he said. "I've had my doubts about him ever since he came. He turned up from nowhere a couple of years back and he's been in jail; you've only got to look at him. We never got anything on him; no complaints of pilfering or petty larceny out Kilskour way or anything of that kind. He's regular at Chapel and he doesn't drink. Too cute to drink, that's my guess. To all appearances he's been running straight, but he's a mystery man and some class of a chancer, I make no doubt. Well, to make a long story short, at 9:55 a.m. this morning, on receipt of instructions, I proceeded to Kilskour and interviewed Mosney, and he didn't tell me anything I didn't know already, but while I was at it I got his fingerprints, without his knowledge, and here they are for whatever they're worth." He opened a tin box and disclosed a cigarette carton. It was quite a dramatic moment.

There wasn't much to see beyond a portion of one print. Those who crowded round to look at it needed no warning not to touch. Powdering would bring up the rest, with luck, but even a fragment of a print is often enough for identification. Lancey handed the box to a fingerprint expert who was eager to do his stuff.

While he was away Healy went on with his review. The housemaid who had left the Fennellys so suddenly had to be followed up. She had taken her night things in a bag and had not yet sent for the rest of her luggage, and had not left an address. But it seemed likely she would reappear. Unlike Mosney, she had come to the Fennellys with excellent references, rather too many of them and covering somewhat brief periods of employment, but accounting for her movements for some six years back. She was well known at the Registry Office from which Mrs. Fennelly had engaged her and seemed to be a girl of good character, as characters go in these days.

Mrs. Mulhall likewise had served with the clergy and nobility and kept herself unspotted by the world.

But as Sergeant Nolan suspected it was otherwise with Mosney. The fingerprint expert came back in high fettle. He had found good prints on the box and had proceeded to classify them. For the untrained eye this would require the help of photography; an enlarged reproduction facilitates the counting of loops and whorls. But the expert was a fellow who knew his papillary ridges and had no need to wait for such aids. He laid before Superintendent Lancey a sheaf of papers which everyone recognized as a dossier from the Habitual Criminal Records.

Mosney was not Mosney; he was Geraghty, and what he had gone to prison for was selling telegraph poles.

Now a matter like this was all in the family, and several of those present knew the story already. It provided some light relief. Mosney, or Geraghty, had gone round calling on farmers in backward parts of the country, representing himself as an official of the Department of Posts and Telegraphs. He had explained that the old telegraph system on poles and wires had been rendered obsolete by a new invention, and that the department was selling off the standing stock cheap to anyone who would remove what they bought. Timber was scarce for fencing or fuel. Faulty telephone wire, as the farmers knew, was often sold for farm or garden use. The story went down well

Geraghty gave everyone receipts for cash, and everyone was satisfied until the time came that some of the farmers began cutting down the telegraph poles they had bought. Then the Guards stepped in, laborious enquiries put them on Geraghty's trail, and he was arrested in another part of the country, under another name and telling a different story. Somebody had noticed that he had a mole on the back of one hand, which mark of identification handicapped him for a life of crime.

Perhaps it had been a lesson to him and he was running straight. On the other hand, perhaps it was not just out of sheer philanthropy that the Gandons sheltered an ex-convict.

It was encouraging to feel that they were getting somewhere. Healy and Lancey agreed that the Gandons' house must be searched. A search was already being conducted at the Fennellys; it was still going on, for to comb a house thoroughly for something so easily concealed as a small supply of arsenic is a lengthy process. The Fennellys had freely given their consent; it had to be done, but nobody expected anything to come of it.

Mrs. Gandon had refused to authorize a search of their own house without her husband's sanction. This looked bad, but Healy said fair-mindedly that it was natural for her to dislike the idea of such a thing taking place when she herself was miles away in Dublin. The best thing would be to wait a little while in the hope of getting Gandon's consent. If a refusal was persisted in they would have to lay the evidence before a district justice and apply for a search warrant, all of which took time. But before they went to extremes something might be brought to light by discreet enquiries on the spot.

At present they had no suspects but Mrs. Gandon and Mosney alias Geraghty. Healy asked about other visitors to the house and the Gandons' relations with people in the village. As to the latter, Nolan had nothing out of the ordinary to report. They owed money in the village, but nothing unusual; they were the kind of people who never seemed able to bring themselves to pay a bill completely off, but gave all the shopkeepers something on account from time to time. The last payoff had been just after Christmas. They just bought the usual things for household requirements. Gandon didn't spend much on drink except when he had a visitor staying there. The only thing that had struck Nolan as out of the ordinary was that they seemed to consume huge quantities of eggs.

"They had an order at Scanlan's poultry farm for a dozen a day, and they must be fresh new laid. It was the time eggs were up to seven shillings a dozen, so it wasn't for waterglass, whatever it was. One week they cleaned Scanlan out and he had no eggs for us at the barracks."

Nolan spoke diffidently as he felt it might be too trivial to mention, but the Dublin detectives sat up. With one voice they exclaimed

"Black marketing!"

"Have you had much work with that in Clogh?" asked Healy.

Nolan shook his head. "Only the usual. Farmers' wives paying two shillings an ounce for tea at the harvest time, and all the tractor owners selling petrol and the like of that. We never had any suspicions of big-scale racketeering." He kept his fingers crossed as he spoke. He had done well over the fingerprints, but if it were to turn out that Gandon had been running some big food racket under his nose without him getting wind of it, well, even his wife would understand why he didn't get promotion.

District Superintendent Healy said to Lancey: "Could you send us down some fellow with special experience of the black market to nose around a bit?"

Lancey suggested an Inspector Devlin, and sent a man to fetch him.

"What about this visitor the Gandons had staying?" asked the metropolitan divisional superintendent. "The time they got in extra drinks. Who was he?"

Nolan was ready for that. "Another artist by the name of Patrick Purtill with an address in Dublin. He came down to paint and, we used to see him and Gandon sketching around. That was in June last year, and again for a bit in October."

"Gandon had attacks both those months," said Lancey, referring to a list of dates given him by the doctor. "At least in June he began to feel ill off and on; no date he can be sure of. On October 7th he had his first real collapse, and Purtill and Mrs. Gandon got the doctor. Purtill was there again at the Fennellys' two days before this last attack. What do you think? Could there be a connection?"

The general opinion was that it would be no harm to look Mr. Purtill up, especially as what they wanted most was more light on the Gandon family, its habits and its finances. The same difficulty that prevented an immediate search of the Gandons' house operated in the matter of inspecting Fergus Gandon's bank account. Even if he had not poisoned Gandon himself, Mr. Purtill might be worth a visit.

Another man to visit was Arnold Silke, the dealer, who appeared to manage all Gandon's professional affairs. Mr. Silke's name was well-known at headquarters, not that there were many art lovers on the staff of the Detective Branch, but because Silkes' Galleries had been the first in Dublin to install a new type of burglar alarm. It was worked by an invisible ray: the smallest thing crossing the path of the ray was enough to set the alarm ringing in Dublin Castle, and twice already the Flying Squad had been called out in the middle of the night by mice.

These Dublin jobs were entrusted to Detective Inspector Grace, a staff man, assisted by Detective Officer Lemon.

This completed the general picture of the case and covered all the individuals who were so far implicated. The chairman again stressed the importance of uncovering the underlying motive for the crime. Then the conference turned to consider the means by which it had been committed, and these were hardly less mysterious when they came to look into the circumstances of Gandon's last attack.

The most recent attack was the only one concerning which the police had full information. It differed from the previous ones in having occurred at the Fennellys'. Another remarkable point of difference was that the victim had this time been on his guard.

He had felt the pain soon after lunch, so soon that it hardly seemed possible that his lunch could be responsible for it. Before that he seemed to have touched nothing since breakfast. Although the police had not yet got a statement from the patient himself, he had told the doctor that he had not taken any pills or tonic or eaten sweets or anything else in the course of the morning, having been totally absorbed in his work. He had breakfasted with the Fennellys.

The analysis of all foodstuffs found in the house was still proceeding. According to reports so far received everything was harmless, including the butter sent from the country by Mrs. Gandon. Scraps of lunch recovered from the pig pail contained no trace of arsenic. On the other hand, arsenic had been found in sediment taken from the bathroom waste-pipes and the bend below the hand basin in the spare bedroom. Also in the patient's excreta. No post mortem was necessary to prove that arsenic was what Fergus Gandon had taken.

The members of the Fennellys' household had all been searched, except the missing Irene. They had consented freely to undergo this ordeal. No arsenic had been found on anybody's person and, as already mentioned, the search of the house had so far been unproductive. Lancey was thorough, but he had little hopes of anything turning up in that direction. The Fennellys kept no fireworks, flypapers, artificial flowers, Scheele's green, insecticide or weed killer on the premises. If they had ever bought any, the fact might emerge from a routine check of poisons books kept by all traders on the register. This had been ordered and would continue, making extra work for hundreds of local sergeants in Dublin city and county and in Clogh and all towns and villages in adjoining counties. If necessary it could be extended to cover the whole of the Twenty-Six Counties. Superintendent Lancey felt a quiet satisfaction in being able to start all this by just giving an order through the regular channels. There was an aesthetic pleasure in being able to produce such immense activity so simply. If only the activity itself would produce something!

But the most exasperating feature of the case was that, even supposing the purchase of poison were traced to one of the suspects, even supposing a packet of arsenic were actually found in his possession, the defense would still have a strong case unless it could be shown beyond all doubt exactly how the poison had been administered to Fergus Gandon.

Now an idea which may be in the reader's mind already had occurred some minutes earlier to Detective Officer Lemon. It felt as if his vest tickled him, and as soon as he could catch the eye of the chairman he came out with:

"Suppose the chap sucked his brush?"

The conference had to have its laugh. Somebody made the inevitable remark about Gandon in that case being a proper sucker. Sergeant Nolan said it was a thing he was always telling the kids off about; if there was arsenic in paints they'd have been dead long ago. An argument arose as to whether a real painter like Gandon would not use oil colors, watercolor being a kids' game. But Detective Officer Lemon had seen the picture on which he had been working that morning, and it looked like watercolor to him.

"It looked like nothing on earth to me," said the metropolitan divisional superintendent, and raised another laugh.

The superintendent of the technical bureau, however, thought there might be something in the idea. He did not believe there was any danger to the Nolan kids in the kind of paints they'd have, but there might be special kinds available to professional workers. At any rate they ought to check up on it.

"Would he ever take enough that way to poison him?" asked Healy.

The superintendent of the technical bureau shrugged his shoulders. "The minimum fatal dose of arsenious oxide for man is about 0.06 to 0.18 grams according to his weight. Say between 1 and 2 milligrams per kilogram. Is Gandon a hefty chap?"

Oddly enough, as the victim had been too ill to be interviewed, the detectives on the case had no clear idea of him as yet, but luckily the sergeant from the local barracks remembered seeing him out one day with Mrs. Fennelly. Gandon was not a big man, though he was athletic and wiry. The sergeant guessed him at about ten stone.

"Well, say he's been getting repeated doses off the end of the brush whenever he's been painting. I suppose in that way he might have absorbed a gram. Enough to make him a pretty sick man." The superintendent of the technical bureau had seen stranger things in his time.

"Better get hold of that box and get the paints analyzed," said the chairman, cocking an eye at Lancey. The O.C. investigation agreed. Detective Officer Lemon was instructed to fetch the box from the Fennellys'.

"Smart of you to think of it," said the metropolitan divisional superintendent to him as he went out.

Detective Officer Lemon did his best to look modest.

CHAPTER 8

HAVING followed the details of the investigation from the police angle, the reader is in a position to imagine its repercussions on the peaceful home life of the Fennelly family.

The search of the house, which went on all night and next morning from the moment when Fergus was removed to hospital, far outdid any turning out ever attempted by Hester's maids. The spring cleaning was almost due, so that there was plenty of dust in corners, which the search party stirred up and removed by somewhat *ad hoc* methods. If Irene had been there Hester would certainly have followed up their operations with a proper cleaning and polished all the furniture and wiped down the paint, but as things were she could not attempt such a thing, and it went to her heart to see all this upheaval go to waste. The search party looked behind all the books and went through all the drawers, not forgetting to examine the backs of drawers, where packets of arsenic had been found in the celebrated Armstrong case. They took up carpets and even floorboards. Listening to the tapping and hammering that went on, generally accompanied by whistling and humming in and out of tune, Mrs. Mulhall remarked sunnily that it reminded her of having the decorators.

Later, as the search went on and on, she declared more solemnly, " 'There is nothing hid that shall not be revealed.' "

But in the end the only find was a silver thimble of Hester's which had lain two years in a mousehole.

Mrs. Mulhall was in her element. Her spirits rose with every fresh complication. She invented difficulties in order to surmount them. She carried gallons of water up from the greenhouse because the house supply was to be turned off for a quarter of an hour. Preferring Irene's work to her own, she went to work vigorously on the carpets with the vacuum cleaner from which the detectives had removed the bag.

Best of all she enjoyed dancing attendance on the detectives, fetching everything they wanted, from Mr. Gandon's paintbox to Mr. Fennelly's garden coat, and continually pressing them to step into the kitchen for a nice cup of tea.

The comings and goings of a number of strange men and the removal of a patient by ambulance had not passed unnoticed by the Fennellys' neighbors. Several of them rang up to ask if anything was wrong. Mrs. Mulhall rushed to answer every call and gave such ambiguous replies that the wildest rumors spread. The old lady next door climbed up a ladder to ask over the garden wall whether or not it was true that Mrs. Fennelly's jewels had been stolen and Mr. Fennelly shot by the escaping thief. Barbara, who had come out to cut flowers, was the one to be caught and had not the least idea what to say, except that there must be some mistake.

"I wish she'd asked me," said Nell Gandon. "I'd have told her cat burglars had taken a tiara that had been in the family for generations. You might as well give people something to keep them happy."

But the Fennellys shrank from prevarication. Hester thought people might as well know that her brother had been taken ill and that the police had provided an ambulance to take him to hospital. "Some form of poisoning" was a formula to allay the curiosity of the medical-minded.

After the search was over there came a lull. The inspector in charge asked Hester and Paul if they had any complaints, and apologized very civilly for causing them so much trouble.

"And really it is we who have caused them trouble," said Barbara.

All the detectives went away, except one who stayed to guard the premises, or watch them—nobody was quite sure which. The family saw the police station wagon depart and went back indoors feeling rather as if they had been sucked into an electric suction cleaner, whirled round in the bag and thrown out on the ash pit.

"I told you what it would be like," said Nell.

"I'm afraid dinner will be a little late again," said Hester to Paul.

"My God, Hester," said Nell, "can you think about nothing else but meals?"

"Somebody has to," said Hester.

Paul said it did not matter about dinner. He began wandering about the house looking for something. His old garden coat was not on its usual peg.

The women had given it to the police.

Nell Gandon was allowed to visit Fergus in hospital, but only with a nurse in the room. They would not let her do anything for him. When he began being sick she stepped forward, having had plenty of practice, but the nurse swept her aside. Nobody seemed to agree with her that a wife's place was by her husband; they hardly seemed to think he required a wife at all.

The only contribution she could make to his comfort was to remove a facetious calendar and a bunch of Cape gooseberries. The calendar was the property of the hospital; the Cape gooseberries had been left behind by the last occupant. Nell put them all on the fire when the nurse's back was turned. It made a very bad impression.

After forty-eight hours the news of Fergus was still that he maintained his strength. Nothing more definite could be hoped for, at least for several days to come. He was by no means out of danger. With arsenic it may happen that recovery is made from the first effects, but death occurs days or weeks later from exhaustion or from secondary causes.

Nell kept trying to imagine all that Fergus was going through, as if she believed she could help him by sympathetic suffering. She harangued Hester on the subject, standing in front of her in the upstairs passage down which Hester was trying to pass with a pile of linen or a dustpan; halting her on the stairs on her way down to pay the gardener. Hester was striving to preserve a semblance of normality in the house, believing that the worst trials were more endurable within the framework of a civilized existence. With one maid short it meant that she was almost continually moving from one job to the next and carrying so many things in her head at once that she had little time to brood. Nevertheless she felt that she had as much right to make herself miserable over Fergus as had Nell. She would have been sorrier for anyone else whose husband was ill; anyone whose husband was not also her brother; anyone, too, who was herself above all suspicion of having directly or indirectly helped to bring him to this pass. Nell thought Hester very heartless, but Hester kept wondering if Nell's distress was not overdone. Was it that she could not control her feelings, or that she felt bound to work them up?

All this was in the air on the third afternoon when the sisters-in-law found themselves alone together in the study. By this time Hester's domestic difficulties had been relieved through the helpful intervention of the local Civic Guard sergeant, who had recommended a charwoman to do Irene's work. Hester all of a sudden had nothing much to do. Had life been normal she should have been at a charity bazaar selling egg cozies and book-markers to people who incredibly preferred being landed with such things to merely parting with a subscription. She might have reflected on this small piece of good blown by an ill wind, but instead she was worrying about where Barbara was, for she had gone out without saying where, and whether Paul would be late, for he had telephoned that he would not be back for tea, and what the police could be doing, and when she would be allowed to see Fergus. They might let her in once, she thought, if he could see Nell.

The cure would have been gardening, but the weather had turned unpleasant; gusts of sleet rattled from time to time on the window. Hester got out the table mats she was embroidering, and had sat for about ten minutes with her work lying in her lap when she heard Nell coming in from town and hastily picked it up. She was stitching busily when Nell came in a minute or two later, bare-legged and bedroom-slippered, and carrying a wet pair of shoes and stockings which she arranged to dry steamily in the grate. Then she sat down in Paul's chair, and there they were *tête-à-tête*.

What with the strain in the atmosphere, Hester could not say anything about drying stockings over the hot towel rail in the bathroom or shoes in the kitchen, for fear it would be interpreted as a reproach. The next remark that sprang to her lips seemed to her comparatively harmless, though to be sure it did betray a certain wish for the presence of a third party.

"Barbara never mentioned where she was going, did she? I suppose she does mean to be back for tea."

"There you go again," said Nell. "Meals, meals, meals. 'Who'll be in for lunch?' 'Whatever shall we do if dinner's late?' Is that really all you think about?"

"Well, my dear," retorted Hester, "would it be better if I thought, 'Let's all make ourselves as miserable as possible? Let's wallow in our emotions? Let's advertise our feelings for all we're worth?' "

Nell looked somberly across at her, a frown making one line of her dark brows.

"You haven't got any special feelings about Fergus, have you? I suppose it's natural, after so many years."

Hester stared at her. "I don't know what makes you say that. How can you possibly tell what I feel?"

"All the same," said Nell, "you'd be different if it were Paul."

The wind blew a puff of smoke down the chimney into their faces. It was a thoroughly unpleasant afternoon. Hester, her eyes smarting, forgot to be kind.

"If it were Paul," she said coldly and distinctly, "I shouldn't have been flirting with another man while he was getting ill."

She hardly knew whether or not she was sorry when she had said it. It had been rankling in her mind a long time. At least she was giving Nell a chance to put her side of the question, and whether or not that was wise, it was only fair. She did hope they could get out of it without having a scene. Hester detested scenes; she believed Nell rather enjoyed them.

Nell cried, "Who told you that?" But it was not a denial.

"It was something Fergus said," replied Hester, speaking more gently. "I know he was worried, or had been."

Nell was a strange woman. After her first indignant reaction she seemed to relax. She sat staring into the fire with her elbows on her knees. Her dark hair fell forward almost hiding her face. Hester did not know what to make of her expression.

"What did he say?" Nell asked. "Was it something about me and Alban? Lord Kilskour, you know?"

"Yes."

"Well, Fergus is a deep one," said Nell slowly. "And I thought he'd never even noticed."

"I'm afraid he did," said Hester in a grave voice. "What else could you expect?"

"But I did expect it," said Nell, looking up. "I thought anyone with a spark of interest in me couldn't have helped it. But he never said a word. He and Paddy Purtill went off together painting, and sat up half the night together arguing, and Fergus hardly came near me unless he wanted food. And when he and Alban did quarrel it was all over art, and nothing to do with me at all."

Hester looked at the flushed indignant face of her sister-in-law and thought Nell might well blush for what she was saying, but it seemed more likely her color came from the glow of the fire.

"You silly woman," said Hester. "Are you telling me that you encouraged Lord Kilskour's attentions in order to make your husband jealous?"

"Oh Hester, what a splendid period remark! Fergus would love that."

Hester bit her lip. What was one to say to her?

"Oh dear," said Nell, clasping her knees, "I wonder can I ever make you see what really happened? It wasn't a bit what you think. Do remember in my favor, Hester, how good a wife I've been to Fergus for years and years and years. Do you think it was much fun for someone like me to be stranded like that in the country? In the days before Mosney came"—she shuddered at the thought of them—"I never had a minute to think about how awful life was. It was just one thing after another, and somehow I kept them all in food and clothing, but I don't know how I did it, physically, I mean. If Mosney hadn't turned up I should have collapsed. Well, since we've had him, I've had time to think of my looks a bit more, and play with the children, and it did seem to me we might have had some fun together—all five. Fergus can be rather good with the children when he likes, though he does tend to look on them as just my little hobby. But Fergus by then had got this new craze, exploring new watercolor techniques, and he had this book to do for Silkes', and as well as that he was painting a grand fresco all over the wall of a garage, and—and other work as well. When Paddy Purtill came down it made him worse. The two of them went off all day painting, or shut themselves up in the studio and sat up all night arguing and drinking, which isn't good for Fergus, and all the use anyone seemed to have for me was to bring food when they yelled for it."

"Well," said Hester reasonably, "men are like that."

"Not all of them," said Nell. "Alban's quite different. Alban's an extraordinarily courteous person. Not attentive, you know, just polite."

"Was that how you came to have an affair with him?" said Hester, not without sarcasm.

"An affair with Alban? Nonsense! I didn't have anything of the sort."

"Well, what did you have then?"

"Just neighborly relations, that was all. We went riding together a bit. I used to ride a lot, you know, and I hadn't been on a horse for years. Alban found one he could hire for me ; it's the sort of kind thing he does. Like taking us all out in his car—the children, too. He would have taken Fergus, if he'd wanted to come. It was so nice to be considered and looked after and to feel that anyhow, somebody enjoyed one's company. I'd been feeling so *passé*. Paddy Purtill always treats me like his maiden great-aunt."

Hester sighed. "Yes, I can see how it all began."

"Began? That was all there was to it, and very pleasant while it lasted. My dear Hester, don't you know Alban? Haven't you met him? You can't suppose he'd be after one's virtue!"

But Hester had a decided impression that aspects of the matter were being glossed over, and she was determined to have it out. She said, "If you never really had a flirtation with Lord Kilskour, why did you, or what did you, expect Fergus to notice?"

"Oh Hester, need you be so stuffy about it?" said Nell. "I should have thought you would understand. It isn't as if you hadn't been awfully pretty once."

"What's that got to do with it?"

"Everything. Even you can't have helped flirting a little sometimes."

Hester wavered. Coquette she was not, but who is going to admit that they don't know the ABC?

"It all depends what you mean by flirting—"

"And whether you both mean the same thing," said Nell. "I've known Alban for years and years. I knew quite well his attentions didn't amount to anything more than a bit of sentiment about the old days. He's one of those simple, sentimental sort of souls. 'Old friends, old books, old wine . . .' You know the sort."

"Old women?" Hester couldn't resist putting in.

Nell made a face at her, and finished, "All I thought was it would do Fergus no harm at all to see I liked to be appreciated."

"I do know Fergus can be exasperating," said Hester thoughtfully. "I can see how you felt. By what you say there doesn't seem to have been much harm in it. Not on the face of it, as Paul says. But how sure are you, Nell, now you see what's happened?" She leaned forward heedless of crumpling her fancy-work. "All this mystery, this attempt on Fergus. Are you quite sure, quite sure there's no connection?"

Nell jumped to her feet. "Oh, but that's fantastic. Are you trying to make out that Alban—a kind of *crime passionel*—oh no, you couldn't think—you don't know Alban." She laughed hysterically. "It would be funny if it wasn't such a horrible idea in itself."

She stared down at Hester and tears gathered in her eyes.

"It doesn't even fit," she said, after a moment's thought. "Alban wasn't even there. Thank God for that! If there'd been the least doubt—if it had turned out that all this suffering Fergus has had to bear was due, even remotely and indirectly to anything I had done—how could I go on living and knowing it? How could I ever punish myself enough?"

The tears brimmed over. "Oh dear," she said, "these days I don't seem able to stop myself crying. I know you think I ought to have more self-control."

Hester's heart melted. It was not that she felt she would ever really understand Nell, or that she could ever have behaved in the same way, but she was convinced at last that Nell did genuinely care for Fergus. She even began to think she had not been as sympathetic as her sister-in-law deserved.

CHAPTER 9

ON the afternoon when her mother did not know where she had gone, Barbara Fennelly was sitting to Mr. Paddy Purtill.

The portrait was intended as a surprise for her mother's birthday. Barbara counted on Hester not enquiring into her movements because there had been a tacit agreement between them ever since she left school that the young had a right to their independence. Parents should not be inquisitive if daughters can be trusted. Barbara's parents never asked what she was doing when out of their sight, and were usually told all about it in the end.

This was one of those borderline cases of conduct when, if consulted beforehand, parents would quite possibly disapprove. When faced by the accomplished fact of a charming likeness of their child by one of the foremost young Irish artists, Barbara felt confident that they would be both touched and pleased.

The commission had been given the day before the tragic happening which had turned the Fennellys' placid existence into a turmoil. Barbara had made the appointment for her first sitting and had forgotten about it, in all the confusion, until it was too late to get out of it. There was difficulty in communicating with Mr. Purtill since he was not on the telephone. You wrote to him, and he rang you up in reply from a call box conveniently placed just outside his door. Barbara could, quite simply, not have turned up and sent a note of apology afterwards, and such was her first intention. But when, as related in the previous chapter, the domestic crisis calmed down and there was no call for her services at home, she saw no reason why she should not go on with the idea. The Fennellys were not seeing people, but Mr. Purtill was not "people"; he was a friend of her uncle Fergus.

The fifty pounds that Barbara had not spent on a putative Van Huysum was still dedicated to art. Indeed, without admitting that her mother had been right in principle that day at the auction, Barbara was glad she had been prevented from spending the money. Since then she had listened to tirades from Fergus on the shamefulness of neglecting living artists while one made a cult of the dead, and she had gathered, from the way Mr. Silke and her uncle talked, that Mr. Purtill was not well off: Fergus had accused him of painting potboilers for money. It was very sad that anyone should be compelled to do such a thing, and it seemed to Barbara that fifty pounds towards helping Mr. Purtill become a better painter would be indeed well spent.

But she was not doing it solely for Mr. Purtill's sake, either. If one is interested in art, one naturally wishes to see a picture painted right through from the beginning, and failing an invitation from an artist to visit him in his studio while he is working, the best way is to sit for one's portrait. One may not be in the best place for watching the brush actually at work on the canvas, but one can follow the development of the portrait through all its stages, and one can profit by the time spent in sitting to talk of painting with one who understands.

When the day came for the first sitting, how glad Barbara was, too, to escape for an hour or two from the atmosphere of mystery and anxiety which had transformed their home to a place of ill omen. Oh the comfort of being with somebody who was quite outside it all!

The Purtills lived in one of a row of lavender-colored houses which had come down in the world through having too many stairs and no garages. Formerly they had been very genteel residences; a stone eagle spread its wings over them from the centre of the parapet which ran along the whole terrace, and there were stucco garlands disposed along the facade. Weedy front gardens, blinds hanging crookedly with tattered lace edges, absence or superfluity of window curtains, unpolished brass doorknobs, showed that no attempt was now made by the inhabitants at what advertisements call "gracious living." In the wind and rain that afternoon the place even looked sinister, and had Barbara not known that Mr. Purtill lived with his mother and sister she might almost have hesitated to knock.

His mother opened the door; that relationship was easy to guess for she was exactly like him only more pugnacious. She wore black and a framed miniature, probably of Mr. Purtill's late father, in a brooch at her throat. Her free hand held a half-darned sock and a half-smoked cigarette, and she seemed anxious to complete both operations, for she shouted upstairs, "Paddy!" urged Barbara on, and went back herself into a room off the hall.

"Do come up," called Mr. Purtill encouragingly down. He appeared looking over the banisters, and seeing that Barbara had a suitcase he politely came downstairs to meet her and take it up. It contained her best evening frock, for in the cause of handing her likeness down to posterity she stuck at nothing.

"Mind where you step," said Mr. Purtill. "There's a canvas there that may not be quite dry."

A number of canvases and a good many other miscellaneous objects were stacked along the walls of the upstairs passage. Mr. Purtill had the best front bedroom for his studio, and as he had to make the most of the space it was kept very bare and tidy, everything not actually required at the moment being stored outside. The atmosphere of the house changed in these higher regions; a smell of paint overcame the smell of cats, and everything up here was orderly to the point of austerity. It was chilly too, at least from the point of view of anyone proposing to change into evening dress. Mr. Purtill plugged in a small electric fire.

"I almost couldn't come," said Barbara, rather surprised at herself for having successfully arrived.

"I don't know that it would have mattered much today," said Mr. Purtill with a grimace at the window. "There's no light for painting, of course. We can settle the preliminary details, and I might just be able to sketch in the outline."

Although he did not seem interested in the reason why she might not have been able to come, Barbara felt it necessary to inform him of the changed state of affairs at her home and their anxiety for Fergus, who had had to be taken to hospital with some acute form of poisoning.

"I'm not surprised," said Mr. Purtill. "I didn't like the look of him the other day. I'm sorry to hear he's so bad, though. No visitors, I suppose?"

"Well, not just yet. As a matter of fact even Mummy isn't allowed to see him, only Aunt Nell."

"Has Nell come up? Then he really is bad." Mr. Purtill seemed to have only just taken it in. "What about the children, are they here too?"

"No, thank goodness. The man, Mosney, and somebody called Mrs. Conarchy-at-the-lodge are looking after them."

"God help the poor chislers!" was Mr. Purtill's comment on that. "Tell me, though, do the doctors think he might die?"

"He nearly did," replied Barbara, "but we hope and trust that as he's still alive he may be all right now." She raised large serious gray eyes to Mr. Purtill, and Mr. Purtill gazed gloomily back.

"He'd be a loss," he said, "with a wife and three young children to leave behind."

"And a loss to Art too," said Barbara.

"Er, yes," said Mr. Purtill. There was a pause, required by decency before turning to material matters, then the painter roused himself to attend to business with: "Ah well, let's see what you've got in the bag."

Barbara cheered up as she opened her suitcase and spread before him the folds of her evening frock. It was of gray watered silk and flowed out of the suitcase like a river all over the studio floor. Barbara's hands touched it with loving pride, and she took up a pink rose from among the ripples and held it against the stiffer silk of the bodice. "I generally wear this here," she explained. "It's cut rather low."

"I'll have to fetch up the larger electric fire," said Mr. Purtill. "You'll be cold in that."

But he was pleased to approve of the dress and fetched armfuls of draperies to try as background to it, flung over a screen, and finally flung them all down and decided on the screen itself, which was dark green. Barbara would sit on a gilt armchair with scrollwork arms, and the picture would be a harmony of green and gray and gold. Should she, or should she not, hold something in her hands? Her evening bag was too large, a cigarette was too small; besides she did not smoke. And nothing could be more banal, according to Mr. Purtill, than a dance program, which was Barbara's suggestion. After a long discussion they decided that her hands might lie idle in her lap.

Barbara slipped on the frock for Mr. Purtill to see, in his sister's bedroom across the passage. This was a cold-blooded business, for though she had the benefit of the small electric fire while Mr. Purtill went off to find the large one, there was not time for it to make very much difference to the temperature. The greenish mirror was also discouraging, making Barbara look colder even than she was. So the great moment when she appeared to the painter in all her glory was not all that it might have been. But Mr. Purtill seemed to be satisfied, and as the weather had cleared and the light somewhat improved, and the room was beginning to warm up, it seemed as if he might be able to sketch in an outline. Unfortunately, just at that moment they were interrupted.

"Paddy!" called Mrs. Purtill from downstairs. "Two men to speak to you."

Mr. Purtill swore under his breath and went out, and Barbara could hear him trying to repel invasion from over the banisters. He came back looking cross.

"I'm sorry," he said, "I'm afraid we might as well pack it up for today. The light won't be good for more than half an hour, anyway. I have to see these fellows, though I can't imagine what they're after. It's a couple of plain-clothes detectives."

"Detectives!" said Barbara. She was jerked abruptly back to all the things she had been so happy to forget.

"Yes, blast them," said Mr. Purtill, "so do you mind?"

Barbara rustled back to Miss Purtill's bedroom, and as she began to change heard the tramp of heavy feet on the stairs.

Detective Inspector Grace and Detective Officer Lemon were calling on Mr. Purtill in accordance with instructions received after the police conference. They had been working together on this case since the police conference. The name of the senior of the two Branch men was appropriate for Inspector Grace had once been just about the handsomest man in the Force. He had been teased about it and had developed a forbidding expression to counteract the effects of his alleged fatal fascination. Now he was getting a bit on the heavy side, and the betting was that he would soon get married—within three years if not two; not that there was any particular lady in question, but experienced colleagues thought they saw signs of a disposition to settle. If Grace had realized how they discussed him behind his back he would hardly have been able to keep on in the job, but nowadays idle tongues were awed by his presence. Even Detective Officer Lemon suppressed a comment on the glimpse they had of Barbara vanishing as they came upstairs. Mick's first thought was that here was a slice of the real *Vie de Boheme* which he knew of from opera. He was disappointed to realize that it was all quite respectable.

"I think you're a friend of Mr. Fergus Gandon?" Inspector Grace asked Purtill. "I don't know if you've heard the news of him lately?"

Purtill looked surprised. "That's his niece, Miss Fennelly, who went out as you came in. I just heard from her he'd been taken to hospital. I knew he was ill, of course. I hope there's nothing worse?"

"They hope he'll pull round all right," replied the detective. "The news today is he's comfortable."

"Whatever that means," finished Purtill. "And what's it got to do with you fellows?"

Inspector Grace cleared his throat. "There are some peculiar features about the case which call for enquiry. Now we don't want to trouble the relatives more than we can help at a time of such anxiety for them, not if his friends can help just as much. The way it is, you see, by helping us you can help spare them. What we were hoping to get from you was a picture of Mr. Gandon's circumstances—home life, professional standing and so on, and also we'd be glad of anything you could tell us relevant to the first appearance of his symptoms. Our information is you were staying with him at the time he first became ill."

"So somebody was poisoning him after all," said Purtill.

"What makes you say that?" replied the inspector guardedly.

"He told me so," replied the painter with a shrug of his shoulders. "I didn't believe him, but it seems he knew best. One should never disbelieve a story on the grounds that it's unlikely. Next time anyone says they're being murdered I'll pay more attention."

"When was it he told you this?"

"On a Christmas card," said Purtill. "Seasonable, wasn't it? I've got it still. I'll show you." He opened a table drawer which was as tidy as all his other arrangements and took from a folder a large card similar to one they had seen on a mantelpiece at the Fennellys. The front conveyed nothing to the detectives. On the back was scribbled:

*Doctor now thinks I may have been doped. What do you
know about that? Greetings from F.G. not moriturus I hope.*

"His question," remarked Purtill, watching them read, "is purely rhetorical. I knew nothing about it, and I didn't believe a word of it. I thought he was just showing off."

Inspector Grace felt bound to remark that for all they knew yet it might be an accident.

"Oh surely not," said Purtill. "That would be such an anticlimax. Ah well, it's no time to be flippant. What do you want from me? Fifteen-minute talk on Fergus Gandon, his Life and Art?" He felt for cigarettes and offered them round. " Excuse me, I think I hear my sitter on the landing. I'll just see her out."

When he came back he appeared to have reflected further on the situation and was looking serious. He shut the door behind him, took up a position with his back to the empty fireplace, and proceeded to hold forth.

Fergus Gandon's former pupil had plenty to say on the subject of his art, but his hearers found some of it bewildering. They gathered that the younger painter had been to some extent disillusioned about the older one since the days when he had sat at his feet. Purtill said he had seen nothing then. Later, just after the war, he had managed to get abroad and travel a little round galleries and private collections, and had been struck by the fact that the work of some painters of the twenties—Kandinsky, for instance—seemed to be, like Hamlet, all quotations. Only like Shakespeare, there seemed no doubt that Kandinsky was first.

"Fergus' stuff is damnably derivative," he said. "That's the politest word for it. Rude people might talk about plagiarism."

They gathered he meant copying.

"Do you mean he can't really paint or draw much at all?" asked Inspector Grace, feeling that that explained the Christmas card.

Purtill stared at him. "He can paint and draw like nobody's business. There's nobody here can touch him for sheer technique."

"But—er—what more do you want, then?"

"What, indeed?" sighed Paddy Purtill. It was all they could get out of him in the way of an answer.

"But don't people take notice of it? Those in the know, I mean?" pursued the detective.

"You don't suppose anyone in Dublin knows anything about the moderns," replied Purtill with a sweep of his hand that abolished a whole class of cultured citizens and knocked a piece of chalk off the mantelpiece. Detective Officer Lemon picked up the chalk and handed it back. Inspector Grace said he was not thinking so much of the public as of the dealers.

"It suits their book," said Purtill darkly.

Then he grinned. "You needn't write that down," he said to Detective Officer Lemon. "Don't mind me when I start ranting; I get carried away. Gandon's been doing some rather interesting work lately—technical experiments with watercolor. He paints on all kinds of grounds: newspaper and wrapping paper even; he took a special fancy to a strong kind of wrapping paper with canvas threads in it that gives an interesting texture. Another thing he does is to draw on white paper with wax crayons—the lines don't show till you put a wash of color over them, and then they come out white. And he tries varying the medium with all kinds of things: gum arabic, glycerine, starch, pure alcohol, laevulose (that's something you get out of honey), sarcocolla, megilp—I don't know what else. L-a-e-v-u-l-o-s-e," he repeated helpfully. Mick Lemon, faint but pursuing, thought what an eye-opener all this would be for Sergeant Nolan's kids.

Inspector Grace saw that his subordinate was dying to ask something, and as Purtill did not touch on the point, he put the question himself. Did Mr.

Purtill know if Mr. Gandon was in the habit of sucking his brush?

"I've no idea," said Purtill, brought back to earth when about to embark on a discussion of the divergent traditions in watercolor in England and abroad. "I shouldn't think so. Why?"

"Some artists do, don't they?" said Inspector Grace.

"I shouldn't think there'd be any advantage in it," said Purtill, "unless to get a nice point. It's a kid's habit. Where was I?"

The detectives listened to a good deal more about art. Inspector Grace believed in letting people talk. When he had had about all he could bear and they did not seem to be getting anywhere useful, he tactfully steered the conversation to Gandon's financial circumstances.

"He's never borrowed money off me," said Purtill. "Perhaps because I haven't got any. But though he's not very well off I don't think he's seriously hard up either. He has those rich relations, and Arnold Silke backs him up like anything and buys his pictures. Look here, that's the very man you ought to see. He can tell you all about Gandon's markets."

Inspector Grace thanked him, without mentioning that they had called at the Galleries already and made an appointment with Mr. Silke's secretary. "Now," he said, "about Mr. Gandon's home life and the beginnings of his illness—"

But Purtill was not able to add a great deal to what they knew already. He could not recollect many details about the attacks Fergus had had when he himself was at the Gandons'; it was all so long ago. All he could say was that the food had always been plain and wholesome. He had got tired of mutton and stewed apple, but had never felt the slightest twinge of indigestion. He described the Gandons' home life as happy. The inspector delicately approached the subject of the relations between Mr. and Mrs. Gandon, hinting that wives do sometimes poison husbands, but Mr. Purtill refused to encourage such a line of thought.

"You were there when Lord Kilskour was over, weren't you?" asked the inspector.

Purtill saw the connection of ideas, but he shook his head.

"There was nothing in that," he said. "Don't you listen to silly gossip. Now is there anything else? Because if not—" The painter glanced rather pointedly at his watch. Detective Officer Lemon, at a nod from his superior, put his notebook away. Purtill thriftily extinguished the electric fire and saw them out.

Barbara Fennelly, walking home through the wind and rain with her hands deep in her pockets (she had left the suitcase at the studio to save carrying), pondered the incident of the detectives' arrival, which she felt pretty sure was more than a coincidence. Would they all now be haunted by detectives wherever they went? She glanced round from time to time to see if she was being shadowed, and though she could see nobody following she could not feel sure.

Had the detectives' visit to Mr. Purtill any connection with her own, or had they other things they wanted to ask him? She had herself been careful not to tell even this friend of her uncle's what was really the matter, but now she supposed he would know. Perhaps on her next visit she might venture to talk to him about it. It would be such a great comfort to have someone she could talk to outside the family.

Busy with cogitations she turned the corner into the Fennellys' own road and saw the old lady from next door coming towards her under an umbrella. Fortunately she was having a struggle with it in the wind that gave her less attention to spare for girls whose mothers' jewels might or might not have been stolen. Barbara hurried past with her head down. At that moment she felt in sympathy with all hunted fugitives but one, the one who had planned the whole devilish business and brought them all to this.

CHAPTER 10

WHEN Inspector Grace and Detective Officer Lemon had called at Silkes' Galleries at 9 a.m. that morning they had found a window protected outside by an iron grille and draped inside with gray velvet curtains. As they arrived an assistant came out to take down the grills, and they were in time to see the curtains swing apart and loop themselves up at the sides in the mysterious fashion of theater curtains, without anyone visibly pulling them. Inside, against a gray velvet background, was displayed according to the best traditions of window dressing just one example of what the establishment had to sell. Instead of a hat, as in a shop across the street, it was a head in greenish bronze. The head gazed wistfully across at the hat as if longing to try it on, and it would have been interesting to try the effect of the hat on the head, if anyone could have afforded to buy them both. An ingenuous person might have inferred from this sparse window dressing that both the shops had little to sell, but it implied of course just the opposite: that everything they had was extremely precious, and not to be exposed casually to the gapers.

The assistant handed the two detectives on to a lady secretary who seemed amused that anyone should imagine Mr. Silke, with his wealthy and leisured clientele, kept the same hours as a common tradesman, or that they should expect to see him without an appointment. She consulted a desk diary and suggested that they should return at five.

They went back as soon as they had wound up their conversation with Mr. Purtill. This time they were shown in to the office of the head of the firm, who gave them a much more cordial reception. As he paid a secretary to say "no" for him, Mr. Silke's own manner was always charming. He gave his visitors chairs and cigarettes. They noted that artists smoke Gold Flake, but art dealers smoke Abdullas.

The room was not like an office, being perfectly clean and furnished with pieces that though old looked new. The pictures hung about in themselves created an individual atmosphere. There were feminine touches (for which the secretary was paid) such as a bowl of snowdrops on the desk. The rug on the floor made Grace and Lemon uncomfortably conscious of muddy boots.

Mr. Arnold Silke, sitting at his desk, a trim dark figure in a very good suit, looked as if he would be at home with any degree of luxury, but also as if he had a good head for figures.

He let them tell him all about it, and sat looking very grave, as anyone might. After the proper conventional expressions of regret and horror at such news of a valued client, he remarked:

"This could not have happened at a worse time for us."

"I beg your pardon?" said Inspector Grace.

Mr. Silke explained that the firm had been preparing a Gandon exhibition to take place late in March. It would be an event in the art world, as it was a long time since Gandon had held a one-man show. "Several important collectors are coming over," said Mr. Silke, and he might have meant either from England or America. "It is time people saw what he has been doing in watercolor," he said, making them feel that the public could not bear to be kept waiting much longer. "But now who knows what may happen to upset our arrangements?"

The men from Dublin Castle were impressed. Hearing about Gandon from his relations and his old friend, Mr. Purtill, they had not gathered that he was a person of any particular importance. The tone of Mr. Silke's voice as well as what he said put the man in a new light. Inspector Grace wanted to be clearer about this and mentioned that they had been informed that Gandon's work was not original at all.

Arnold Silke looked several degrees more shocked than when they had told him that the man was being poisoned. He could not believe it, except that every great reputation was a target for calumny. "Jealousy," he said. "You have no idea how far people will go out of sheer spite. But have you never seen a Gandon?"

There was a large picture hanging on the wall to the dealer's right, from which both the detectives had instinctively been averting their eyes. Mr. Silke now invited them to contemplate it, and did so himself with the air of one giving himself a special treat.

It was a large picture, about three feet by two, painted in vivid colors with black scribbles over them. There were bright green vegetation, violet crags, and a flat orange desert modulating into pink in the distance. There were also two pink figures in the foreground among the vegetation, meant for human, and not only naked but wearing their insides outside.

"At present," said Mr. Silke in reverent tones, "Gandon seems to be moving from abstraction towards realism, but without sacrificing his linear rhythms or his unique mastery of the whole keyboard of color. The great question is, can he integrate this vital interior humanism with the syntax of his exterior composition?"

The only bit of this that Inspector Grace fancied he understood was "interior humanism," and that he did not like. If he had cherished any hope of being able to form his own estimate of Gandon's work, it was abandoned at this point. One thing he could say was that in spite of Mr. Purtill's allegations he for one had never seen anything like this in his life. He was inclined to think Gandon must be a genius to be able to get away with it, for surely nobody would spend good money on a thing like that unless they saw something in it that he did not.

Detective Officer Lemon, speaking out of turn under the spell of the master work, asked: "What is it?"

"Gouache," said Mr. Silke. "That is, a combination of chalk and gouache on a basis of ink and watercolor."

"Oh, that's gooash, is it?" said Detective Officer Lemon, pleased, because he had just acquired the word from Mr. Purtill. "But I didn't mean that; I meant what's the name of it or hasn't it got one?"

" 'Adam and Eve'," said Mr. Silke, "if you feel it matters." He turned from the picture and inspected Detective Officer Lemon with some curiosity.

"And what do you want me to tell you about Gandon?" he then said, addressing them both. "I am not fond of discussing my clients' business out of their presence, but this is exceptional. Pray ask me anything you think might help. I must confess that I myself cannot imagine how you are to set about discovering anything in this case, though I know you have your methods."

"Well," said Grace, "one thing we always have to look into is the question of a money motive. 'Money is the root of all evil,' you know, or at any rate ninety percent of it. From what you've been telling us, I suppose Mr. Gandon does pretty well out of his work?"

Mr. Silke regarded the two plainclothes men with eyes that were beautiful and sad. "The rewards of art," he said, " are not comparable with those of leading men in other professions. It is the hard lot of genius to be compelled to wait for posterity to pass the final judgment. Work like Gandon's stands at the bar of time. Fifty years hence it will probably fetch five or ten times what it does today, but the fact so far is grasped only by the few."

"Then he doesn't sell so many, after all?"

"Ah," said Mr. Silke, "that is where we come in."

"You buy his pictures from him?"

"We have given him a contract. It is often done in the case of a man with a future. We pay him so much annually for the full rights in all his work. It means, you see, that he has a feeling of security and a completely free hand."

"And he doesn't let you down?"

"A completely free hand," Mr. Silke repeated, ignoring interruptions, "apart from occasional commissioned work which is paid for separately, such as a book he is illustrating for us now. Since his illness we have had hardly anything from him, nevertheless the usual sum has been paid on the first day of the year. We can look to the future for our dividend."

Grace remembered that shortly after Christmas the Gandons had paid off part of their debts in the village, but not all. As the dealer had so far avoided mentioning figures, the detective was obliged to be crude and ask:

"How much?"

"Five hundred a year, paid quarterly. Commissioned work might come to a hundred or two more."

"Thank you very much, Mr. Silke," said Inspector Grace. "That certainly helps to clear the ground. It doesn't seem as if money could be the motive in this case, or not in a direct way. You don't think, though, that he's in any financial difficulties?"

"If he were, I should have been the first to know. Gandon would come to me. Why should he hesitate? What is a dealer for?"

Dealers, they gathered, were in this art business simply for their health. It made them feel good to buy works that nobody else would and support individuals who were incapable of earning an honest living. They saw before them Gandon's fairy godmother. But Mr. Silke would have had to wave a powerful wand before either of his visitors could find any attraction in the picture of "Adam and Eve."

Detective Officer Lemon's fascinated eyes kept coming back to it in the brief pauses when he was not taking shorthand. He slipped his superior officer a pencil note. Grace grinned as he read it.

"And that's another point on which perhaps you can enlighten us, Mr. Silke," he said. "Your firm sells colors too, I believe? Well now, a green like that," he pointed at the cabbage plants in Gandon's Eden, "that suggests arsenic to my eye. Would arsenic be an ingredient in the kind of paints they make nowadays?"

Mr. Silke's eyes narrowed as if the smoke of his cigarette was getting into them. "My dear sir, we have advanced since the Middle Ages. You are thinking of paint as a possible form in which arsenic could be obtained commercially? Not in this country or in England. If it were so we colormen would be obliged to register, should we not, and keep records of such sales? But it is just possible that it might be obtained abroad in such a form. There are still certain Continental manufacturers who cater for clients with antiquarian notions and supply such colors as orpiment according to the old traditional recipes. We have never imported any of our stocks from the Continent, and I imagine there might be difficulties in the way of obtaining a license which would deter your hypothetical poisoner. If he were to go abroad himself, of course, he could smuggle a supply of arsenic home fairly easily in any form. The ordinary man in the street would hardly be likely to know anyone who had real orpiment in his paintbox. I'm sure Gandon hadn't; he gets all his colors from us."

"Does he so?" said Inspector Grace. "Then that's that, I suppose. We did have it suggested," he glanced out of the corner of his eye at Detective Officer Lemon, "that a man might poison himself accidentally if he was in the habit of sucking his paintbrush." He laughed. "No idea too farfetched for us to look into it, you see. I don't suppose a real professional like Mr. Gandon would have a habit like that."

Mr. Silke smiled too. "He might, Inspector, he might. Surprising how some men cling to childish habits. What an ingenious idea! But I am afraid I must debunk it for you. Arsenic has been found to darken in watercolors, and has not been used in their manufacture for many years."

"He wouldn't have had some old paints lying around?"

"They would have to be centuries old."

"Well, that's just too bad," said Grace. "Thank you very much again, sir. I don't think we need take up any more of your time." He nodded to his assistant and Detective Officer Lemon put his notebook away and stood up, a trifle pink about the ears.

"Call on me at any time, Inspector. If I can help you in any way, or inform you on any point, I am entirely at your disposal. A shocking business! We must hope for the best, but at present I'm afraid it hardly looks as if you would soon come to the end of your labors."

"Don't say that, Mr. Silke. We may get a break any moment."

"I sincerely hope you will. But I do hope too," the dealer's earnestness here became intensified, "that you will be able to avoid publicity. Nothing could be more undesirable. It might draw morbid crowds here to his exhibition."

The detectives were let out through the iron grille, which was in place again as the shop had closed. The gray velvet curtain had fallen between Silkes' and the common world.

They walked in step down Grafton Street, a thing you can only do on a wet evening when there are no crowds. Inspector Grace said kindly to the young man at his side,

"Well, there you are, Mick. Better luck next time."

Detective Officer Lemon said, "The Old Masters used it, didn't they? He said they did."

"If they did, what about it?"

"They're dead anyway," said Mick with a grin. But he did not intend to try that one on Superintendent Lancey.

CHAPTER 11

IT was all very well for the O.C. Investigation to decide that the Gandons' house must be searched as the Fennellys' had been. Mrs. Gandon still refused to give permission, and as everyone who knew Fergus Gandon agreed that the bare mention of the Civic Guard would send his temperature up, Dr. Colville was not yet prepared to run the risk of letting them in to interview him, although he was a little better.

Superintendent Lancey complained of all this to Chief Superintendent Healy, who said cheerfully that any trail down at Kilskour must be so cold that a few days more would be no matter. Healy took Sergeant Nolan and Inspector Devlin back with him in his car after the conference. They discussed the case all the way down in the car. By the end of the journey Healy was able to give a betting forecast as follows: 9-1 Mrs. Gandon, 15-2 Mosney and Lord Kilskour a 100-1 chance. This of course was merely the Chief expressing his view of it in his own language, with no money passed.

Next morning early Nolan and Devlin belted themselves into mackintoshes and set out on bicycles for Kilskour, to find out anything they could without throwing their weight about. They made an odd pair. Nolan was the big St. Bernard dog type of Guard, all patience and caution. Devlin was nobody's idea of a policeman, and the mystery was how he ever came to join the Force. He had the strong point for detective work of being one of those people whose appearance it is almost impossible to remember; there was nothing in it to strike you except the fact that he had ill-fitting false teeth. Sometimes he took them out, so he told Nolan, when he wanted a simple kind of disguise. He had a great fund of stories, and beguiled the way with talk about sides of bacon hidden under floorboards, turkeys stuffed with gold watches, geese wrapped up in shawls and carried like babies, and nylons found wound round the waists of portly commercial travelers, till Nolan's blood ran cold at the thought of what this man might find in his village. Nolan could not help respecting Devlin both for his past exploits and for being in such good training that he could talk about them without stopping while bicycling to Kilskour through muddy lanes, uphill all the way and against the wind and rain. The unpleasant weather—just subfreezing—which spread towards Dublin by afternoon descended earlier on Clogh and Kilskour.

About ten o'clock, the earliest hour at which it would have been any use to arrive, they dismounted at the great gates of Kilskour Castle. These massive fortifications had been erected about 1840 to give employment in one of the famines before the Great Famine. They and a pair like them on the far side were the only ways in and out of a demesne covering about two square miles, encircled by a twelve-foot-high wall in good repair. The Dower House, where the Gandons lived, was inside the gates, enclosed with the castle in a private world. Nolan told Devlin that the gate on the far side was kept by the brother of the lodgekeeper here, and between them the two lodges should know all about everything coming in or out.

The lodge was built all over and each side of the gate, in two two-story octagonal turrets joined by a Gothic arch. Four octagonal rooms in the turrets and an up and down room in the arch housed the Conarchy family, who were all, however, quite ordinary shapes. The husband, Tim Conarchy, was Lord Kilskour's head gardener, and it was Mrs. Conarchy who assumed the chief responsibility for opening and shutting the gates.

There was no difficulty in getting the lodge woman chatting, for she was consumed with curiosity as to what was happening at the Dower House since Mrs. Gandon left. What brought the Guards up there? First Sergeant Nolan and Eugene Roche from the barracks at Clogh, then a red-faced old fellow in a car with someone to drive him (that was the chief superintendent) and now Sergeant Nolan back again with a man Mrs. Conarchy never saw before. She thought they could hardly do more if it was murder.

Naturally she had been at Mosney to tell her all about it, but Mosney was a queer, shut-mouthed man, and whether or not he knew any more than she did he was very yorky about saying anything at all.

The Guards did not tell her much either. The fact was few people ever would tell Mrs. Conarchy anything. People who would not refuse a drink to a dog or a cat that was thirsty yet instinctively withheld information from a person so openly inquisitive.

Devlin put a few questions about visitors and vehicles passing through the gates, which brought on him a lament for the good old days when there was more life in the place. The hunt used to meet at the castle then, and old Lady Kilskour had her annual sale of work. There was nothing like that now. Mrs. Conarchy envied her sister who lived in Clogh and saw life. Her refrain was "Nothing ever happens here."

Extricating themselves from this conversation, Nolan and Devlin rode out from under the archway and got their first view of the big house and the small one. The Dower House was down a side avenue in a grove of evergreens. The castle, a conglomeration of dwelling and outhouses, spread out right and left beyond a stretch of pasture dotted with large old trees.

Sergeant Nolan on his last visit had been only as far as the Dower House, but this time they slid past the entrance to the side avenue and rode on up the main drive to the castle. It was Devlin's idea that his trained eye might pick out something significant if he let it wander over those sprawling outbuildings. He was thinking of a case when over a thousand pounds weight of lead had been removed from the roof of a gaol. You never knew what it would be next.

In any case one of their main objectives was in the stable yard. Fergus Gandon had his studio there, well away from his family, in a converted loft over a garage. They knew which it was because the door was padlocked. All the other doors were on the latch or wide open, waiting for farm horses which were all out at work. Beyond the stable yard there was a farmyard with pigsties and cow sheds, and beyond that again, on the way to the walled gardens, a space with tool sheds and potting sheds, a manure heap, and a five foot high compost heap, scientifically constructed on the Indore method.

The rain was coming in gusts, and the going underfoot was what you might expect of a farmyard in February. Devlin led Nolan in and out of sheds and stables, but all the roofs seemed in good repair, and everything uninteresting and innocent. It was dull work.

"Mind you, Lancey isn't really expecting anything in your line," said Nolan. "He's just a terrible thorough man.

But Devlin was probing the compost heap with a stick. He asked Nolan to get him a crowbar he had seen in the tool shed.

When Nolan had the crowbar in his hand it occurred to him to stir up a box of litter, old seed packets and such rubbish, which Conarchy kept in the shed, he being a tidy man. Devlin had been in there but he might have overlooked it. The crowbar struck metal, and up from the bottom came an empty tin labeled Poison. It had contained arsenate of lead for spraying fruit trees.

Such tins are common and might turn up in any garden except one belonging to a man like Lord Kilskour. Sergeant Nolan well knew his lordship's disapproval of the use of chemicals in agriculture. His theories were much discussed in the district. The subject came up whenever an old farmer's middle-aged sons wanted him to lay out money on things like superphosphates. Though Conarchy had a fairly free hand, he would never buy stuff like this without reference to his employer. This was an interesting find indeed. If only there were fingerprints on it, the tin might turn out to be the lynch pin of the whole case.

Nolan called Devlin and explained to him all the wheels within wheels. They wrapped the tin carefully in clean paper, of which they had brought a supply, and noted down the time, place and history of the find. Devlin was disappointingly calm over it. It was not his find, and it was not as if Lord Kilskour was likely to have bought such a commodity in the black market. The Dublin detective was not sufficiently in touch with agriculture to understand what principles were at stake. It spurred him on, however, to further efforts on his own account. Nolan turned round, after carefully depositing the tin in a locked bag he had on the carrier of his bicycle, to see Devlin in the stable yard trying the strength of the staple which held the padlock on the door leading to Gandon's studio. The screws were rusty and it looked as if the whole thing might come off at a pull, and Inspector Devlin was pulling.

"What do you think you're doing?" asked the sergeant in a shocked voice. "I suppose you know that's breaking and entering?"

"No need for that, Sergeant. Sure, I have the key here," said a chirpy voice. A monkey-faced man carrying a large umbrella had come quietly into the yard through the arch from the main drive.

This was Mosney, the Gandons' ex-convict factotum. Anyone could see it was meat and drink to him to catch the police at a disadvantage. But the man from the Detective Branch was not so easily put down. He said sternly,

"This fastening ought to be screwed on properly. Look at the state of it! All falling to bits. How do you expect the police to protect people's property if they don't keep it in repair?"

"It'll protect itself a while yet," said Mosney, "if nobody goes out of their way to make it worse. Did you want to get in, by any chance? I seen you pass and I came down after you from our place, because I knew there was nobody around to keep an eye on you."

Sergeant Nolan in the course of years had accumulated a fund of patience for dealing with people like Mosney. He replied civilly that they had just been taking a look round to see if there was anything in their line, but that he supposed the demesne wall was a great protection in itself and not many unauthorized persons would get this far. Then he asked,

"Is it in here Mr. Gandon has a picture painted all over the walls, that his lordship didn't like? I was telling Mr. Devlin here about it."

"Interested in pictures?" enquired Mosney with the air of a dilettante and acknowledging the introduction to Devlin with a slight flicker of his eyelids.

"Oh, just curiosity," said Nolan. "And we'd like another word with yourself."

"I'm afraid I can't spare much time," said Mosney affectedly. "The house you know, and the children. There's baby up there all alone till the two older kids come home from school. But I'll show you the murals as you're so interested."

He unlocked the door and sent it flying back on its runners. The garage inside was a spacious one with room for at least three cars. At present it was empty, and yet the visitors' first startled impression was that it was full of strange presences.

The large expanse of the walls, smoothly finished off by the builders with white plaster, had proved irresistible to Fergus Gandon. He had executed thereon an enormous design in primitive colors, black, yellow and terra cotta.

It was a kind of hunting scene, in which centaur-like beings with subhuman faces, accompanied by vaguely canine monstrosities, pursued a variety of smaller creatures all over the wall surface. The design was subtly repetitive, but no detail ever recurred in quite the same form, for Fergus was fertile in invention. The simple color scheme made it gay and even attractive from a distance, but a close-up was disconcerting. There was something nightmarish about the half repetitions and the dominating theme of flight and pursuit.

Mosney, knowing what was coming, had fixed his small sharp eyes expectantly on the Guards' faces. Nolan's came best up to expectation. The big sergeant turned quite pink and shuddered. "Oh God," he said, "it'd give you the bull horrors!"

Inspector Devlin from Dublin remained impassive. "Any more like it upstairs?" he asked.

Mosney hesitated. The fact was he had not been able to resist showing off the murals, but he did not much want to let the Guards in any further. But they were not to be put off once they had got their feet in the door. Mosney protested that he really had not the time, whereat Nolan suggested that he should return to his baby-sitting and leave them to follow. As he did not like that either, they all three climbed the ladder that led to the upper floor.

The upper room had been converted to a painter's use by blocking up the windows which had opened at floor level in the days when it was a hayloft, and by letting skylights in to the roof. It was a large place, but fantastically untidy, choc-a-block with junk. At one end was a dais with a model throne, and at the other a work bench with a stone for grinding colors, also three Primus stoves and a litter of saucepans, palettes, brushes, bottles and jars. Among miscellaneous objects lying about the room in heaps, the visitors noticed a human skull.

"What's in all these?" asked Devlin, indicating the things on the work bench.

"You wouldn't understand if I told you," replied Mosney. "Glues and varnishes. Grounds of different kinds. Size. Gesso, if you know what that is."

"What's the smell? " asked Devlin. "I don't mean the oil paint. The smell like something gone bad."

"Might be some smell you brought with you," muttered their cicerone. They told him sternly that he should watch himself or it might be the worse for him, and he sulkily suggested fish glue.

"It's more like egg," said Devlin sniffing.

"It could be egg," said Mosney. "He's had plenty up here from time to time. I suppose one got overlooked."

"What was he doing, picnicking? " asked Devlin sarcastically.

"Ah, not at all. He uses the eggs to paint with. New laid, they have to be, and only the yolk. There was hundreds used in that job below," Mosney's finger jabbed at the floor. "Mrs. Gandon makes the white into meringues. Sure we lived on them at one time. Sick and tired of them we were. I wish now I'd thought of sending some a present to the barracks." He grinned at Sergeant Nolan in a way that might or might not have been intended to conciliate him.

The investigators by now were prepared to believe any wickedness of a man like Gandon, but the studio revealed no traces of felonious activity to the superficial glance. The skull was only the innocuous kind of exhibit to be found in the rooms of medical students. The pictures upstairs were mostly unfinished, and though some were sketches for the mural below they were considerably tamer than Gandon's final working out of his conception. Devlin peered underneath the dais. Mosney called to him that there was nothing in there but rubbishy old canvas. The detective pulled out something in a long roll, and thought for a moment that the establishment had been caught out at last, but it was only a picture, taken out of its frame and rolled round a stick. There were several others. Devlin pulled them all out and let them unroll with an air of doing it accidentally that deceived nobody, but he found nothing inside. They were nicer pictures than the others in the studio, and it seemed a pity to leave them rolled face outwards among all the dust and dirt, but Mosney said they were only old stuff Mr. Gandon bought. He picked them up cheap for the sake of the frames.

While Devlin rooted about, Nolan made it his business to observe Mosney's reactions. The man puzzled him. He had an actor's face; it was sallow, pinched, and deeply lined, all its life in the eyes. He was clean-shaven and looked neat although his clothes were ragged. He might have been any age from thirty to sixty.

Whatever had made him reluctant to let them into the studio seemed to be off his mind now. He had ceased to pretend he heard the baby crying, and stood looking on and grinning to himself. Had they missed something, or was there after all nothing there to find ? Feeling that the time had come to give the man a jolt, Nolan said,

"Do the Gandons know you've done time, *Geraghty?*"

Mosney never blinked. He replied, "I wondered how long it would take you to get around to asking that."

"Come on, quit stalling," said Nolan. "You heard what I asked you."

"Sure they know. They've known this long time."

"Was that why they took you on?"

"It was not. I got engaged on my merits, because I had an honest face."

"How did they find out, then?"

"I told them myself when I seen what a nice broad-minded gentleman Mr. Gandon was."

"What do you mean, broad-minded?"

"Opposite of you," said Mosney.

"Listen," said Nolan, "tell me this. Did the Gandons take you on to help you run straight, or did they take you on to help them run crooked?"

Mosney looked indignant. "You've no reason at all to make those kind of insinuations. If you want to know, I was taken on because nobody else offered for the job, and I stayed because I liked the family and the freedom from petty interference."

He sounded sincere, but he was a twister if ever the sergeant saw one.

"Do they pay you wages? " asked Nolan.

"Two pound a week and all found," said Mosney. "It's the best they can do. There's not much money in pictures, not his kind."

"Damn the penny I'd give for them," said Nolan, "but he's well known up in Dublin."

"I'll tell you what it is," said Mosney. "It isn't what way a picture is painted that matters; it's how you sell it. That's where the art comes in."

"Like selling telegraph poles, eh?"

"Harder than that," said the ex-confidence trickster with a shameless grin.

"And do you do the sales talk?"

" Ah, not at all, that's Mr. Silke's job. The stuff's all sent up to his place in Dublin. He's in touch with all the right class of buyers—more money than sense."

"And what does he get out of it?"

Mosney did not know the exact nature of the arrangement between his employer and the dealer.

"Whatever it is," he said, "Mr. Gandon thinks it's more than his share. I heard him say so a couple of times. But what I say is, it's at Mr. Silke's end that the brains come in."

"Did they fall out over it?" asked Nolan, pricking up his ears.

"Ah not at all, it was only Mr. Gandon grumbling to himself and the mistress. You know how it goes. The producer abuses the middleman and vice versa. That happens in all trades. Hello, who's this?"

Mosney's ears, accustomed to the noises of the locality, had been the first to hear a car stopping at the big gates.

They could not see out through the studio skylights, so he dropped down the ladder into the garage and went out through the yard to the drive. Sergeant Nolan followed, while Inspector Devlin was left in possession of the studio to his own great satisfaction.

Nolan and Mosney watched the car. It had been to the Dower House, and was emerging now from the side avenue and coming towards them up the drive. It was an Austin A40 with a Dublin registration, driven by a chauffeur. It drew up on the gravel sweep in front of the castle, and a man got out of the back.

"More of your lot?" Mosney asked the sergeant out of the side of his mouth.

Nolan shook his head. You never know what may turn up in plain clothes, but they do not usually have that kind of chauffeur.

The stranger approached, feeling in an inner pocket of his dark overcoat. He wore pince-nez and a bowler hat. Ignoring the uniformed sergeant he addressed Mosney, at the same time producing a letter. "An introduction from Mr. Gandon," he said, "but I'm afraid I've come at an inconvenient time. My name is Fringley Pole."

A name like Fringley Pole might belong to a black marketeer as well as anybody else, and the fact that he looked an innocent sort of a man was, Nolan knew, nothing to go by. However, the letter he had brought from Fergus Gandon, which Mosney let the sergeant see, said that all he wanted was to look at pictures in the castle, and there seemed no reason why he should not. It would have been hard on him to be turned away after coming down from Dublin on purpose.

It was one thing after another for Mosney, but for the investigators it was a bit of luck. The sergeant said that he too would like to see over the old house; he had never been in it in his whole time at Clogh, and Mr. Devlin also might be interested. Devlin had joined them; ten minutes to himself in the studio seemed to have satisfied him. He said he would be interested to see the castle, very interested. Nolan suggested that they should take the keys and go in with the gentleman and release Mosney for other duties, but Mosney said the dinner could wait for once, and as he could not hear baby crying she must be asleep.

Mr. Fringley Pole might have looked more pleased at having so much company, but he accepted the sergeant and the plainclothes man very civilly. He evidently took Devlin for one of the locals, as he remarked to him in a man-to-man way that he supposed the rain would be good for the crops.

Kilskour Castle consisted of a central block and two wings. It had four stories, six staircases, between fifty and sixty rooms, not counting cellars and attics, and one bathroom. (In the matter of sanitation Lord Kilskour's principles reconciled him to earth closets.) A suite of rooms was kept ready for his lordship. The rest of the house had long been uninhabited, and was furnished only with pieces too cumbersome to move: huge old chests and cupboards fit to hold any number of sides of bacon. The walls in places were three feet thick, and the chimneys were wide enough for a man to go up and down. An illicit still might be working there and no one any the wiser. To search the place, in the strict sense of the Manual of Criminal Investigation, would have required an army corps. The most Devlin hoped was to find evidence to justify an application for a search warrant. He moved doggedly on from room to room, with Mosney opening doors and disclosing ever further possibilities. Far from obstructing the police in the performance of their duties, Mosney seemed anxious to egg them on.

Sergeant Nolan, however, remained with Mr. Fringley Pole, who did not offer to accompany Devlin on a tour of inspection and obviously thought his curiosity ill-bred. Mr. Fringley Pole had come to see the pictures, not to pry into the home life of the aristocracy. He took root in the first floor drawing room, where there were pictures all over the walls. There was also a nice turf fire burning, which Mosney said was lighted on wet days by Mrs. Gandon's orders, for the good of the grand piano. By contrast with the rest of the house it was agreeably warm. Sergeant Nolan felt glad that his duty called him to this post and not to go the rounds with Inspector Devlin. He sat down on a dust-sheeted sofa, smoked a peaceful cigarette, and counted thirty-five pictures in all, some nearly as good as new, some nothing but dirty patches of canvas inside fancy frames. It seemed funny anyone should come all that way to look at them, but there was no doubt Mr. Fringley Pole took a genuine interest. He wandered round and round, stooping and stretching and getting quite a lot of exercise, and coming back to his favorites over and over again. When a cloud of smoke blew down out of the chimney the man got really worked up about it because, he said, it was ruination to the pictures. He declared it was a disgrace the way art treasures were neglected in country houses, and that he should make it his business to write to Mr. Gandon about it.

Sergeant Nolan was good-naturedly trying to smooth the man down, in the interests of peace, and out of a feeling that Mr. Gandon had troubles enough already, when they heard shouts outside. Also the violent ringing of a bicycle bell. Looking down from the high windows they saw a bicycle coming up the drive, carrying two passengers—a small girl in slacks with flying pigtails, who sat on the saddle pedaling energetically, and a small boy perched on the bar. They careened full tilt up to the steps and there the small boy fell off and evidently hurt himself, for he yelled louder than before, while the small girl, entirely unsympathetic, proceeded to scold him and shout him down. Mr. Fringley Pole's chauffeur got out of the car but stood looking on helplessly. The sergeant rapidly explained to Mr. Fringley Pole that these were Mr. Gandon's children, and they both hurried downstairs to pick up the pieces. As they came out on the steps a window above them opened and Mosney's voice floated down. It was inaudible in the uproar, but menacing, and it had an effect. The small boy stopped crying and joined his sister in a chant of:

"We want din-din-dinner. We want Mos-ney! We're STARVING!"

"Stop bawling then," called Mosney. "You'll get no dinner if you go on like that. Disgracing my upbringing. Hold on, now, and I'll be down to you."

A minute later (the children meanwhile continued chanting in more subdued voices) Mosney clattered down the main stairs and appeared in the big doorway. The small girl hurled herself at him. The small boy sat still at the bottom of the steps and announced to Sergeant Nolan:

"My leg's broken, I do believe."

It was not, however; merely grazed. Mr. Fringley Pole's chauffeur became really helpful and produced a first-aid box, and between them they dabbed disinfectant on the wound and tied a pad over it. The child bore this stoically; his crying out before had been mainly showing off. But he suggested that it might be bad for him to walk back to the Dower House, and he had better have a lift in the car.

The small girl clinging to Mosney's arm explained to the sergeant:

"We were afraid you had arrested him, and then we shouldn't have got any dinner at all."

"You should know me better than that, Miss Grania," said Nolan. It was long past his dinner hour, too. He thought he and Devlin had done about all the detecting they could in this direction, and was ready to support the suggestion of a move for home.

Mosney called into the house, "I'll have to lock up here now, Mr. Devlin," and the last member of the party emerged reluctantly, with a lingering look at a suit of armor big enough to hold a half-dozen of whiskey hidden in its warlike breast. He tapped it as he passed, but it rang hollow, so he came away with the others.

Grania Gandon sped back on the bicycle, and her brother, Colm, had his wish and rode back in state beside the chauffeur. The two Guards fetched their bicycles from the yard and walked back with Mosney. At the Dower House they met the third and youngest member of the Gandon family, Faustine, or Fossy. She was sitting up in her pram outside the door, hurling toys out on to the path. Guard Eugene Roche, one of the three members of Sergeant Nolan's staff who had been placed at the Dower House to protect and watch it, was picking up a woolly rabbit with the air of one performing an action for the twentieth time.

"Look at that now," said Mosney delighted. "Ah, you're very bold, Fossy, to plague the poor policeman. Sure he has enough to do without you to vex him."

Roche stood to attention with a wooden expression. The sergeant felt glad to think his relief was due in about an hour.

Mr. Fringley Pole leaned out of the car to thank Mosney for all the trouble he had gone to and gave him a tip before he drove away. Sergeant Nolan and Inspector Devlin also said good-bye but omitted the tip. They told Mosney they would be back one of these days and meantime he had better watch his step.

There was still Conarchy the head gardener, whom they had to find and question on the subject of spraying apple trees with arsenic. Nothing had interfered with Tim Conarchy's dinner hour. He was just buttoning his waistcoat and preparing to come away from the lodge again when the Guards called there to ask for him. He and Nolan were old acquaintances, but few people knew Tim well; he was as silent as his wife was talkative. Whether this was by nature or the consequence of living with Mrs. Conarchy, Nolan had not known them long enough to say.

They showed him the empty tin, warning him off touching it, and asked him if he could explain what it was doing in his tool shed. Tim shook his head. His one reply to everything they asked him was the ambiguous phrase, "I couldn't say." He could not say who had bought the tin or how long it had been there or what had become of the contents, or even whether or not he would consider it the right treatment for some of the old apple trees if his employer would permit the use of it. His mind seemed completely blank.

"That man knows more than he'll say," said Nolan to Devlin, as they cycled wearily back to Clogh. "You wouldn't get it out of him by any amount of cross-heckling, but we're on to something there. Well, we've got something to send to Dublin anyway."

They had also some samples from the studio. When left alone there Inspector Devlin had seized the opportunity to extract small quantities of white powders or pastes which he found in several of the jars on Fergus Gandon's work bench. They might turn out to be arsenic, or something else equally interesting.

It was arranged for Devlin to go up by the evening train and bring all the exhibits up with him. Sergeant Nolan had plenty of duties to keep him at the barracks and would not attend the next conference unless he had special orders to do so. But he wrote out his own report for Lancey and made it clear by whom the tin had been found. He thought Devlin was the sort of fellow who might forget to mention it.

CHAPTER 12

"AND have the police anything to go on? Do they keep you informed?" enquired Mr. Arnold Silke, glancing round the faces of the three Fennellys and Nell Gandon. He had come straight out to see them after the detectives had left him and had found them all assembled in the study.

They realized now that they ought not to have left Fergus' man of business to learn the news first from the Civic Guards. Mr. Silke had reason to feel hurt but was able to be magnanimous. He had paid this visit partly to express his sympathy, partly to discuss the prospects for the Gandon Exhibition. They owed it to him to put him in possession of all the facts.

"They never tell us anything," said Nell. "They suspect us all."

"They are always very busy and in a hurry," said Hester. "One doesn't like to bother them with questions."

"That's only to put you off," said Nell.

"What makes them think it was anything but an accident?" Mr. Silke asked. "They came to me talking about motives. I did not like the trend of their questioning at all."

"Oh, they have to explore all the possibilities," said Paul in his reassuring way. "I don't think they have formed any theory yet. They are still collecting data."

"But their idea of data!" The dealer wore a pitying smile. "Tell me, did they ask to see his paintbox?"

"They took it away," said Hester. "They take all kinds of things. I've given up asking them why."

"I know," said Mr. Silke sympathetically. "The time they must waste on trifles! The paintbox was because of some marvelous theory of the dangers of sucking one's brush."

Nell and Hester looked at each other. "Fergus does," said Nell. "I'm always telling him not to. Could it have been that?"

"He's done it all his life and he's never been ill before," said Hester.

Mr. Silke nodded. "I am afraid the solution is not so simple. But one knows what can happen. A panic starts about poisonous paints. The thing comes up in court. Experts are required to testify, and representatives of the manufacturers have to be brought over from England. A number of busy men with real work to do have their time wasted." He sighed. "I said what I could to prevent such extravagances."

"The police are certainly thorough," said Paul. "But very considerate on the whole."

"But not, perhaps, very open to suggestions?" ventured the dealer.

Paul smiled. "Well, you know, I rather believe in letting people alone to do their own job in their own way."

"Oh, quite," said Mr. Silke, but he looked dissatisfied, and as if he felt there was danger of mismanagement.

Then he came to the other purpose of his visit, which was to impress on Nell, as regards the Gandon Exhibition, that the show must go on. Nell was ready to agree. The trouble was that if the exhibition was to consist only of canvases and watercolors already at Silkes' Galleries, it would be a bit thin. They had been counting on Fergus' completing other work that he had in his studio, and now, however good his recovery, there was no hope of that.

Nell thought she might find three or four extra items at home, either old work, or even work that Fergus himself would not have passed as finished. She and the dealer had before now conspired to steal away pictures which still to his eye wanted touching up, or studies that he had not intended for exhibition.

"There are the designs for the hunting mural," said Nell. "The one he painted on the garage walls for fun. It's finished now, Arnold, and it's the best work he ever did. It makes me cry to look at it; it's so wasted in a place like that. You ought to send somebody down to photograph it and write it up. You'd better do it soon, or Alban will have it whitewashed. He got frightfully cross over it. It must have jabbed him right in the subconscious. That shows you how good it is."

Mr. Silke cast an appealing look at the Fennellys. "These artists! Just having fun and games, when they might be painting something that would sell. I don't know about the photographer, Nell. It'd cost something to send one all that way. Get me the designs and I'll think about it."

"I can't go home yet," said Nell. Her eyes filled with tears again. "I can't leave Fergus. He's still in danger."

Hester put her arm round her sister-in-law. Mr. Silke, looking alarmed, rose to his feet.

"No need to distress yourself," he said. "There's no such urgent hurry. The sooner the better, of course. You know what it's like. There's the framing, and the catalogues. One must allow for delays at the printers'." He stood looking at Nell anxiously, evidently torn between a wish to spare her and anxiety to get ahead with his arrangements. "Ah well," he concluded, "we must hope for better news in the course of the next few days."

Another reason for Nell Gandon to return to Kilskour was provided by a letter which came next morning, addressed to Fergus, from Mr. Fringley Pole.

"What tiny finicky writing!" said Nell, spreading out three half sheets on the dining-room table. "What's it all about?" She proceeded to read aloud:

" . . . *feel I must draw your attention at once to a matter of which you are doubtless unaware, the smoking of the drawing-room chimney at Kilskour Castle. Today, the weather being wet and windy, black clouds of smoke came billowing into the room with every gust. I need not point out to you the danger to the pictures, especially as none of them is glazed. The blackening of the surfaces by smoke in this way will inevitably necessitate cleaning, and may even prove to have done irreparable damage.*

"The poor lamb, God help him!" commented Nell, casting her eyes heavenward.

"How sensible of him to tell you," said Hester. "It's so easy not to know about things like that. I daresay it's only a matter of getting it swept."

"M'm, yes, I daresay," said Nell, reading on. "The next bit's more interesting. He's seen a picture he thinks he'd like to buy. 'The flower piece hanging on the right of the fireplace.' Yes, I know the one. I suppose he thinks he can find a safer place to put it."

"I suppose Lord Kilskour will sell?" said Hester. She remembered Fergus saying something about it.

"Oh, that part's all right. A hundred pounds, he says. I think he might make a better offer."

"He seems to collect flower pieces," said Hester. "He bought one just the other day." Nell had not yet heard the story of their first encounter with Mr. Fringley Pole at the auction. She listened with more interest than she usually showed in her sister-in-law's conversation and asked to have the picture described to her.

"Only fifty," she said at the end of Hester's account. "That was dirt cheap."

"Don't let Barbara hear you say so," said Hester. "Anyhow how can you tell, just on description?"

"Oh, I'm only guessing," said Nell. "It must be some good or he wouldn't have bid for it. But collectors will go any length. I shall ask him two hundred pounds."

"And he'll beat you down to a hundred and fifty, and you'll say 'make it guineas'," said Hester laughing.

"That's how it goes," said Nell. "Business is business. I'll write about it now and post it on my way to the hospital."

That day the doctor decided that Fergus Gandon was well enough to be told about the Civic Guards, and if he survived that, he might be able to talk to two of them for not more than ten minutes. The fact was, Dr. Colville was getting tired of being rung up morning, noon and night by Superintendent Lancey.

Nell took a poor view of it and insisted on being present when the subject was broached. Dr. Colville did the broaching. Nell flung herself on her knees by Fergus' bed and fixed her eyes on his face. But the critical moment went by quietly. Fergus made no fuss. Either he realized himself that this was inevitable, or he was too ill to care.

"Darling," said Nell, "it isn't my doing. I tried to stop it, but nobody listens to what I say."

A pale smile showed fleetingly in Fergus' beard.

"Darling, do you forgive me?" said Nell.

"What for?" whispered Fergus.

"For not being a protection to you."

"What could you do against Destiny?" said Fergus. "Kiss me, you idiot."

Nell kissed him. Dr. Colville stepped forward and took his pulse.

"Don't excite him, Mrs. Gandon," he said. "I think he might as well see them now and get it over. Will you wait outside?"

"Let 'em loose," said Fergus. "I hope their boots don't squeak."

Dr. Colville took Nell out. Inspector Grace and Detective Officer Lemon came in with catlike tread.

The detectives found Fergus Gandon more amenable than they had expected. He apologized for his wife. He said she meant well, but she had exaggerated his prejudice against the police. They might search his house if they liked, and if they could throw any light on this business of the arsenic he would think better of them in future.

He himself could not even give a guess at the identity of his enemy nor suggest any motive for the crime.

He was obviously a very sick man and in no condition to be cross-questioned. Inspector Grace rose at once when the doctor came forward. He was satisfied to be able to bear back to Superintendent Lancey the permission to search. But at the last moment Gandon said something more, in a voice the inspector had to bend down to catch

"You'll keep your fellows away from my studio. Nobody but me goes there. It's not near the house."

Inspector Grace pointed out that it was no use doing things by halves. They must search everywhere if they searched at all.

"But I can't have my studio pulled to pieces," said the painter. "It's not as if I could be there to keep an eye on things. It isn't necessary, either. The studio is my own place. Nobody would have the nerve to hide things there."

Seeing the inspector inclined to argue, the patient raised himself on his pillows. The doctor begged the detectives not to excite him. The inspector begged Gandon to reconsider. The patient started being sick. A nurse, who had been effacing herself in a corner all the time, suddenly magnified herself into an outraged guardian angel and turned everybody out.

Fergus had his own methods of obstructing the police in the performance of their duties. Inspector Grace said at the next police conference that he wished the murderer had made a better job of it. What were you to do with a body that was dead but wouldn't lie down?

Contrary to everyone's predictions, the little bit of excitement seemed to have done Fergus good. Later in the day he saw Nell and Hester together. They did not stay long, or talk much about the investigation, but they came away feeling happier. The fact that he knew the worst now was a weight off their minds.

Nell was silent most of the way home. Then, when Hester was taking her hat and coat off, her sister-in-law came in and announced

"I think I ought to go back to Kilskour. The Guards will be there turning everything upside down, and there are those pictures to see to, and Mr. Fringley Pole's picture, and I don't like to leave the children to Mosney too long. He's wonderfully good with them, for an ex-convict, but it isn't quite the same as a mother."

Hester saw an opportunity to do her sister-in-law a kindness and seized it, for she was filled with compunction now for her attitude in the past. The journey to Kilskour by train was tedious and comfortless. She offered to drive Nell down and bring the pictures back.

Nell jumped at the offer, and Barbara also was glad to come as spare driver. If they started early she and her mother could get there and back in the day, with time to spare to see her uncle's studio and the art treasures of the castle. Barbara would have gone further than eighty miles with such inducements.

"You see, Aunt Nell," she said, "if one can't paint pictures oneself, it seems to me the next best thing is to form a good collection. I do wish Mother had let me buy that one she told you about. I grudge it to Mr. Fringley Pole."

"She was jolly well right," said Nell. "Don't you go thinking you know better than your mother, at your age."

After what Nell had said to her earlier about the picture having gone cheap, Hester had had moments of self-reproach about her action. She was surprised and touched by this warm support. She fancied it might be only Nell's way of showing gratitude for the drive.

CHAPTER 13

THE second police conference was smaller than the first. The only VIP present was Chief Superintendent Healy, summoned from the country by Superintendent Lancey relentless in the cause of duty. Fresh news had come in which indicated that the case was moving Healy's way, and he did not like the look of it.

The metropolitan divisional superintendent was busy with a real murder. The superintendent of the technical bureau was attending a case in court. Sergeant Nolan's duties, as we know, kept him down in Clogh. Inspector Devlin and Inspector Grace and Detective Officer Lemon were all there, and one or two other detectives who had been employed on minor enquiries, and a fingerprint expert, and an officer acting as assistant to Superintendent Lancey, who helped to carry the growing pile of manila files. Behind these members of the

Civic Guard actively at work on the investigation may be envisaged an army of clerical workers, laboratory workers, fingerprint specialists, photographers, to say nothing of all the local police checking poisons registers, and this gives some idea of what Fergus Gandon's misfortunes were costing the taxpayer.

The various officers who had been employed on enquiries had all made written reports, and these had been typed and stenciled and copies, still wet, were available for the conference. The fingerprint section had had Sergeant Nolan's find to play with and had found on it some smudgy fingerprints and one big beautiful thumbprint. These could not be identified with any prints in the records. The tin had been sent to be photographed. The analysts' reports on the various samples sent to them from the Fennellys were beginning to come in at last. Lancey's assistant was still sorting the copies and getting them into the proper files.

The piece of news which had brought poor Healy to Dublin on a day when he might have been hunting had emerged from the check on the poisons registers. Superintendent Lancey was gratified; he loved to see the system produce results so promptly, like putting a penny in a slot. A message had come in from a Dublin station to say that in July of the previous year a seedsman in Dawson Street had sold a tin of arsenate of lead to a customer who gave his address as 9, Evelyn Gardens, Dublin. There are no such gardens, a fact which aroused suspicion. The customer had signed his name as "A. Hering." The shop assistant whose name was entered as the seller could not remember anything about him or her, and none of the staff knew the name. But Superintendent Lancey knew that Hering was the family name of Lord Kilskour. He put through a trunk call to Chief Superintendent Healy and said: "I think this looks fishy."

Healy groaned, and Lancey, who was innocent of intent to pun, thought the chief superintendent must be very much upset at the idea of Lord Kilskour being implicated.

Lancey sent for the Poisons Book in question and had the signature photographed. He also sent a man round the most likely banks with a vague tale of suspected forgery and secured a specimen of Lord Kilskour's usual signature. The bank's specimen was "Kilskour" not "Hering," but it looked like the same hand.

One other contribution to the case had also come direct to headquarters. Mr. Arnold Silke had rung up and asked to speak to the officer in charge of the Gandon enquiry. He had had some second thoughts about his interview with the detectives who had called the previous afternoon.

Lancey, a copy of Inspector Grace's report in his hand, took the call. Mr. Silke said he wanted to raise a minor point—a point so trivial that he would not have troubled the police with it if it had not carried an imputation against his own firm, which he would not be thought to have deliberately sidetracked. The detectives had asked him if there was any possibility of watercolor paints being poisonous, and he had pooh-poohed the idea and declared, as a dealer in artists' materials, that there was absolutely no danger of anything of the sort. But on thinking the matter over—Mr. Silke must have been lying awake in the small hours—it had occurred to him that arsenic was indeed a possible contaminant of low-grade gelatin, and that gelatin was used by some makers to give viscosity to paint wash colors. He was disturbed in his mind about this, for as far as he knew Mr. Gandon purchased his materials entirely at Silkes'. He frankly admitted that he was not solely ringing up in order to be helpful but also in the hope of relieving his own mind.

The analysts' report on the paintbox had not yet come in. Even if it had Superintendent Lancey might not have parted with any information; he was a firm believer in silence being golden. He thanked Mr. Silke very much for ringing up and said he would make a note to enquire about it, and rang off, indifferent to the thought of an art dealer on tenterhooks.

These fresh developments gave the second conference a hopeful start, but then, as often happens in detective work, other information turned up and the pieces of the puzzle which had seemed about to fit in to each other were all spilled again, and more patience required from all concerned.

The first snag was that the analysts' reports on the patient's excreta did not correspond with the formula for the contents of the empty tin.

The tin had contained a powder intended to be mixed with water for the purpose of spraying fruit trees. It was by no means pure arsenic: the actual arsenic content was only fifteen percent. Roughly speaking, it would take at least a teaspoonful to ensure a fatal dose. Lancey's first thought on working this out was that this must be the explanation why Gandon had never, at any one time, taken enough arsenic to kill him. Little as the chief superintendent might like the idea, it seemed to look like a case. Then science stepped in and insisted that what the patient had swallowed was sulphide of arsenic with absolutely no trace of lead in it at all.

"Looks as if your bally tin was nothing but a coincidence," growled Healy, thinking wistfully of his day's hunting.

"It could be a coincidence all right," agreed Lancey politely, "but what about that business of the signature? That was very irregular."

"Might be sheer absentmindedness."

"A man would have to be very absentminded to forget his own name."

"Hering is his own name."

"He's been Lord Kilskour this twenty years."

"Oh all right, have it your own way," grumbled the chief superintendent. "If it wasn't a coincidence it might have been a practical joke."

Superintendent Lancey looked really shocked.

"Beg pardon," interposed Inspector Devlin, "mightn't it be a kind of a practical joke with a purpose? Something to set us off on a wrong track."

"It sounds to me," said Healy, "the sort of thing that fellow Mosney would get up to."

"They aren't Mosney's prints this time," said Superintendent Lancey.

"That fellow Conarchy, the lodge man, knows something," said Inspector Devlin.

"I think Lord Kilskour should be asked about it," said Lancey, firmly but deferentially, to Healy. "It's a nuisance he's in England; we'll have to trouble the Yard. We can mark the form 'Discreetly'."

"For heaven's sake see you do," said Healy, and watched Lancey's assistant make a note of it.

Healy had time to simmer down while Lancey proceeded in his methodical way to tidy up loose ends. No arsenic had been found in foodstuffs taken from the Fennellys, or anywhere except where it was to be expected: in sediment from the W.C. drains and the wastepipe of Gandon's bedroom handbasin. The housemaid, Irene, had been traced. She was in another place already, and had sent promptly for her luggage, thus saving the police all trouble in finding her address. Irene had simply glanced through the day's "Domestics Wanted," answered the advertisement offering the highest wages, and walked straight into the job. Her new employer not only gained an excellent maid but the first rights in a thrilling item of gossip. She felt herself favored of heaven, and as she knew plenty of people who knew the Fennellys she was spreading the story far and wide. The detective who called, having sized her up, cramped her style a bit by hinting at the chance of an action for slander. But there was no doubt people were talking, and the case could not be kept out of the newspapers much longer. Irene did not behave in the least as if she might be guilty, and was not able to add anything to what they knew already.

It seemed as if the idea of black marketing might as well be abandoned, There could not be much to find out if Inspector Devlin had not been able to find it. The large-scale purchases of eggs by the Gandons were explained, and nobody thought any the better of Gandon for wasting good food spreading paint on a wall, but it did not seem as if this could be his guilty secret. They were even beginning to wonder if, after all, he had one.

"Remember this chap's an artist," said Healy. "It's natural him wanting to keep everyone out of his studio. It's probably just a kind of mania with him. He gave permission to search the house freely enough."

It may as well be added here, though the results of analysis did not come till later, that the samples taken from the studio by Inspector Devlin were all harmless and proved to be legitimate ingredients of the painter's craft.

Some hopes had been entertained of the enigmatic figure of Mr. Fringley Pole, but a few straightforward enquiries sufficed to strip him of all mystery. Mr. Fringley Pole was a partner in a firm which sold ecclesiastical furniture and so had been led to art by way of business. Pictures were his one extravagance. He was married but childless. His wife never did anything but good works on which she spent little herself.

Then they tackled the Dublin end of the case in detail. The conference by now was working up an intensive fug. Everyone was smoking, there were two electric fires on, and the weather outside had suddenly turned from cold to stuffy, a way it has in Dublin. Mick Lemon, a fresh air lover, almost longed to be out on a beat instead of stuck in here listening to Healy and Lancey and the rest going over and over all the facts. And then, as sometimes does happen, out of the fog and welter of discussion a new line began to open up. Suspicion began to gather round a new figure. The conference was asking, "What about Mr. Paddy Purtill?"

What seemed to lend this man significance was the fact, emerging from a fresh review and comparison of everybody's statements, that he alone had been on or near the scene at every stage of Gandon's illness. Neither the Fennellys nor their maids had ever been to Kilskour. None of the Gandons, nor Mosney, nor Lord Kilskour, had been at the Fennellys. But Paddy Purtill, though not obvious in the general picture, had been staying with the Gandons when Fergus Gandon first fell ill, and he had called at the Fennellys two days before his final collapse.

Inspector Grace gave it as his impression that Purtill was not such a friend of Gandon's as he made out. He was certainly not a wholehearted admirer. He had some hard things to say about Gandon's work, which, according to Mr. Silke the dealer, were quite unjustified. Grace had been struck by Mr. Silke's allusion to professional spite and jealousy among artists.

"He didn't mention Purtill, did he?" asked the chairman.

Grace shook his head. "Mr. Silke's not the sort to mention names. But he might be able to tell us more if we asked him."

"I suppose we can take Silke's word for it Gandon is a genius," said Healy. "It might make a difference if he wasn't. Purtill might not be doing any more or less than tell the truth."

"Purtill's only a painter," said Inspector Grace, "and not in much of a way of business either, by the look of things at his place. Now Mr. Silke knows a whole lot about art. Takes it all round, so to speak, and makes it pay him, too. Mr. Silke says Gandon's the goods. There's another thing about Purtill too. He could have got hold of arsenic if he wanted any. He's been abroad not long ago."

"You have something there," said Healy. "And we can't afford to neglect anyone."

It looks as if Mr. Silke could be helpful to us," said Superintendent Lancey. "Both knowing about art and knowing the Gandons like he does. I think Grace had better drop round there again and ask him if there's ever been bad blood between Gandon and Purtill. Better perhaps not to go about it too direct. Make some kind of an opening out of this paintbox business."

"What's all this holdup over the paintbox?" demanded Healy. "What do the analysts think they're playing at?"

"They didn't get the box as early as the other stuff," said Lancey. He told his assistant to ring through and try to hurry them up a bit.

"I had an idea of my own about that business," remarked Healy conversationally. "Why wouldn't someone have mixed arsenic with his paints on purpose? Isn't that more likely than accident? I mean to say, he wouldn't have got this habit of brush sucking if it wasn't pretty safe in the normal way."

There was a murmur of interest, and one or two forgot themselves far enough to whistle. Junior members of the conference had to admit that to be a chief district superintendent implies having some brains, though to look at Healy you would never suspect him of it. Mick Lemon had been drooping like a flower someone had forgotten to water, but now Detective Officer Lemon squared his shoulders and sat up.

"And you see the implications of that?" Healy was saying. "The trap could be laid by anyone at any time. It means we must widen the field."

Lancey frowned. "It would have to be someone who knew Gandon sucked his brushes and who had access to the box."

"It's the kind of idea that would occur to a man like Purtill," said Inspector Grace. "A man who was a painter himself."

"Wait now," said Lancey, rustling papers, "It says here in Mrs. Fennelly's statement that Gandon got a paintbox sent him by post the day he was taken ill. It was sent by Mrs. Gandon."

"Mosney could have put the poison in it," said Inspector Devlin, "or even Lord Kilskour, months before."

"It wouldn't have come out of that tin we have, anyway," Lancey reminded them. "That might be the analysts now." The telephone bell had broken in on the discussion. It was not the analysts yet, however. It was a message from Mrs. Gandon, notifying the Guards of her intention to return to Kilskour on the next day but one.

"We can't stop her," said Healy. "Will they be done searching by then?" Lancey said a party had gone off from the technical bureau the moment the news was received that Gandon had given his consent. Healy then asked if the Branch could spare a couple of good men to watch the Dower House. Sergeant Nolan's young Guards at the barracks were new to work like this, and besides, the necessity for keeping two out of the three of them always at it in turns left him dangerously short handed.

When the chairman came to sum up, or as he put it, when he had done calling over the card, Mrs. Gandon retained her place at the head of the quotations at 9 to 1; Paddy Purtill advanced to second favorite at 100 to 7; and Mosney dropped back a few points to 20 to 1. Lord Kilskour's price was slashed from 100 to 1 to 22 to 1. But there was room yet for surprises before the final calling over.

Lancey was left to decide who should be sent over to interview Lord Kilskour if it should seem advisable when they heard from Scotland Yard. Inspector Grace was instructed to make further enquiries about Purtill's relations with Gandon. The check on Poisons Books would be continued. That disposed of the chief business of the meeting, and all in all, Lancey was not dissatisfied. They had made some progress in three days, and at any moment something might turn up—in connection with that paintbox, for instance—to give them a clear lead.

Before the conference broke up they rang up the analysts again, and Superintendent Lancey himself conveyed a few winged words over the wires. A patient voice replied that since this case began they had been flooded with specimens, they only had a limited number of retorts and burners, testing for arsenic took some time, and there were fourteen paints in the box. So far, it added, results had been negative.

The final report did not come in till next morning. The paints in Gandon's box were all completely harmless.

Superintendent Lancey never swore. He told his assistant that every possibility you eliminated was a step in the right direction.

CHAPTER 14

IT was the day after the second police conference and the day before Nell Gandon was to go back to Kilskour. The gale had blown itself out and left the sky clear as one limpid wash of cobalt blue; watercolor, not gouache. There was sunshine, bringing thoughts of Easter in mid-Lent. Outside Fergus Gandon's door in hospital was a row of vases of snowdrops, violets, winter irises, and forced daffodils and tulips, all sent by sympathizers to Fergus, who would not have any of them in the room. Fergus was well enough for Nell to sit with him the whole afternoon, though the nurse stayed on guard. To let them take full advantage of this, Hester Fennelly went shopping for her sister-in-law, with a long list of requisites for the Dower House.

It was a good light for painting and for looking at pictures. Paddy Purtill was doing the one and Inspector Grace and Detective Officer Lemon the other. It was a day when women whose thoughts dwelled in external things and vanity set out to buy new spring hats. It was a day that pierced Barbara Fennelly with thoughts of the transience of flowers and spring and beauty and youth, and of the haste that artists feel to translate it all into paint, they being transient themselves. Barbara often felt sad like this in spring and sorry also for people who did not.

She had another sitting that afternoon, and she picked a bunch of forsythia and polyanthuses for Mr. Purtill's mother. The old terrace houses had nothing much in their gardens, except a few yellow crocuses with which spring pushfully established a footing, though snubbed by the immortal garlands in stucco and the stone eagle which laid no eggs. Mrs. Purtill was also occupied with thoughts of transience; she was spring cleaning. She wondered if she could darn the hole in the sitting-room carpet and how she could persuade her son Paddy of the necessity of replacing worn-out chair covers. Her furniture was all out in the hall, with pails of water, and there was nowhere to put the flowers brought by Miss Fennelly, but still Mrs. Purtill was touched by them; she had not a bad heart. She asked affectionately after Nell Gandon, who she seemed to feel was more to be pitied than Fergus. She could sympathize more with the relations of invalids than the invalids themselves, for her experience was all of nursing, rather than being nursed. She also thought women more to be pitied than men, on general principles.

Barbara climbed past the stacked chairs and the mops and brushes to the serener heights. This time she found the studio warmed up—ready for her. Mr. Purtill had lighted the larger electric fire beforehand, not so much out of consideration for his sitter's comfort as concern for her flesh tints. The stately armchair stood ready in front of the tall screen on a small raised platform. There was a chalk mark on the floor where the sitter's feet had rested last time.

Barbara's tweeds and her everyday self lay on the bed of Mr. Purtill's sister. She swished across the bare studio and ascended her throne, and sat with her gray silk gown billowing out all round her, full of reflected lights. She felt she had the strangeness of a princess visiting a factory, or flowers in a hospital ward.

Mr. Purtill, however viewed her prosaically, and went to enormous trouble to get her into the same position as last time. She was to sit relaxed, but upright, looking straight in front of her and sideways out of the picture. It sounds simple enough, but they spent fully fifteen minutes turning bits of her this way and that, raising her chin, lowering her knees, bringing her hands apart or together, and when at last Barbara saw the painter stand back looking not so much satisfied as resigned, she could not believe she had ever spontaneously fallen into such an unnatural pose.

There was nothing for her to look at but Mr. Purtill himself, no flowers, pictures or bric-a-brac here. Draped in a smock, with a bunch of brushes like knitting needles in one hand and a palette in the other, the painter walked to and fro in front of his easel frowning, and looking very like his mother. Barbara did not think they were really the same kind of person, and she felt sad for him. She knew how one may suffer from being identified with one's relations. She hoped he too would understand that she was different ; she ate the food and wore the clothes provided by her family, but her inmost self lived in a dream that was other than theirs. She was conscious of being more serious, more mature than she looked. Mr. Purtill must not take her for just a rich man's child.

He surveyed her critically, and she wondered whether perhaps he was really seeing her for the first time.

"Could you look past me, not at me?" said Mr. Purtill. "A little further round, and lift the chin a little. Yes, that's what I want. See, I'll chalk something up for you to keep your eyes on." He snatched up his useful piece of chalk from the mantelpiece and drew on the wall a lightning caricature of his own face (he had standardized it by many repetitions). Barbara smiled fleetingly, but soon became pensive again.

There were so many things she wanted to say to him. He gave her permis-

sion to talk while he rectified his first sketchy outline, and she set herself to
make the most of it.

She said, "You don't know what an event it is for me to come into a real
studio. Oddly enough I've never seen my uncle's. They live so far away, we've
never seen as much of Uncle Fergus as I should have liked. I do so wish I had
known him when I was young."

Mr. Purtill grinned. "Yes, Fergus can be surprisingly good with children,
though I think his own are a bit much for him at times."

"I shouldn't have expected him to play with me," said Barbara. "I've always been good at amusing myself. We might have looked at pictures together sometimes; he might even have let me watch him paint. But if he had
never taken any notice of one at all, it would have been something to have him
there and hear him talk."

"Lift the chin a little," murmured Mr. Purtill. "Not too much! Sorry, I
interrupted you."

"I've never had anyone to talk to about art," said Barbara. "You can't
imagine how little my family care. Mother used to know lots of artistic people
before she married, but she hasn't bothered to keep up with them. That's Father's
fault of course. He's never taken the least interest in pictures, and if he looks at
Uncle Fergus' work it's only to make fun of it. I'm afraid you must have found
the atmosphere at home rather trying, didn't you? I mean, a person like you,
who has devoted their whole life to art, must find it hard to have patience with
the Philistines."

"Oh I don't know," said Mr. Purtill. "It's worse when people go all
soulful."

"Yes, in a way," said Barbara, "but at least it means something to them."

"Not much, it doesn't. How many of them ever buy a picture?"

Barbara congratulated herself inwardly on having passed this acid test. For a
moment she had been afraid that by soulful people he meant her.

She sighed delicately, careful not to disturb her facial expression.

"Their values are all wrong, you know," she said. "Mother's so busy keeping accounts and planning menus and thinking what to wear, and Father's
awfully particular about food and having first-class fruit and vegetables from
the garden. All their lives are spent on things like that and it just leaves no time
for really important matters such as art."

"Lift the chin a little," murmured Mr. Purtill with a brush in his mouth.
"Stop! Not too much. Please try not to jerk about." Barbara was not aware of
having jerked, only raising her head about a quarter of an inch. She sat as still
as she could. Mr. Purtill said reproachfully that it took two to make a good
portrait.

He picked up another brush and began to paint quite fast. Presently he
stood back and looked at his canvas and looked at her and again asked her to
lift her chin a little. This time Barbara did not move at all. "That's better," said
Mr. Purtill after a moment, and went to work again, frowning so grimly she

dared not speak to him. At long last he stood back and took the brush out of his mouth. His frown relaxed. A crisis seemed to be over. He asked her if she had said something.

"I said art was more important than food and clothes and money and all the things most people spend their whole lives on."

"I don't know about it being more important," said Mr. Purtill. "It's an elaborate process for converting paint into all those other things. The trouble is it doesn't work fast enough."

"You don't mean that," said Barbara. "If art's anything at all it's the communication of a vision."

"Don't cod yourself," he replied. "It's ten percent religion and ninety percent racket."

"Please don't be cynical. You wouldn't be an artist if you really thought that."

"I don't paint to communicate visions," said Mr. Purtill. "I paint because I damn well think I can paint, and I shouldn't be the least good at anything else. That's how it goes. You ask your uncle Fergus."

Barbara was prepared to argue, but he apparently was not, for he started to paint again with concentration. She could not resent this, it was what they were there for, but it was a pity it took up so much of his attention.

Presently she ventured to ask his opinion of Fergus' work. "Please say what you really think," she added.

"I used to admire him tremendously," said Mr. Purtill. "I've learned a lot from your uncle in the past. I worked under him, you know, at one time."

"I know," said Barbara. "But what do you think now?"

"Bit too much of the Bauhaus," said Mr. Purtill.

This left Barbara none the wiser.

"Mind you, it'll pass off," said Mr. Purtill. "Cubism, abstractions, surrealism—nothing ever lasts long with Fergus."

"He admires your work very much," said Barbara graciously.

Mr. Purtill actually stopped painting. "Did he say so? He gave me to understand that it stank in his nostrils. And so he tells the world."

"Oh no, I'm sure he doesn't."

"He told Arnold Silke so anyway. I don't know quite how much attention Arnold pays to him, but lately he's gone off my stuff. Canceled arrangements for a show. And it's not easy to find another gallery."

Even Barbara saw that she had hit on a sore subject.

"What a shame!" she said. "I'm sure Uncle Fergus had nothing to do with that. He told mother you were the coming President of the RHA."

Mr. Purtill said nothing.

"I'm afraid Uncle Fergus can be terribly tactless," said Barbara. "Even we find him rather trying sometimes. It would be easier to make allowances if one was quite certain he really was a great artist."

"And aren't you?" asked Mr. Purtill.

Barbara hesitated. "Mr. Silke thinks he is. But you don't."

"How can one tell?" asked Mr. Purtill. He pointed reproachfully at the chalk drawing on the wall, and Barbara, who had moved her head, meekly moved it back again.

"Keep the lips firmly pressed together," said Mr. Purtill.

At the end of the sitting Barbara came round the easel to look. The portrait was not very recognizable yet. The face was painted though far from finished. There were dabs of green on the background and gray on the dress. It all looked rather smudgy.

There is always the feeling about having one's portrait painted that perhaps the seeing eye of the artist will reveal beauties in one's appearance, and even in one's character, that have remained hidden from one's nearest and dearest, who are far too ready to assume that they know one through and through. Also if one is a young girl and the painter happens to be a young man, it becomes interesting to discover how one looks to him. Barbara did not quite know what she expected for her fifty pounds— perhaps that everyone would at last see her as she really was. These dabs on canvas held as yet no message. It was too soon to tell if Mr. Purtill had anything to communicate.

The embarrassing thing about criticizing one's own portrait is that whatever one says about it is liable to sound like a reflection on one's own looks. It will hardly do to suggest that the painter has not done one justice. Best to lie low and say nothing, like the Mona Lisa.

Mr. Purtill remarked that the damn things often looked best at this stage.

Detective Inspector Grace and Detective Officer Lemon had not intended to devote the whole morning to art. It was because Mr. Silke was out but expected back at any moment that they waited an hour in the Galleries improving their acquaintance with the works of Fergus Gandon and other masters.

All the Gandons in the possession of Silkes' were propped face to the wall in the side room devoted to contemporary exhibitions. In between shows the entrance to this room was roped off from the big room where there was always a mixed exhibition of modern work. These two galleries were on the ground floor behind the art materials department in the front shop. Old pictures were upstairs. It was not Silkes' way, like meaner dealers, to hang pictures all the way upstairs and along the passages. Every work was treated with respect, and fluorescent lighting shed its calm effulgence on all alike.

Fergus Gandon's one-man show was not immediately imminent. The side room was closed for longer than usual owing to a change in the arrangements with Paddy Purtill. The reopening would be all the more of a social event. In the meantime a screen across the opening prevented anyone seeing that there was nothing to see. Mr. Silke's secretary seemed to feel that the place for two detectives was behind the screen, but Inspector Grace lingered in the mixed exhibition. He thought it might help if he could find out a little more about this modern art.

He tried to get the secretary to explain it to him. She was classified by that connoisseur, Detective Officer Lemon, as an educated dame. She wore glasses, but she had them with pink rims and her nails tinted to match, showing that she did not lose heart. She had a permanent too, and her figure was not bad, but her manner was standoffish. There was no give and take about her at all.

Inspector Grace thought his best line of approach was to ask about prices, to get an idea which works were the best. The secretary said that one man's work was priced far below its merits, the artist being altogether unmercenary and not caring about money. He refused for idealistic reasons to take more than what would pay for his time and materials, and Silkes' apparently went for nothing in the matter. She recommended this artist as an investment. Another set of paintings was priced staggeringly high, but, the secretary assured the detective, even at that high price they were rapidly snapped up by all the best people, and she reeled off a dazzling list of famous names which she had at her tongue's tip. As Inspector Grace remained unimpressed she showed him some other work, by a man who was not, she said, everybody's taste, but who was represented in one or two extremely choice collections. It seemed that people bought pictures to be in the fashion, or to be different, or to sell again at a higher price, but whether anyone really liked them, or why they liked them was not for the secretary to say.

Many of the works on view were by young artists, of whom she said that they each had a great career before them. When it was a case of an elderly painter who could hardly win more fame since everybody knew all about him long ago, she managed to suggest that now was the time to buy his works before he died and the supply ran out. Also before death turned him into an old master. Having gathered that it paid Silkes' rather than otherwise for artists to die, Inspector Grace forbore to correct the slip when the secretary happened to allude to the coming one-man show as the Gandon Memorial Exhibition.

When clients began coming in the secretary excused herself, and the inspector joined his junior officer in the room that was closed to the public. Mick Lemon had been passing the time by examining the Gandon pictures. He looked at the fronts and then tried to guess the titles which were written on neat labels pasted on the backs. He had only scored one right in ten. At least he had guessed "Atomic Bomb Explosion" and the title on the back was "The World of Atoms," but it was near enough. He would have liked to bet Inspector Grace couldn't do any better.

The dates were written on the backs as well as the titles. Fergus Gandon was curiously methodical about some things. Mick pointed out that the more recent dates roughly corresponded to Superintendent Lancey's list of dates when Fergus Gandon was taken ill. It would have looked like corroboration for the paintbox theory, if only that had not been abandoned. "Coincidence," said Inspector Grace. "I've known it play the devil with evidence. You can't go against the analysts. Science always has the last word at our job."

The paintbox was the first thing Mr. Silke enquired about, when eventually he arrived. Mr. Arnold Silke's eyelids were a little weary that morning. He fidgeted more than usual and seemed to be itching to use his pocket magnifying-glass on a clue. "Have you yet arrived at any conclusion about the chance of an accident?" he asked. "Was my theory anywhere near the mark?"

Lancey's instructions, as will be remembered, were that the paintbox was to be made the excuse for the detectives' visit, and instead of setting his mind at rest they proceeded to ask the dealer for more information, or rather for the same information as he had given on the telephone all over again so that Detective Officer Lemon could write it down. It was hard on Mr. Silke, but he bore it with patience and seemed only anxious to be helpful, even if he did fish for a little information in return.

"I suppose you are also engaged in drawing up lists of suspects," he said. "You cannot afford to assume that it was an accident at this stage. I do trust you will be able to spare the family annoyance. I am in their confidence, you know. We have acted for the Gandons for years, father and son; my father acted for Fergus Gandon's father."

"Did he so?" said Inspector Grace. "You would be able to tell us, I daresay, if the man had any enemies."

"Not one in the world, I should have thought," said Mr. Silke, "since he and Paddy Purtill made it up again."

"And had they fallen out?" asked the inspector. "Nothing serious, I suppose, as they seem to be on good terms at present."

"Oh, nothing serious," said Mr. Silke with a laugh. "If there had been I don't know that I should have mentioned it. At least not without seeing Paddy about it first. It was just an explosion of temperament on both sides. Artists, you know! For a while each of them was the worst of the worst, according to the other, but I was delighted to find they had got over it. Purtill was there one day when I was, just a day or two before poor Gandon got so ill, and they were on the best of terms again."

"Do you happen to know what caused the falling out?"

"Oh nothing, Inspector; nothing. Some divergence of taste or outlook. Jealousy of each other's work. Artists can be very childish at times."

"Purtill isn't as well thought of as Gandon, is he?" asked Inspector Grace. He had not seen any Purtills in the Gallery, and when he asked the secretary about them she only replied that he had a certain following in some quarters, nothing about having a great career before him, though he seemed to the inspector young enough to qualify for that section.

"Hardly!" said the dealer smiling, in reply to the question. "You must not think I meant to suggest they were in any sense rivals. Paddy was Fergus Gandon's pupil at one time, believe it or not! Now he has struck out a line of his own, and his former master may have been a bit hard on him. There you have it in a nutshell. I assure you I am not keeping anything back from the police, but I see I can't expect any *quid pro quo."*

The inspector looked as if he did not understand Latin, but thanked the art dealer with sincerity for the help he had given them. "I don't know who's who at all in this art business," he explained, "and we have to find out all we can about everyone even remotely connected with the case."

"Well, I don't think you'll find poor Paddy deserves hanging," said Mr. Silke.

"Not even in your Galleries?" said the inspector. Mr. Silke protested that he did not mean it in that sense, and they parted pleasantly.

When Grace and Mick Lemon reported to Superintendent Lancey he said it was a pity they had been so long about it as it was too late for them to see Gandon that morning, and now he would be asleep till after four. He thought they had better go and sound Gandon out about Purtill before they started on Purtill himself.

A telegram had come from Scotland Yard, in reply to the form marked "Discreetly," to say that Lord Kilskour was in Liverpool where he was booked to lecture that night on "Decomposition, not Putrefaction." It was followed by another telegram to say that Lord Kilskour had canceled his engagement and was crossing to Ireland by the night boat. His ticket was booked through to Clogh so that he should reach Kilskour the following afternoon.

CHAPTER 15

IT was early in the year for a long country expedition, but the party who set out next morning in Paul Fennelly's Alvis found themselves rejoicing in the release from town and from all the heavy sorrows and petty worries of the last few days. It was blessed to be fifty miles from the telephone and from Mrs. Mulhall and the sense of surveillance by the police and the inquisitive glances of the neighbors. Never before had Hester found such an attraction in the lonely midlands. The sun was shining; it glowed in the red branches of willows and struck gold from the gorse. Blackthorn was out in some hedges, and there were very young lambs.

Barbara had the joy of driving the Alvis. The car which she and her mother shared for their own was a small Morris, but Paul had lent them his for the long drive. She pressed on fast, though at times it was difficult to pass the great slow lorries which make up so large a part of country traffic. There was the inevitable cattle fair, completely blocking the main street of one market town, with cattle being driven to or from it along the roads, causing more delay. But they had started early and bore with obstacles patiently, commenting amusedly to each other on the slow pace of country life.

They traveled faster out on the bog roads, where cultivation was only a thin fringe on the edge of the broad brown waste. There were no more fairs, hardly any farms, only an occasional turf development scheme or an attempt at forestry, to give employment in the wilderness. Everyone working near the road stopped to stare at a strange car driving past. In the village of Clogh, beyond the bog, the turf stacks were as big as the houses. The only buildings with two stories were the school, the general stores, the barracks and the dispensary. Sergeant Nolan, in the doorway of the barracks, saluted the car as it passed.

"Checking up on us," said Nell. It was the first reminder of the investigation. They were still in the police net.

After Clogh they left the main road and climbed through four or five miles of lanes to the higher ground about Kilskour. Hester counted three cottages in two miles.

"Have you no neighbors at all?" she said to Nell. "I find that rather frightening."

"There are more people than you'd think," said Nell. "Nice old folks who don't bother us. Of course everybody over school age and under sixty is in England or America."

"But I mean, educated people?"

"What do you mean by that? The sort who compel you to make up bridge fours? We're better without them."

Though Hester knew quite well that the Gandons saw few people she had not grasped that there was nobody at all for them to see. Most country villages, even remote ones, maintain one or two necessary functionaries : a bank manager, a schoolmistress, a Protestant clergyman and his family, and a Catholic priest. But Clogh was too small to have a bank or a Protestant church; the priest was a recluse, and the schoolmistress—though she spoke Irish fluently— would not read banned books, so she was not what the Gandons called educated. "You might as well be on a raft," said Hester.

There was Dr. Caraway, and that was all. He lodged at a farm the other side of Clogh and had another village dispensary to attend, further away again. Nell said he was a great improvement on the real dispensary doctor, who had gone in for politics and paid Brian Caraway to do his own work for him. It suited Brian till he could get something better; he liked country life with a chance of fishing and shooting. Having a car he was not quite so restricted for company as the Gandons were, and he managed to hunt if there was a meet anywhere within fifteen miles (it was the same hunt that the chief district superintendent followed when his duties would let him).

They met a horseman coining down a lane, and it was the young doctor himself. He waved and reined in, and Barbara edged the Alvis up a grass bank and wound down the window beside her and stuck out her head in her little fur cap. It was not such a coincidence as it seemed; Dr. Caraway had been looking out for them. He knew they were coming, because Nell Gandon's simple method of communicating with the Dower House was to telephone to the doctor and ask him to send someone with a message. So he had ridden out to see a patient in that direction, and back the way he knew the car would come.

He said the countryside was ringing with the news of the Civic Guards being at the Dower House. He heard a different story from every patient. The number of Guards at Kilskour was given as anything up to a hundred, and some said there were troops in it as well. It was generally believed that Mr. Gandon was in prison instead of in hospital and that he was a secret agent of Russia.

"I don't bother contradicting them," said Brian Caraway. "It seems a pity to spoil it."

"Come back and have lunch with us," said Nell. "I'd like to talk to you about Fergus."

Dr. Caraway seemed pleased to be invited.

He trotted on ahead of them, and as the Alvis overtook and passed him, Nell explained that his landlady at the farm was not much of a cook and that it was a Christian duty to give him a good meal now and then.

And so they came to Kilskour, a walled stronghold in a wilderness. They drove along the high wall for the last mile. Then the Gothic gates towered over them and Mrs. Conarchy came rushing up to the car to clasp Nell by the hand.

"I'll come down and tell you all about it later, Mrs. Conarchy," Nell promised, and nudged Barbara to drive on.

At the Dower House they were almost deafened with the enthusiasm of their reception. Grania with a dinner gong and Colm with an old motor horn of the rubber bulb kind stood at the gate to welcome them, and Faustine yelled in the arms of a uniformed Civic Guard. Faustine liked a uniform, and her old friend, Dr. Caraway, and her nurse, Mosney, were nowhere at all beside Guard Eugene Roche in his dark blue.

Mosney was wearing brown corduroy trousers and a gray pin-striped coat, and though he wore no collar or tie his hair and chin were smooth and his hands clean, and he held open the door like a butler born. His small, pinched face looked to Hester too demure to be honest. The thought of his having been alone in charge of the children for nearly a week filled her with dismay. There were no visible signs of their having suffered, but the dangers to their minds and morals were simply incalculable, and they certainly had got thoroughly out of hand.

"The children wouldn't go to school when they heard you were coming, ma'am," said Mosney. "We'll be having an attendance officer down on us, but what do they care? And how did you leave the master?"

Nell, swarmed over by her family, had begun as usual to cry.

They lunched, mainly on cooked food that had been brought down from Dublin, and things became a little calmer. The Fennellys felt they could spare an hour or so before they need start for home, so Nell sent Mosney to let them into the castle while she stayed with the children. Mosney was to pack the picture for Mr. Fringley Pole and the works for the Gandon Exhibition, while the ladies inspected the art treasures. Dr. Caraway also was in no hurry, and said that he took a great interest in old houses and pictures though he did not profess to know much about them. Throughout the year and a half he had been in the district he had been able to curb his curiosity about Kilskour Castle, but when such an opportunity as this presented itself he felt it was not to be missed.

Dr. Caraway had one at least of the attributes of a good doctor; he was an excellent listener. This made him an ideal companion for Barbara, who became animated when confronted with so much art. Since he admitted he knew so little, she felt it a mission to open the doors of enjoyment to him by pointing out every detail that charmed her, and the large, blond, normal young man listened most seriously to all she said about the pictures and looked at her glowing face under her fur cap a good deal more than at them.

Hester sat on the sofa, as Sergeant Nolan had done a day or two earlier. The drawing-room chimney was still smoking, just a slight puff every now and then, and she agreed with Mr. Fringley Pole that something ought to be done about it and wondered if anything ever would. Such of the pictures as could still be seen under a deposit of dirt seemed to her commonplace enough: there were such scenes of everyday life in old Holland as soldiers chucking servant girls under chins in inns, or boot-saddling-to-horse-and-away. Barbara was enchanted with the painting of the lace collars which the cavaliers so unpractically wore over everything else and with a cat lapping up some milk which had been spilled during chin chucking. Dr. Caraway also said he liked that kind of picture, with a bit of a story to it.

But the most interesting picture of all was the flower piece coveted by Mr. Fringley Pole. It was extremely like the one he had bought at the auction; quite surprisingly so. Indeed, the more they looked at it the more Hester and Barbara became convinced that the two pictures must have been painted as companion pieces.

The first one had been full of the promise of early summer: spring flowers—auriculas, guelder roses, hyacinths, narcissi, the inevitable tulips, and roses still in bud—rioted over the stonework of their vase and shed their petals over the skull resting at its base. The symbol of death was subordinated to the symbols of resurrection and joy. The Kilskour painting seemed to say that ripeness is all. Instead of the skull there was an hourglass, with the sand still full in the top, and among dahlias and fullblown roses were clusters of reddening blackberries, twining hops, and ears of wheat. The two pretty allegories were obviously intended to complement each other, and moreover the flowers in each picture leaned over as if they called for something more to balance them, so that the one was incomplete without the other. The frames too, Barbara thought, though Hester could not remember, were exactly alike.

The two pictures must have been painted to hang in adjacent panels of a wall, or one each side of a mirror or bureau. It was no wonder Mr. Fringley Pole felt called to reunite them. He had probably read Bodkin's *Dismembered Masterpieces* as well as Barbara. But more than that, the second picture threw light on the authorship of the first and increased its value, for it was signed in one corner: Jan Van Huysum,* 1737.

Barbara's regrets knew no bounds. Dr. Caraway was appalled to hear that they had let the other picture go for a mere fifty pounds to a man who was willing to pay three times as much for the second one.

Hester said little, but she regarded the picture in a critical spirit. Mosney had taken it down from the wall and turned it to the light. Barbara pointed to a snail in it, crawling up the stem of a dahlia, and wondered why it gave her so much more pleasure than a real snail would do on a real plant. Dr. Caraway suggested that it was because it showed that the chap who painted it must be fond of nature. But Hester stood in a trance, not an ecstatic trance like Barbara's, but a grim trance from which she emerged with a purposeful frown. There was something queer about the picture, as will have been apparent to the reader even from a written description.

Hester said she must have a last word with Nell before they left, and they would soon have to be going if they were not to do the last part of the journey in the dark. The room was still flooded with the silvery light of a fine spring afternoon, and Dr. Caraway pointed out that the roads were dry and they would be able to drive fast. The eighty miles would only take about an hour in the Alvis, he said, but even Barbara hesitated to accept this estimate. Hester proposed to walk on ahead of them to the Dower House, trusting Dr. Caraway, she said, to keep an eye on his watch and not let Barbara linger too long over the treasures of the castle. When you are eighty miles from home it is too easy to lose count of time.

Mosney insisted that first they must all see the mural painting in the garage; he would not let them miss that on any account. Whether it had so greatly impressed him as a work of art, or whether the idea of painting the walls of a garage appealed to him as original, or whether he simply rejoiced in this novel method of annoying one's landlord, he was intensely proud of this production. Barbara also begged hard to be allowed to look into Fergus' studio. So they let Mosney lock up the castle and all went down with him to the stables, taking the flower piece with them. Another man loomed up in the stable yard and added himself to the party. He was in plain clothes and wore an air of sociability rather than surveillance. He must have been getting very bored with no company but his own.

It was a startling transition from the mellow old genre pictures of the Dutch School to this work of the twentieth century vanguard, revealed when Mosney pushed the doors aside. The plainclothes man, who was having his first introduction to Fergus Gandon's work, looked as if he could not believe his eyes. He glanced anxiously at the others as if wondering whether they saw

---

* "Son, pupil and assistant of Justus Van Huysum. Jan acquired the highest reputation as a painter of fruit and flowers, and he was likewise a landscape painter. After a very successful career he died in his native city of Amsterdam on Feb. 8, 1749." -*National Gallery Catalogue.*

what he saw. Dr. Caraway's healthy face wore an expression most unlike itself, as if he had bitten on a nerve. Barbara spoke first and said hopefully that she was sure she would come to appreciate it better than she did now. Dr. Caraway said he hoped not. The plainclothes man ventured to comment that it was "a bit gaudy looking," and Mosney turned from him in contempt.

Hester said, "If that isn't just like Fergus!" but what she meant was, how like Fergus to waste his work like that. It was brilliant of its kind, but if Fergus wanted to paint like that, were there no walls left in Paris? Why plaster poor remote reactionary Ireland ?

Hester had no desire to see the studio; she had seen enough of studios in her time. And there was something she had to say to Nell. She left Mosney to do the honors for the plainclothes man and the doctor and her daughter and set off alone for the Dower House, the crisp earth of the drive ringing under her determined tread.

Nell also wanted to talk to Hester. She was just sending the children in a band to the castle to tell the party to hurry up. It was not possible to hear oneself speak so long as the children were present, so Hester encouraged her to speed them on their way, and she and Nell watched Grania proudly wheel out the pram, Colm going ahead with the motor horn to sound at dangerous bends, not that there were any on the drive. It seemed just possible that they might all arrive safe without overturning the pram, and anyhow the doctor would be there, in case of need.

The sisters-in-law retreated to the Gandons' living room, one of two bow-windowed parlors on either side of the hall door. It differed from Hester's own drawing room in that everything had stripes instead of patterns. On the walls were pictures given to the Gandons by Fergus' contemporaries and friends, including a small Purtill, a lovingly painted study of some old tin cans.

Hester sat on a chair with a seat made of colored rope, and Nell squatted on a pouffe by the fire. Nell said, "What do you think I've just heard from Mrs. Conarchy? The Guards found a tin of arsenic in Tim Conarchy's tool shed. It's the stuff you use for spraying, but what makes it jolly queer is that Alban, as you know, is dead against anything like that."

Hester was surprised for a moment out of her own subject of thought.

"Doesn't Conarchy know what it was doing there?"

"I don't think he does. Mrs. Conarchy's awfully upset about it, and of course now she knows what did happen to Fergus. I mean she knows he was poisoned, not just ill in a normal way. Hester, what do you think it means? I don't like the look of it."

"Perhaps somebody gave Conarchy a present of it and he tried it out and doesn't like to admit it," said Hester. She searched in her mind for reassuring remarks. "It's all to the good that they have found something. All that searching seemed such a waste. Now they have something to work on and perhaps the whole thing will soon be cleared up."

"But don't you think that Alban—?"

"I don't see that it makes things any worse than they looked before. After all, we always knew there must have been arsenic about."

Hester would have been prepared to discuss the news at more length if there had not been another matter on her mind which she was anxious to clear up before they were interrupted. She said, "We do no good by guessing. We must leave things to the police and hope for the best. Forgive me, Nell, but there's something else rather urgent that I want to talk to you about. That picture's no more by Jan Van Huysum than it's by me. It's the most obvious fake I ever saw."

Nell looked up with her hair in her eyes. "What picture?"

"Mr. Fringley Pole's picture."

"What makes you think that?"

"Well, it looked wrong to me in the first place, and then of course I realized about the dahlias. The picture's dated 1737. There couldn't be dahlias before 1789. They were first introduced into Europe from Mexico in the year of the French Revolution."

"Oh ye gods," said Nell, "you gardeners!"

"It's one of the few dates I can remember," said Hester. "I like to wonder which gave people the most satisfaction. Not that I care a lot for dahlias, but they do come in when there isn't much else to pick. And some are lovely things. But Jan Van Huysum can never have seen one; he must have been dead long before."

" 'He should have died hereafter,' " muttered Nell.

"But quoting Shakespeare won't do for Mr. Fringley Pole."

"Is it necessary to do for him?"

"Nell, we haven't time for this," said Hester. "Do, for goodness sake, tell me what I'm to say to the man."

Nell looked genuinely surprised. "Why say anything?"

"But you can't let him buy it under false pretenses."

"He isn't. I'm not. He had every chance to examine it and he made an offer for it off his own bat. He ought to know, if he knows anything, that a signature isn't anything to go by. He probably likes it for its own sake."

"If so you needn't be afraid of telling him it isn't authentic."

Nell made a face. "Much better leave well alone."

"The curious thing is," said Hester reflectively, "that it's very like the other picture he bought, the one Barbara wanted. They might have been designed as companion pieces. Assuming the other is genuine, this might have been based on an older original, or perhaps the faker had seen the other and it suggested the subject for his counterfeit. The two pictures certainly can't have been independent of each other. It's odd we should come across them both within a few weeks."

"Amazing," murmured Nell. "I do wish I'd realized he had the pair to it; I could have asked him double. I suppose it's too late now."

"My dear, you'll have to let him have it at his own price if he takes it at all."

"Oh nonsense, Hester. Look here, suppose Mr. Fringley Pole was rummaging in a secondhand bookshop and found a first edition of Yeats or something in the sixpenny tray, do you think he'd point out the value of it to the bookseller? This is just the same only the opposite. All's fair in collecting. *Caveat emptor.*"

Hester frowned. Although she had by this time acquitted her sister-in-law of the crime of husband-murder, she could have wished her to be more strict in other ways.

"He is sure to find out in the end," she said. "Someone will point out the anachronism, even if he doesn't notice it himself."

"I don't see why he need ever know, if no interfering gardener goes and spoils it for him. It looks very convincing, you must admit."

"Not once you start wondering," said Hester. "Oh, it's cleverly done, as you say. The crackling looks natural. I daresay it may be a good many years old. It must have been in the castle for a long time. Lord Kilskour may know where it came from originally. I suppose the best thing to do will be for you to write to him first, and I must make some excuse to hold Mr. Fringley Pole at bay till we hear what is to be done."

Nell cried out, "Hester, for the Lord's sake, need you make such a *thing* about it? Forget you ever saw the thing. We'll hand it over to you all wrapped up and all you need do is to give it to Mr. Fringley Pole just as it is, with my love."

But Hester was quite determined not to wink at this shady transaction. Nell, kneeling on the hearthrug fiddling with the logs, with her hair falling over her face and her underlip jutting out, appeared to her sister-in-law in the light of a sulky child with whom one ought to be firm.

"Nell, I'm afraid you'll have to take this more seriously," she said. "One simply can't do that sort of thing."

Nell sat back on her heels.

"Forget it," she said. "Forget it, Hester. Why stir up trouble? It might turn out a deal more serious than you think."

Her tone and expression, even more than her words, conveyed a warning. Hester wondered what exactly was at the bottom of all this. It was easy to see the Gandons were in some kind of scrape. Nell had not been much surprised that the picture was a fake. She must have known more about it than she let on.

"Good heavens!" said Hester, light suddenly dawning. "Is it by Fergus?"

"Yes, of course it is," said Nell.

The revelation was not incredible if you were well acquainted with Fergus Gandon's work, however much of a spiritual hiatus there might seem to be between the putative Van Huysum and the Picassoesque mural on the garage wall. Fergus had always been addicted to painting in other people's styles. It is a knack, like parody, but to him it had been a fairy gift ; there was a snag in it. Even when he was most himself in his work there was always a critic somewhere to breathe the word "derivative." Nothing made Fergus so angry, but if brought in time to recognize his debt he would promptly start deriving from somebody else. Arnold Silke, in organizing publicity for his exhibitions, was accustomed to signalize a change of manner every two or three years. Nothing that anyone else did with paint was beyond Fergus' technique. He had technique, but he lacked something less easily definable; not personality, he had plenty of that. Perhaps it was stamina. He could not bear to be himself for long.

"What induced him to start adding to Lord Kilskour's collection?" asked Hester, amused.

"Alban's collection!" said Nell with scorn. "Alban doesn't know anything about pictures, he never had any collection. All those up there are by Fergus."

"Nell!"

"Don't look so horrified. It's only a method of salesmanship. They look well up there in the drawing room, don't they? We have to send most of them away in the end, but we get better prices when we can sell them here."

"But do you mean you and Fergus are systematically swindling the public?"

"Nothing of the sort. It may not be in accordance with narrow bourgeois ethics," said Nell, "but there's nothing dishonest about it. People see what they like and like what they get. All we do is to create an atmosphere. They come to us not knowing good from bad or fake from genuine, and turn up the whites of their eyes when we show them Fergus' best work. So instead we give them the kind of art that will look good among their sham-Oriental rugs and reproduction furniture. Nobody need buy if they don't want to, but they just eat it up. Fergus can turn his hand to anything—genre, landscape, still life, even portraits. He specializes in minor Dutch because there's so much of that about in Ireland ever since William of Orange. The flower pieces always sell. Interior decorators have started a craze for them, and you know how some women are forever doing flower arrangements. Unfortunately Fergus has got quite sick of flowers and now he won't have any in the house."

Hester recalled many stories of Italian dealers palming off spurious antiques on collectors by displaying them as part of the furniture and decoration of old houses, where the setting lent them an appearance of authenticity. She saw that in Ireland the chance of carrying off the deception was even better. Italian noblemen are apt to be suspect, but Irish country gentlemen are generally assumed to be unsophisticated and innocent of culture. They might not be trusted in horse dealing, but they would over works of art. She asked faintly,

"Are you hoping to sell the lot?"

"Oh yes, in the end. We don't depend on the chance of people coming here. We send them to auctions sometimes. You know those big Fine Art auctions where they sell up the contents of a dozen old houses at once. The dealers advertise beforehand that they can include any items anyone wants to dispose of. All that's required is a descriptive note for the catalogue; you can say what you like and the auctioneers print it whatever it is, and nobody guarantees anything. It's quite safe and not a bit dishonest, because everybody knows some of the attributions are quite mad, and if it makes the buyers happier to fancy they might have a Van Huysum or a Gerard Dou or a Breughels or what have you, why spoil their fun?"

"But surely any dealer or auctioneer would know these were fakes at a glance?"

"Who's going to worry? The auctioneers don't care so long as they get their commission. The dealers needn't bid unless they like. Nobody's going to bother unmasking a fake unless it goes for big money. That's where Fergus is so sensible. He doesn't profess to be a Van Meegeren and paint Vermeers, only to supply the steady demand for nice old pictures at modest prices. But he's pretty good at it, you must admit. He's done a lot of research and experimented with all kinds of ways of making them look old. I think even dealers are generally ready to give them the benefit of the doubt."

Hester could not help asking to know more of how it was done. After all, but for the chance of knowing about the dahlias, she would have been as much deceived as anyone. She listened in painful fascination while Fergus' wife expounded his methods of turning fresh oil paintings into old masters. The first essential was to produce realistic cracks in the paint. Fergus had found a quick drying varnish which would break up the surface paint all over. Sometimes he applied glue over the varnish; the stiffening of the glue improved the crackle and the glue could be wiped off afterwards. But freshly made cracks are fine and hardly visible; the next stage was to open them and let the dirt in, and to this purpose they were rolled face outwards and stored in the dusty space under the dais in the studio, which might have been made for it. Finally the framed canvases were hung in the drawing room to mellow in the smoke that poured out of the wide chimney, the chimney that Mr. Fringley Pole so mistakenly advised Fergus to have swept.

"Damp turf is splendid for them," said Nell. "I often think we might tell the Turf Development Board."

"May I ask," said Hester, "if Lord Kilskour is in the plot?"

"Oh, dear me, no," said Nell. "Alban would be scandalized. When he comes home we pack all the stuff away in an attic and hang up the mirrors that always used to be there in the old lady's time. And now you see of course why Fergus didn't want to let the Guards in. As it turns out we needn't have worried." Nell laughed. "It isn't as if they knew anything about art."

The thought of the police nosing out Fergus' unofficial output made Hester feel quite faint. Nell went on gaily,

"Mosney has just been telling me two of the Guards were actually up in the studio, where they had no business, and they sniffed all round Fergus' special glues and varnishes for making the paint crack, and even pulled some canvases out from under the boards, but they never saw anything wrong with them. Mosney said he was in kinks of laughter at them. So after that they can all go where they like."

"But you can't go on like this," said Hester. " Doesn't Fergus ever make any money honestly?"

"Not much, but I keep on telling you it's not dishonest, it's showmanship. You have to have that if you want to sell anything nowadays. If Fergus showed stuff like this as his own work the critics would kill it. And anyway they're not his real work, only what he does on off days. Fergus would never lower himself to painting slick little potboilers and signing them with his own name as if they meant something. That's all right for Paddy Purtill, but Fergus has more respect for his integrity as an artist."

Nell spoke with such pride and conviction that Hester exclaimed, "Upon my word, you make me think black's white."

"So it is," said Nell, "in the realm of the absolute."

"We aren't in the realm of the absolute."

"No?"

"No," said Hester, "and it's got to stop."

"But we've got to live."

"But surely Fergus isn't dependent on what money he makes by this?"

"Not entirely," said Nell, "but all the same he can't afford to give it up. I won't go into all the ins and outs, but you know yourself, Hester, that everything's twice as dear as it was before the war, and the children are getting older and will have to go to proper schools. They'll need more clothes, and bicycles and lots of things, and there'll be fares to pay as well as school fees. Fergus' illness has been frightening from the standpoint of money as well as everything else. We must save up a bit, if we can, in case it ever happened again. And we ought to pay Mosney more, I don't know what we'd do if he left. This is no time to talk about giving up anything there's a bit of money in."

"No, Nell, it's not good enough. I'm not arguing about whether it's honest or dishonest, I'm saying it's too risky. Any day the Guards may notice something, or somebody else who knows a bit more may put them on the track. Fergus might find himself in prison. You must make him put a stop to it, and if you don't I will."

"You know quite well Fergus does what he likes. He wouldn't listen to either of us."

Hester said, "I should think he'd listen to me if I told him I should write to the four or five leading auctioneers in Dublin and to Lord Kilskour."

Nell wriggled like a bird in a net. "You can't, you shan't. Those pictures up there," she gestured towards the castle, "are what we depend on to pay for Fergus' convalescence."

"But my dear, Paul and I could help."

Nell shook her head. She said that Fergus would not accept it. It seemed that, against all probability, Fergus still remembered the share that Paul had taken in clearing up their father's debts. It had hurt his pride at the time. Hester had thought Fergus would never want for anything from not liking to ask for it. Perhaps she did not know him so well after all.

"He'll never let me tell you if we're hard up," said Nell. "We had a bad winter once during the war, but then Fergus started the old pictures and we began to get along quite well. I'd never have told you if you hadn't more or less found out for yourself. Please don't tell Fergus I told you, and don't go and scold him till he's well enough to defend himself."

Hester was touched at this unexpected glimpse of Fergus in a noble light. Nevertheless she might have gone on arguing if she had had the chance, but the hooting of the motor horn interrupted them, and broke it to them that Colm and the rest were back. Hester had lost count of time while they were talking, just as she had warned Barbara and Dr. Caraway not to do, and now they were all later than they had meant to be, and the Fennellys could not stop to have a cup of tea, for the kettle was stone cold and the kitchen fire had gone out.

Mosney had already placed Mr. Fringley Pole's picture in the car, and the other pictures, and spare pajamas for Fergus, and a box of books, and two jigsaw puzzles, and a box of fresh eggs from Mrs. Conarchy's hens. Also a bookmark worked in cross-stitch by Crania, a painting by Colm, and a one-legged teddy bear dear to Faustine, which she knew would be company for the invalid.

Dr. Caraway was already to horse and away, managing his horse capably in spite of its indignation at the motor horn. There was everything to please Barbara's aesthetic tastes in the gallant picture he made as he rode off.

Hester kissed Nell and promised not to do anything drastic till Fergus was well enough to talk things over. Then she slipped in beside Barbara, who was already in the driver's seat, and the Alvis, silent and efficient, slid away and out under the arch of the gate.

"What a place to live," said Barbara, wearing her faraway expression. "Do you know what it reminds me of?

" '...and then comes Death, and with a little pin Bores through his castle wall.' "

She shivered at the sound of it.

"Don't!" said Hester. She was thinking as usual on more material lines. She did want some tea, and well she knew that money could not buy any till they were much nearer to Dublin. The Irish main roads are a tealess hunger belt.

"What ever made you let the fire out?" said Barbara, as if she too had some material thoughts. "You and Aunt Nell must have been having a great conversation."

"We had a great deal to discuss," said Hester. "What a long time you were up there at the studio! What kept you?"

"Oh, talking," said Barbara. "Uncle Fergus' studio is simply grim. Not a bit like—er—anywhere else I've ever been. Full of all sorts of things. He even has a human skull."

"Oh yes," said Hester. " I remember it in one of his pictures."

CHAPTER 16

LORD KILSKOUR had told his secretary to send word of his coming, and the secretary as usual had written to Mrs. Gandon. Telegrams were impracticable owing to the distance from Clogh; there was a large delivery fee to pay, and the postmistress had difficulty in finding anybody to send such errands. Unfortunately, owing to the suddenness of his lordship's journey and the number of excuses and alterations that had to be made at short notice, the secretary's letter missed a post and Lord Kilskour arrived before it. There was nobody at the station to meet him, and he was faring forth into Clogh to look for a vehicle he could hire when Hester and Barbara Fennelly came down the main street on their return journey.

The negotiations for a vehicle were being conducted in the middle of the main street by Lord Kilskour, Sergeant Nolan, the owner of the general stores who had a Ford but with two tires punctured, and various sympathizers, all occupying the roadway, so that the Alvis was obliged to pull up. Sergeant Nolan, an Irishman with all the instincts of a host, took it for granted that the Fennellys would like to meet Lord Kilskour of whom they had heard so often. Hester in any case had recognized him, and with prompting, he remembered Hester. They all engaged, therefore, in civilized conversation, nobody giving away what they really felt.

Sergeant Nolan felt embarrassed because he knew that some time that evening the chief district superintendent would be coming to call for him, to drive out to Kilskour Castle and interview its owner about the awkward business of the tin of arsenate of lead. The subject was much too delicate for him to open in full hearing of the village gossips. Lord Kilskour wanted to know what the police thought they were doing persecuting Tim Conarchy. He had had a letter from Tim with an extraordinary story about Fergus Gandon, but Tim was not good at explaining himself on paper, and his employer felt he had to find out more of what was happening before he took the matter up with the authorities.

As for Hester Fennelly, she was mentally in turmoil. What with Nell's earlier confidences about her summer flirtation, and with the recent news that the police had found a clue at the castle, she would not much have cared to meet Lord Kilskour in any circumstances. Now she was flung into a panic by her own guilty conscience at the way Fergus used this man's house for his own shady purposes, and still more by the thought of all the pseudo-Dutch pictures hanging in the drawing room all ready to give the owner a surprise. A short time ago she had been threatening to expose Fergus herself. Now she was wondering how on earth she could avert discovery of his ill deeds. So she smiled at Lord Kilskour and remarked that it was many years since they had met, with the quiet heroism that in women so often passes unseen, unguessed.

She remembered his face quite well, an Edwardian face with the aloofness of a survival from another era. His heavy dark mustache and thick dark hair were grizzled, but otherwise he had scarcely changed at all. He was still thin, and he always had stooped a little. Hester, who envied thin people, reflected ruefully that she herself must have changed a good deal more.

Hester made up her mind rapidly. There was no way now of warning Nell, or of preventing the wretched man from getting home, if not in the punctured Ford, in some other emergency conveyance. But if she were there too she might be able to help, and at least she would know the worst at first hand, and when the inevitable row began she could lend Nell moral support, if moral was the word. So she offered to turn the Alvis and drive Lord Kilskour back. Barbara looked surprised, but she could not help that. She reinforced her offer by inventing something she had forgotten at the Dower House, and pretended that they would have had to turn back anyway. Hester was, after all, *née* Gandon, and had a gift of obliquity only waiting to be developed by the occasion.

They piled up all the parcels on one side of the back seat, and edged in the grateful nobleman beside the large flat package which theoretically contained an heirloom of his family only he did not know it. Hester would have felt more comfortable with him sitting on a case of gelignite.

As soon as they were clear of the main street he began telling the Fennellys about Tim Conarchy's letter.

"Very sorry indeed to hear such bad news of poor Gandon," he said. "I hope he's going on better now."

"Yes, thank you," said Hester. "Indeed, I almost think we may consider him out of danger, but we can't feel easy in our minds about him until we know just what happened to cause his illness."

"You mean, all this about poison? There is something in it, then? Not just Tim's lurid imagination?"

"Oh yes. I'm afraid there's no doubt at all that Fergus has somehow managed to take quite a large quantity of arsenic."

Hester was so used to the idea now that she was able to make the statement calmly, but Lord Kilskour was profoundly shocked.

"Arsenic?" he said. "Good God! And I take it you don't mean by accident?"

"I'm afraid not," said Hester.

"Then you have some idea who—?"

Hester shook her head. "No, indeed, I only wish we had. As you can imagine it's all extremely embarrassing and worrying. The police don't tell us much of what they are doing, and we hardly like to ask. They may know more than we do."

"You think they are getting somewhere?"

"They've found a clue," said Hester. She only mentioned it in order not to appear too pessimistic, but it was an unfortunate reference and seemed to set Lord Kilskour's teeth on edge.

"If by clue," he said, "you mean an empty tin that once held a spraying powder consisting of lead with a small admixture of arsenic, and which was removed by detectives from my head gardener's tool shed, I am afraid that is not likely to take them very far."

It was not easy to find the right reply to this. Hester ventured to remark that Lord Kilskour had been away a long time.

"Yes. Yes, I have," he said. "They can hardly suggest that I knew anything about it." He brushed the idea off as absurd. "I just came over to see what poor Conarchy's trouble was. It would have to be something serious to make him take to the pen. It wasn't exactly convenient, and I must get the night boat back tomorrow, but I don't suppose there's likely to be anything to keep me longer."

"Oh no," said Hester. The matter of the fakes, she thought, could be dealt with by his solicitors.

Barbara all this time was concentrating on driving as fast as she could. She was obliged to drive "on the horn," and the Alvis rushed noisily up the narrow lanes.

"Trying time for poor Nell Gandon," observed Lord Kilskour presently.

"Yes," said Hester, and added, with the ulterior motive of giving him a hint for himself, "she's so completely devoted to Fergus."

"Extraordinary, isn't it?" replied Lord Kilskour. Then it must have occurred to him that it might seem less extraordinary to Fergus' sister, for he cleared his throat and remarked that he supposed modern art was all right for those who could understand it, and it took all sorts to make a world. He also asked if Fergus was allowed grapes, and Hester said he was, only his nurse had to skin them.

And so they came to the great gates of Kilskour, and Mrs. Conarchy scuttled out of the lodge and flung up her hands in horror when she saw who was in the car. Indeed nobody was more put out than Mrs. Conarchy by Lord Kilskour's unexpected arrival. There was nothing for his dinner and no sheets on his bed. It was like the Last Judgment.

The lack of preparations at the castle gave Hester an excuse for driving first to the Dower House. Once there, she felt, the situation would be out of her hands.

Nell was in the living room with the children, preparing for tea. They had the kettle on the fire in there, and Grania was making toast. It made a cozy picture seen through the window. The family as usual were intensely occupied with their own concerns and did not seem to have heard the car, but Guard Eugene Roche, on the *qui vive* for murderers or higher police officials, stalked up to investigate and then rapped peremptorily on the kitchen window for Mosney.

Mosney said, "Welcome back, your Lordship!" and let them in with a poker face.

"What, back again?" said Nell. And then: "Good heavens! Alban!" She exchanged a swift glance with Mosney. She looked at her sister-in-law with wild surmise. Luckily the children created a diversion. Grania got up from the fire and shook hands with great formality. Colm said, "What have you come back now for?"

"Sit down by the fire," said Nell, recovering herself. "You must be perished, Alban, after your journey. Hester, you and Barbara will have to stay for tea now. You might as well; it'll be dark anyway in another hour. Mosney, go up to the castle and see if you can give Mrs. Conarchy a hand to get things ready. I know she's all unprepared."

"Yes, ma'am," said Mosney, the perfect butler.

Nell encouraged Lord Kilskour to wash and make himself at home, and soon he was seated on the living-room divan (an affair of mattresses and cushions) with Hester beside him on guard, much as she would have preferred to sit on something higher. Grania was toasting again and Barbara was cutting and buttering; Colm and Faustine were interrupting as little as possible; the kettle was boiling; Nell was making tea and pouring out, and Mosney was trudging up the drive to the castle.

It was an admirable arrangement. It was much pleasanter for the lonely traveler to be received into the family circle instead of his own cold empty mansion. He basked in warmth and welcome after his long chilly journey and bleak arrival with nothing to meet him. It gave Mrs. Conarchy time to put sheets on the bed and kill a chicken. It gave Mosney time to take down thirty-five pictures and put up four large mirrors and six small ones, and carry the pictures up to the attics.

"Stay as long as you possibly can," murmured Nell in Hester's ear as she handed her a cup. Hester nodded. The thing was to keep Lord Kilskour talking.

But they had hardly had the first round of cups when there came another knock at the door. Another car had drawn up outside, unheard in the living room. Sergeant Nolan was there, begging Mrs. Gandon's pardon, but, if Lord Kilskour was inside, the chief district superintendent was in the car and would like to have a word with him.

"Bring him in here," said Nell, but hospitality was not enough. The visit was official and business was business. Lord Kilskour got up and thanked her for his tea and entered the car of the chief district superintendent, and they drove off together to the castle.

Nell stood looking after the car with a face of vexation. "One of those days," she muttered. "Everything's against us. Why couldn't they come just half an hour later?" She looked at the castle chimneys. Smoke was rising from two well-separated stacks. Mrs. Conarchy had got a fire going by now in his lordship's study. The other chimney was over the drawing room.

"Please God, they go in by the small door and then they won't go near the drawing room," said Nell. "Stay with the children, Hester. I must go and warn Mosney and give him a hand."

There was not much use in Hester protesting. She was wedded to complicity by now. Nell pulled on an old mackintosh and hurried off.

Hester went back to the fire and had her second cup of tea, and saw the children through their tea and then made them clear away and wash up. Grania and Colm were used to this and quick about it. When they had finished, as Nell still hadn't come back, Hester put on another kettle for a bath for Faustine, and bathed her by the living-room fire and put her to bed. They had just successfully brought this domestic operation to an end when at last they heard laughter outside and Nell saying, in a stage voice, to Mosney

"I just had to make sure the bed was aired. Poor Mrs. Conarchy so loses her head in an emergency."

Thus much for the benefit of Guard Roche. But in the living room she said to Hester:

"Oh my dear, you've been marvelous; you've saved all our lives. Oh Hester, it is good to know I can count on you." She kissed her fondly. "You can go home now," she said, "and tell Fergus not to worry. Everything's in hand at this end."

It still was not quite dark when the Alvis got away for the second time. It was half light, the worst possible for driving, and there was a mist hovering over the fields which meant there would be a real fog on the bog roads.

Hester felt she owed Barbara an explanation. So did Barbara. The child was completely mystified by the afternoon's proceedings. After her mother's haste to be off the first time, to linger so long, to let her Aunt Nell disappear like that after tea, making them an hour later than they need have been, with eighty miles to drive and her father already probably beginning to worry about them—it was not the way the Fennellys did things. Every time Barbara had murmured anything about it getting late her mother had either pretended not to hear or appeared not to mind. What on earth had come over her?

They drove in silence for a time, the air heavy with mystery and misunderstanding. Then Hester decided reluctantly to tell Barbara the whole story. She knew so much already that she would be certain to let fall some hint in just the wrong quarter unless she was warned not to. Hester hated to have to disillusion her daughter about Fergus' character, but she felt disillusionment was inevitable sooner or later. And one thing that encouraged Hester to indulge in a revelation was the thought that at last Barbara would have to admit that her mother was a better judge of old pictures than she was.

She was not afraid of Barbara giving Fergus away. She was a sensible child who could be trusted not to chatter. And though her education had been up to date in most ways, she had not been brought up to think she knew better than her mother in such matters as when to break, or not to break, the law.

The mist crept up round the Alvis and it nosed its way cautiously across the bog as Hester talked. Barbara could not take her eyes from the road ahead, but it was evident that she was deeply shocked, especially to think that she had been so completely taken in herself. But at last she said, "Surely it shows that Uncle Fergus is every bit as good a painter as the Old Masters. After this, even Father will have to admit that he can paint."

"It only shows he can copy," said Hester. "And I think Father had better not know anything about it just yet. Poor Father has such a lot to worry him just now."

"You're afraid he might tell," said Barbara who, if she lacked perspicacity in some directions, at least knew her mother well.

Hester admitted it. Her first intention had been to confide in her husband and trust entirely to his judgment, as she did in most matters. But then she wondered if that would be fair to Paul. She saw that the strict business integrity she admired in him had its dangers. Paul was almost certain to say that Fergus must cease fabricating Old Masters. He might even want him to own up and make restitution where possible. Then Fergus might go bankrupt and even be sent to prison, and Paul would find himself supporting Nell and the children indefinitely.

With the uprightness of her husband on the one hand and the crookedness of her brother on the other, the path for Hester was the middle way. If only she knew what it was!

"Father might feel he ought to tell," she said, "and I'm sure he wouldn't want to. I do think it's kinder not to leave it to him to decide."

"Thank goodness," said Barbara, "we're coming out of the fog."

Alas, in some ways they were deeper in!

CHAPTER 17

LORD KILSKOUR led the police in by the small door. It was the door to the estate office, at the far end of the main block. It stood wide open, and a lamp inside showed the way to the staircase leading up to Lord Kilskour's personal suite of rooms, from which bumps and thumps could be heard. The rest of the main block was all dark and shuttered. The massive front door when closed looked forbidding enough to daunt even the owner of the house. There was nothing about it to indicate that any living soul ever passed through, or that Mosney had gone in that way with the stable step ladder five minutes earlier. This was best for the happiness of all.

The estate office was a room dedicated to deed boxes and ledgers and photographs of prize-winning animals. It could be warmed, with toil and forethought, for there was a fireplace, but the fire in it had been laid the previous September and the general dampness of the house had affected the twigs and newspaper, so that when Lord Kilskour put a light to it nothing much happened. And this, too, was for the best, for the chimney, had they but known it, was in the same state as that of the drawing room. The three men kept on their overcoats and sat down on horsehair-padded chairs and looked at each other mournfully across a large inkstained table.

"I'm afraid I have a disappointment for you," said Lord Kilskour. "I know what you want to see me about, but I can assure you that the tin you found in Conarchy's potting shed has nothing to do with your enquiry into Mr. Gandon's illness."

Chief Superintendent Healy opened a handsome silver cigarette case with an inscription on it and offered round Sweet Aftons but got no takers. Lord Kilskour preferred his own, and Sergeant Nolan would have liked a pipe but did not feel it would be quite in place. Lord Kilskour flicked open a lighter but could not make it work. Healy began getting his own out of an inner pocket. The sergeant struck a match for both of them. Lord Kilskour got an ashtray from the mantelpiece and put it in the middle of the table. Then they began again.

"So you know all about Mr. Gandon's illness, my lord?" said Healy.

"I didn't even know he was ill till I heard from my gardener that your fellows were swarming all over the place. Naturally he thought I ought to be informed."

"They had Mr. and Mrs. Gandon's permission to look round," Healy explained, since Lord Kilskour's words seemed to imply that someone ought to have asked his permission. "In any case of this description we have to search the premises as a matter of routine."

"Oh, I didn't mean to criticize your routine," said Lord Kilskour kindly. "You never know, of course, whether or not you'll be wasting your time. As in this case, I'm afraid. That is if this empty tin was really all you found. Oh, don't think I'm fishing for information." He smiled at Healy who was looking noncommittal. " I don't want to know anything that isn't for general publication. My only concern in this is to protect poor Conarchy. I'm perfectly certain he had no more to do with it than I had, and I don't see why he should be subjected to the third degree."

"Nothing to do with the tin being there, you mean?" said Healy, not rising to the last accusation. He knew all the hundred and one ways in which witnesses try to lead a conversation off the point.

"Oh, that wasn't what I meant exactly," replied Lord Kilskour. "I was thinking more of the whole business. It does seem a most extraordinary affair. I haven't heard much about it, you know. Naturally one couldn't question Mrs. Fennelly and Mrs. Gandon, poor women. They must be in great distress of mind, I'm afraid. But it does all seem most mysterious to an outsider. If it's not unfair, may I ask if you are getting anywhere with your enquiries?"

"We hope so," said the chief superintendent with his best air of sober confidence. "The race isn't run in the first quarter of a mile, you know. In this case there are various minor details that have to be cleared up. Things like this tin of yours."

"Well, as I've told you, there's no need to waste time on that."

"No need at all," agreed Healy. "We needn't keep you a moment, my lord. All we want to know is when and where this tin was bought, and who signed for the purchase of it."

Lord Kilskour reached for the ashtray and stubbed out his cigarette. He had smoked it fast; Healy's was only half burned down.

"The answer ought of course to be easy," said Lord Kilskour. "It ought to be down in one of Conarchy's books, only I'm afraid bookkeeping isn't Conarchy's strong point. Unless, of course, I bought it myself." He looked like a man trying to look like a man who is trying to remember. "It's probably entered somewhere as 'Sundries,' you know."

Healy said with an air of trying to be helpful: "We have an entry in a Poisons Register from a Dublin shop regarding a tin similar to this purchased last summer and signed for by 'A. Hering' of Evelyn Gardens, Dublin."

"Why, that must be it, Superintendent!" said Lord Kilskour with every appearance of surprise and relief. "One up to your routine, in fact. The system really works."

"Sometimes it does," said Healy, with a modesty that would have pained Superintendent Lancey. "But if that was you signed the book, my lord, what possessed you to give a fictitious name and address?"

Lord Kilskour's bushy eyebrows drew together. " I don't know what you mean. 'A. Hering' is my name. Oh, I see, did I put 'Evelyn Gardens, Dublin?' A slip of the pen for 'London.' It's the address of my London flat."

"Ah, that explains it," said Healy. "But, begging your pardon, my lord, don't you usually sign yourself 'Kilskour?' "

There was a short pause in which Lord Kilskour sat looking cross with Healy, and Healy remained patient but dour, very like the prize bulls in the photographs on the walls. At last Lord Kilskour began to laugh.

"Have it your own way, Chief Superintendent. I see it's no use trying to lead the police up the garden, ha-ha. You must forgive me, I had my reasons. I admit that there was, shall we say, a fictitious color about the transaction. How enormously one's most trifling irregularities become magnified when seen through the microscopes of the Detective Branch!"

He offered the chief superintendent a cigarette. Healy nodded to Sergeant Nolan to get out his notebook. Lord Kilskour winced but did not falter.

"I'll tell you all about it," he said. "But I don't, surely, have to tell a man like you how one may be put to the pin of one's collar to avoid some kinds of publicity."

He appealed to Healy as one VIP to another.

"Ah, to be sure," said Healy, smoking placidly. "The police often have to do with people who want to avoid publicity." Lord Kilskour shot him a suspicious glance under his eyebrows, but Healy did not mean it sarcastically; he was a simple, straightforward man.

Sergeant Nolan wrote "Statement by Lord Kilskour," at the top of his page. Lord Kilskour leaned back in his chair, in a haze of smoke, and talked as if dictating to his secretary.

"My whole life is dedicated to promoting a saner agriculture. I, and a few others, are doing our best against heavy odds to educate public opinion, and farmers, and governments, against our present crazy methods. This is what happens: the-get-rich quick way is to load the soil with artificial fertilizers, which for a time yield large crops of grain and vegetables. But these crops are inferior in food value to those grown on wholesome natural humus. They lack the essentials on which our populations depend for stamina. Resistance to disease is weakened. The future of the race is jeopardized. And the soil is left impoverished. We are burning our boats. Where modern methods have been in use too long, acres of once fertile tillage and pasture are crumbling away to dust. Does the ordinary farmer think of this? All he cares about is the simplicity of measuring something out of a cardboard packet, as against the labor of saving and composting animal and vegetable waste. Does the city housewife think of this? All she cares about is up-to-date sanitation, and instead of returning fertility to the soil a city the size of Dublin daily empties hundreds of tons of valuable refuse into the Irish sea. But let them beware! Already there are signs and portents. Baldness is increasing. We lose our teeth at an earlier age. How long will the public rest content to be pawns in the game of the great vested interests, the big business gentry, whose factories turn out sulfates and nitrates in insidious packages with specious promises printed on the wrappers?"

Sergeant Nolan labored hard but his pencil dropped farther and farther behind. It hardly mattered, as the passage was to be found in full in one of his lordship's lectures. Chief Superintendent Healy sat passively through a recital of facts calculated to keep anyone awake at night, except at one moment when his hand absentmindedly found its way to the thin patch on the top of his head. When the lecturer paused for breath the chief superintendent brought him tactfully back to the subject of arsenic.

"I'm coming to that," said Lord Kilskour, having got his second wind. "It's all of a piece, don't you see This spraying with chemicals is all part of our superstitious and blind belief in science. Mind you, I don't deny they give results of a kind. But where is the advantage in destroying a few insect pests if in so doing you upset the balance of nature and contaminate the soil? People don't think these things out. They go for immediate results and never reckon on the long-term effects. Do you realize that when once arsenic gets into the soil it stays there for good?"

This was more up Healy's street. "That's right," he said, taking his cigarette out of his mouth. "That's exactly what the murderer overlooks. As you say, he doesn't think things out. Arsenic's the ideal poison from one point of view; it's the hardest thing in the world to diagnose. Your man may die without anyone suspecting it. But once he's dead, there's no getting rid of it again. There it stays, and years later we may come and dig him up and find it in him. It hangs about in or around where it's buried, and if there's no remains left to analyze we may find it in a sample of the soil near the grave. Even cremation wouldn't be safe. It's not what I'd choose to poison anyone with, if I wanted to live in peace afterwards."

"Yes, there are drawbacks to everything," said Lord Kilskour. "So you see my point? It just won't do to let every Tom, Dick and Harry scatter stuff like that about their gardens. Those sort of fellows never measure anything accurately. They just mix up these sprays double strength to be on the safe side, as they think, and slosh them about regardless. I've seen them used strong enough to kill all the grass and weeds under a tree, which means very likely they'd injure the roots as well. These things are dangerous when they aren't thoroughly understood. I've been preaching against them for years."

The lecturer drew a long breath and stubbed out his cigarette which had been burning away to waste.

"So you see, Chief Superintendent," he went on, "it would not do for me to give a handle to my opponents. Suppose my signature in your precious book had happened to catch the eye of some reporter! It would be news, you know. The scientific world would soon hear of it, and you have no idea of the lengths to which certain people would go to discredit my opposition. Some of these so-called experts are capable of anything, and paid for it too. Show me one that doesn't represent some vested interest!"

I wonder you took the risk of buying the stuff," said Healy.

Lord Kilskour spread out his hands. "It was like this, Chief Superintendent. Desperate diseases call for desperate remedies, and there are exceptions to every rule. You interested in pomology at all?"

"In what?" said Healy.

"Apples, man, apples. Every intelligent person ought to take some interest in apples. You eat them, don't you? Then you ought to see that you get the best. I suppose you'd never think of asking for White or Scarlet Crofton, Sam Young, Gibbon's Russet, Cockle and Whitmore Pippin, Cluster Pearmain, Cat's Head, Nonesuch, Hall Door, Cockagee?"

The chief superintendent shook his head.

"Of course you wouldn't," said Lord Kilskour. "You've never heard of them, let alone tasted them. Nobody now grows any but the commercial varieties. Big croppers and poor eaters. A big turnover and a quick sale. That's all your commercial grower cares about. Nobody bothers to select fruit for its flavor; we've almost lost the sense of taste. Nobody takes the trouble to store good keeping apples like Cockle Pippins which you can eat in April; it's easier to import characterless stuff from the Colonies, I mean the Commonwealth. It's better for trade. Vested interests again. It's all of a piece with the modern world."

Sergeant Nolan's pencil slowly overtook the flow of words, while Lord Kilskour lighted another cigarette. The sergeant was not getting it down word for word, but a fair summary. When "vested interests" came in again he skipped it.

"I have one or two very old trees here," said Lord Kilskour. "I'm anxious to preserve them. I may be able to grow some of them on from grafts. There's Tervoider Rennet, and Aclam's Russet, and a Cockle Pippin, all dating from my great grandfather's time. The names are all down in his Orchard Book. The Cockle Pippin still bears a good crop and they keep till April. I don't know where else you'd find any."

He fixed his hearers with a solemn gaze and sank his voice to the level of tragedy.

"What was my horror, two years back, to find the fruit riddled with caterpillars! Winter moth, ruining the entire crop. There was only one hope of curing it. I have to admit my principles went by the board, but do you blame me in all the circumstances?"

"I wouldn't blame you for that," said Healy cautiously, "but this entry in the register, you see, looked rather bad—"

"I'll pay anything you think I should," said Lord Kilskour all too eagerly. "Any fine, I mean, of course." He had seen Healy's scandalized expression. "I don't want you to think I'm trying to dodge the penalty of my misdeeds, but you do see, surely, that the publicity, if there was any, would be damaging quite out of proportion to the crime. Could you not keep my name out of it?"

"That's not a matter for me, my lord," said Healy. "It'll be up to the police in the metropolitan division where the offense was committed."

"Really? Then why do you come to me about it?"

"I'm only concerned with any possible bearing on the Gandon case."

"Oh, that. It's nothing to do with that, no connection at all." Lord Kilskour laughed the idea off.

An idea struck him.

"Will you have an apple, Chief Superintendent? We ought to have some Cockle Pippins still in store. Then you'll be able to understand what I'm talking about."

Chief Superintendent Healy would rather have had a drink. Even with his overcoat on he fancied he had caught a chill. When Lord Kilskour led the way outside the air out of doors felt warmer than the estate office. Circulation only gradually restored itself to the policemen's extremities as they stumped round after their host to the stable yard.

There they found Conarchy, Mosney, and the detective on duty, deep in conversation. This detective was not one of Sergeant Nolan's staff, but a man sent down from Dublin, a studious youth who generally had a magazine digest in his pocket.

"They tell me these hormones are wonderful things," he was saying.

Conarchy gave a deep rumbling growl and spat.

"Hormones, how are ye?" said Mosney. "Take my advice and have nothing to do with the like of them. You don't know what could happen to you. I was readin' the other day about a fellow researchin' into them things, an' d'you know what I'm tellin' you? He developed breasts."

The detective's mouth opened but no sound came. The silent Conarchy, on the other hand, was moved to speech. "Glory be to God!" he said. They all three jumped up as Lord Kilskour and his party came up.

Conarchy had the key of the apple house and let them into a delightfully smelling shed with shelves ranged all round and a space in the middle with a pile of packing boxes. Most of the shelves were now empty, though a few shriveled fruits remained on them from earlier in the season. Some were heaped with late apples in separate kinds but miscellaneous sizes. Some were stacked with trays of open slats on which the fruit was carefully graded and spaced. There were labels with the names Lord Kilskour had mentioned, and others more familiar.

"I want to send a basket down to the barracks, Conarchy," said Lord Kilskour. "Here you are, Chief Superintendent, try that. Help yourself, Sergeant."

The chief superintendent took a bite at his apple, then he looked where he had bit and his expression changed. He was no reader of *Punch* but he agreed with George Belcher's charwoman about finding " 'arf a maggit in a napple." He stepped quickly to the door and expelled a fragment.

"Oh dear," said Lord Kilskour. "I'm afraid spraying hasn't been entirely effective. But you see what I mean, Chief Superintendent?"

"Maybe you'd better repeat the dose," said Healy. "Er, I expect you could get someone else to sign for the arsenic."

Lord Kilskour frowned. "I don't know who I could trust."

They walked back through the yard, picking their way among little smoking heaps of horse droppings on which Lord Kilskour and Conarchy threw calculating looks. The only sign of life in the big house was a flicker in the window over the estate office, showing that Mrs. Conarchy had got the fire in his lordship's sitting room to burn. The police car passed Mosney and Mrs. Gandon walking back up the drive. The chief superintendent stopped the car to say goodnight, and Mrs. Gandon explained that she had been to make quite sure Lord Kilskour's sheets were aired.

The Dower House made a bright-windowed contrast with the castle. Mrs. Fennelly's Alvis still stood at the door. She would have a long drive in the dark.

The chief superintendent dropped Sergeant Nolan at the barracks, with his basket of apples. Then the car took him on to "Bundoran," the red brick villa that he and his wife had built for themselves out of money left to Mrs. Healy by an uncle. Even in winter with the grass uncut and no roses flowering on the pergola, it looked good to Healy. He felt a little hurt that Paddy Purtill had omitted it from all the pictures he had painted in the neighborhood.

CHAPTER 18

WHILE this sequence of events was being run through down in the country, a fresh development occurred in Dublin.

When Superintendent Lancey sent Inspector Grace and Detective Officer Lemon to see Fergus Gandon on the subject of Paddy Purtill, they were able for the first time to have a reasonably long interview with the person most concerned in the case.

They called at the hospital in the evening, the day they had their second talk with Arnold Silke, only to be confronted with a "No Visitors" notice, and informed by the Guard on duty at Fergus Gandon's door that Mrs. Gandon had been in there the whole afternoon, saying good-bye, and the nurse said "that woman" had taken it out of him and he had to rest.

On the following afternoon, however, when all the patient's womenfolk were safely away in the country, he was glad of company, even that of detectives as he was not allowed to see anybody else. They were told they might stay an hour if they did not upset him. The nurse seized the chance of his being in safe hands to slip out for a while, and the three men were left together.

The small room just held a bed, a toilet table, and two policemen. They sat one each side of the bed. Inspector Grace had at his elbow a glass and metal whatnot on which things were sterilizing in tumblers. Detective Officer Lemon was wedged in beside a chair with a wireless set which played soft dance music all the time they talked. Fergus Gandon was propped up on pillows. Copies of the *New Yorker* were scattered over the eiderdown. Detective Lemon tried not to let his attention be distracted by the covers.

"Do smoke," begged the patient. "I've no cigarettes to offer you, but do smoke your own. It helps to kill the disinfectant. Never mind dropping ash on the floor; the nurse can sweep it up." In a short time the room began to seem quite cozy.

"You know what we've been trying to get at, Mr. Gandon," said Inspector Grace. "Any person who might have, or think they had, a grudge against you. Somewhere there's somebody with a motive for putting you out of the way, and that motive's what we need to work on. Now we've had a piece of information about a certain individual who's supposed to have quarreled with you, and we'd like to hear the story from your angle. The name is," he bent forward, lowering his voice, "Mr. Paddy Purtill."

"Funny you should say that," said Gandon. "It's what I've been thinking about myself."

"I'll just run over what we've got about him," said the inspector, anxious to save the sick man from too much talking. "He was staying with you in the early summer of last year, about the time you felt ill first. He was staying with you again in October when you had a serious collapse. He left immediately you were taken ill. He visited you at Mr. Fennelly's house and had tea there, in company with two other guests, two days before this last attack of yours came on. Now, our information is that you and he had quarreled, but had made it up again. That would have been—when, exactly? "

Gandon said, "I suppose you mean the row we had the second time he stayed with us, in October. It was just a flare-up, you know. I didn't think much of it at the time. But I was ill, as you said, and I collapsed in the middle of it all, suddenly like this last time, only I wasn't quite so bad. Everybody got into a flap about me, and my wife sent for the doctor, and Paddy cleared out. Well, I mean, it was no place for a visitor. We never did properly finish the row; it just got shelved. We didn't make it up exactly, but when Paddy came round to see me this last time he seemed to have forgotten all about it."

"Had you no communication in between times?"

"Not unless you count Christmas cards."

The inspector nodded. "I was going to ask you about that. We saw a card you sent him, and written on it was 'The doctor thinks I'm being poisoned; what do you know about that?' I was wondering just what construction to place on that."

Fergus Gandon's eyebrows lifted. "How on earth did you get hold of that? It meant what it said. I thought if he knew anything it might make him play up."

"You had suspicions of him then?" The inspector sounded reproachful.

"Only nor'-nor'-west, Inspector. I think I meant it more as a joke. Anyhow he didn't react."

"So then you thought the quarrel was forgotten if not forgiven. Would you mind telling me now, Mr. Gandon, what was it about?"

"I criticized his work and he resented it."

Inspector Grace looked disappointed. "Would he have taken a thing like that to heart?"

"It's hard to explain," said Gandon, "if you're not in touch with these things. Artists are terribly touchy about their work, you know. I am myself. I knew how to get under Paddy's skin all right. Only I don't think it was that that annoyed him so much as telling him I'd go to Arnold Silke."

"He does business with Mr. Silke too, doesn't he?"

"Not now, Inspector. I fixed him." Fergus Gandon grinned to himself. "He didn't think I could, but I did. That shook him."

"I don't understand, Mr. Gandon."

"I did it for his own good," said Gandon. "You see, it was like this. Ten years ago when that lad came to me as a pupil he was as full of the *zeitgeist* as any of us. He looked to me to be going right on out in front. He was one of the vanguard, but he reneged on us. I don't know if you're familiar with his work?"

"Devil a bit," said the inspector frankly. "I may as well admit, Mr. Gandon, I don't know anything about art."

"How should you, Inspector?" said Gandon kindly. "We all have our own consolations. For all I know yours are more reliable. Well, take my word for it, Paddy's present manner is just too sick-making. Indeed that alone might almost account for everything. Slick, photographic, boring, you couldn't believe! And the worst is, people buy it, and the way he keeps turning it out, a picture a week or thereabouts, soon he won't be able to do anything else even if he tries. He thinks he can potboil for a bit to make money and then go on again and have some more adventures, but it's no go, Inspector. You can't do that. You can't play tip and run with a creative talent. An artist has got to know what he means by his work. If he stops meaning anything in particular the rot sets in at once."

"Don't get worked up, Mr. Gandon," said the inspector nervously, for the sick man lay back looking pale after this harangue. "Now if I have this right, you spoke to Mr. Silke about this man's work, and Mr. Silke broke off dealings with him. Would that be a big loss?"

"He'd feel it in his pocket all right. We all have to listen to Arnold. The power of the purse."

Gandon sounded breathless. The inspector took a minute or two to let him recover. He turned over his notes. Detective Officer Lemon craned his head round and read the top *New Yorker* joke. The wireless played on.

Inspector Grace said, "This quarrel, Mr. Gandon, you say it took place on this man's *second* visit to you?"

"Yes. I know what you mean, Inspector. I had been ill before. But I hadn't been so bad. The first time it mightn't have been more than ordinary indigestion. Do you know what I thought? It might have been me complaining of pains in my tummy the first time that put the idea of poison into his head."

"Yes, that could be," said the inspector gravely. "Now, when he called to see you this last time, Mr. Gandon, was that by surprise, or by invitation?"

"By invitation, but he more or less asked for it. He rang up to enquire. My wife had told him where I was, you see, thinking no harm. She hadn't been told anything about anything. I think she wanted us to make things up."

"And so you did, then?"

"It never cropped up at all," said Gandon simply.

"Like that, was it?" said Inspector Grace. "Our informant drew the wrong conclusion?"

"Who was your informant, Inspector? My sister, I suppose."

"No, Mrs. Fennelly never said anything." The inspector hesitated, for it was against his custom to disclose the sources of his information. In this case, however, the answer was fairly obvious. "It was another person present that afternoon, Mr. Silke."

"Arnold Silke? What else did he say?"

"Oh, it wasn't so much him that said anything as a hint we got in the course of a conversation. We were just making some routine enquiries, you understand. We were asking for a bit of help from somebody who knew about art."

"Arnold doesn't know anything about art, bless you. Knows how to sell it, that's all."

The inspector allowed Mr. Gandon to have his joke.

"Fact, I assure you," said Fergus Gandon. "An art dealer doesn't need to know about pictures, any more than a publisher needs to know about books. He knows what's in demand, that's all."

"But what else is there to know?"

Gandon closed his eyes a moment. "Remind me to tell you another time, Inspector. Or, I'll tell you what, ask my niece Barbara. Now, as I was saying under 'Publishers', a sentimental story sells a hundred times better than a brilliant novel at the first printing. The profits on the sentimental story pay for the loss on the novel. But don't you believe it's all loss on the best work. The novel will be a paying item on the backlist long after the sentimental story's been pulped. *Mutatis mutandis*, Inspector." Gandon waved a thin hand to deprecate the classical tag. "Paddy's work is sentimental twaddle whereas mine's the stuff with a future. What I had to point out to Arnold Silke was that Paddy could be turned into one of his long-term investments if he found his trash was frozen out."

Inspector Grace looked a bit bewildered, but he could think it over afterwards. He saw Mick Lemon getting it all down in his notes. He remarked tactfully that Mr. Silke had praised Gandon's own work up to the skies and enquired for him most anxiously.

"Naturally," said Gandon. "From his point of view, I'm the goose that lays the golden eggs."

"No motive there," murmured the inspector, whose mind tended to run in professional grooves.

The wireless interrupted his train of thought with a sudden outburst of crackling noises. The dance music was torn in pieces. Detective Officer Lemon vainly tried to get it from another station, and finally switched off. "It's some electrical gadget they've started up," Gandon explained. "Reception's rotten here. To enjoy the radio you want to have it where I live-down in the country." They all agreed that it would have been better if progress in electrical inventions had stopped at wireless sets. Then Inspector Grace came back to business.

"If you don't mind, Mr. Gandon, cast your mind back to the day this man came to visit you at Mr. Fennelly's house. Did he bring anything with him? Fruit, or sweets, or anything of that kind?"

"Oh no, nothing. Only a paintbox I'd asked him to lend me."

Inspector Grace's exclamation—he swore by the holy powers—was echoed by a yelp from the far side of the bed, and Mick Lemon's pencil clattered to the floor. Gandon winced and shut his eyes tight. He was not well enough to be yelped at. After an interval of dead silence he ventured to open them and ask what the excitement was about.

They told him.

"All my life," said Gandon, "people have warned me of the dangers of sucking my brushes. To think they were right!"

"If only we'd known to get hold of that box!" Inspector Grace almost writhed at the thought. He veered from hope to despair. "I suppose it's been returned to him?"

"Quite likely," said Gandon. "My sister's the sort who's always returning things to people. Naturally he'll have taken all the poison out of it. You'll never prove anything."

"Don't be too sure," said Inspector Grace, to comfort himself. "It's not so easy removing all traces. Up at the technical bureau—"

Gandon interrupted him.

"Wait a bit, Inspector. Come to think of it, I never did use that box. My own arrived next morning, and I didn't need to borrow after all. If your idea's right, it's my box that's poisoned. Someone's been mucking about with it without permission."

His voice rose on the last words, and his expression gave them to understand that hardly even the crime of trying to poison him could be more heinous than that of interfering with his painting materials. A man who would do that would do anything.

But the detectives' faces were a study in disappointment, and Mick Lemon all but groaned aloud at seeing his promising theory punctured for the second time. They broke it to Gandon that his own paintbox had already been tested without result.

Gandon sat bolt upright.

"You took my paintbox! How dare you? Who gave it to you? No one had the right to do a thing like that without consulting me. Nobody takes my paints without direct permission from me. Nobody, do you hear? Nobody." He fell back, his voice petering out with helpless rage. He looked so white that the frightened inspector rang the bell for the nurse, who came running from the pantry at the end of the corridor. She glared at the detectives, bent over the patient, gave smelling salts, took his pulse.

Gandon recovered speech enough to tell her pettishly that there was no need to fuss, and that if only he could trust people to leave his belongings alone he would be all right. He seemed to hold her responsible but did not dare to abuse her as roundly as he had the police.

"Nobody touched your paintbox, Mr. Gandon," said the nurse. "It's there in the washstand drawer. It's been there all the time." She slid the drawer open, and there it was.

Inspector Grace turned his sternest expression on Detective Officer Lemon, and it looked as if Mick might be the next candidate for the smelling salts.

"She gave it me," he said, several times over. "She gave it me for Mr. Gandon's. I mean that old hairpin up at the house. The cook, I mean, not Mrs. Fennelly. The cook fetched it out to me, but Mrs. Fennelly took a receipt for it herself, and seemed to think it was okeydoke. How was I to tell?"

The inspector had silently handed the box to Gandon, who looked up grinning and seemed to have benefited by the discovery that it was indeed his own.

"It's Paddy's box you've been mucking about with," he said with simple pleasure.

"But that box was harmless," said Inspector Grace. "Not a thing wrong with it at all."

"So what?" said Gandon.

"Now, Mr. Gandon, you must have a rest," said the nurse. "I'm going to turn these two men out, and then I'll make you a nice cup of tea."

Her word was law. In any case Detective Inspector Grace and Detective Officer Lemon felt it was time they went home. The had had all they could take. It only remained to persuade Gandon to part with his own precious paint-box, and he agreed without difficulty, saying that it was reasonable in the circumstances.

The problem passed to Superintendent Lancey and the paintbox to the laboratories.

CHAPTER 19

HESTER and Barbara stood in the drawing room contemplating the flower piece. It was placed on a chair where the light fell relentlessly on its shortcomings.

Knowing what she knew, the sight of it fairly set Hester's teeth on edge. Yet, superficially, it was pleasing enough and, as fakes go, quite a creditable production. There was no crudeness of composition or negligence of detail. The veining of leaves and petals was as minutely rendered as the cracks and other factitious evidence of antiquity.

"Uncle Fergus must have some love of nature after all," said Barbara. "He puts everything in."

"Yes, even the fly spots," said Hester. "Look at them, all painted on, even on the frame."

She was feeling tired after the long drive of the day before, not to mention the varied emotions. She had to fit in a visit to Fergus that morning, and she expected one from Mr. Fringley Pole that afternoon. She did not think she had the heart to speak to Fergus, and she did not know how she could look Mr. Fringley Pole in the face.

Barbara, more thoroughly restored by her night's rest, was serenely prepared to argue the ethics of the case.

"If a picture is good enough to be mistaken for an Old Master, oughtn't it to be worth the same price?"

Hester said: "A bad penny isn't worth the same as a good penny because you can pass it off as one."

"That's different. It doesn't matter how many Old Masters there are in circulation."

"Well," said Hester, "Corot's reputation was nearly ruined by a quantity of feeble productions being sold as his after his death."

"But this isn't a feeble production. It's one Van Huysum might be quite proud of."

"Well, if you feel like that about it," said Hester, "you'll have a chance to buy it when Mr. Fringley Pole backs out."

Barbara blushed and said nothing, and her mother imagined that she had called her bluff, whereas the fact was that, though it was still a secret, Barbara's birthday money was already allocated to art under a different form.

"What shall you tell Mr. Fringley Pole?" she asked. "Not the whole story?"

Hester shrugged her shoulders. "If I tell him anything he can guess the rest."

"No, why should he? Any collection might have one fake in it by accident. It's no business of his where it came from."

"But he'll wonder how I know."

"That doesn't mean you need tell him. Just say that you have reason to suspect it may not be genuine and ask if he'd like to reconsider."

"Then he'll want to have it inspected by an expert."

"Let him. Nobody could tell it was anything to do with Uncle Fergus. Pull yourself together, Mother."

Hester smiled gratefully. It was a new sensation to be leaning on Barbara for support.

It was a disappointment to find that she would not have Barbara's support when Mr. Fringley Pole arrived. She was going out after lunch and might not be back for tea. She did not say where, and Hester thought how mysterious her daughter was nowadays about her comings and goings. But she stuck to her principles and would not allow herself to ask.

Hester found Fergus sitting up and looking more like himself. He was wearing his old red dressing gown and admiring himself in a hand mirror.

"They gave me this for the first time this morning," he said. "It's a good sign when they think you can stand it. I must say, I never knew I could look so El Greco."

Hester thought he still looked too ill to be worried with anything so tiresome as the problem of earning an honest living. She sat down by the bed. The wireless at her elbow announced that it was going to play a melody mixture. She switched it off.

"I say, have you heard the latest development?" said Fergus, before Hester could say anything. He plunged into an account of the discovery of his paintbox. The prospect of the mystery, or part of it, being solved was enough to divert Hester's thoughts for the time being from her brother's past and future. This was something they had to discuss in all its bearings. Fergus poured forth his suspicions of Paddy Purtill. Hester said that Mosney was more her idea of a murderer. She said, "I never saw such a hangdog face."

"Murderers never look like murderers," said Fergus. "Haven't you ever been to Madame Tussaud's?"

Hester knew by now that, whatever circumstantial evidence there might be against him, both the Gandons would resist to the utmost any attempt to deprive them of their domestic help.

"It'll be a lesson to you not to suck your brushes," she said, pointing the moral in a sisterly way.

"I don't know that I shall do much more in watercolor," Fergus replied. "It's nothing but a little hobby after all. Lying here, thinking about death, and what I'd like to leave behind me"—he turned large pathetic eyes on Hester, who nearly wept—"I've decided to lose no time, seeing I've gained a respite. I've been working out an idea for something big, in tempera—"

He lay back on his pillow and described his conception, with sweeping gestures at the ceiling, which he saw simply as so much beautiful blank space to fill. It sounded as if it would take him the rest of his life if he lived to be ninety. It was allegorical, embracing the lost ten tribes and the Congress of Europe, Atlantis and the Apocalypse. Hester, with her mind more on the material than the creative aspect of his career, reminded him that he would have to complete the set of illustrations commissioned by Arnold Silke, at which Fergus looked oppressed, slave-driven, exploited. He was not the kind of artist to whom the prospect of being paid is an inspiration in itself. He might in the long run carry out commissioned work, but he would do everything else first.

The time passed so quickly in conversation that Hester suddenly found she must go, and she had not yet said anything yet about the Old Master situation. She mentioned, watching Fergus for any signs of a guilty conscience, that Mr. Fringley Pole was coming for his picture that afternoon.

"Good work," said Fergus. "Don't give it him till you get his check."

She looked at him, hesitating, but the time was not ripe. He asked her to switch on the wireless again before she left, and she went out quietly to the strains of a herdmaiden's dance.

Mr. Fringley Pole's chilblains were better but he had a cold in his head, and his eyes were watery behind his rimless glasses. He stood in front of the picture and blew his nose. He gazed at it so long that Hester fancied his suspicions must be aroused and became anxious to get her word in first.

"It's only fair to warn you that my sister-in-law cannot guarantee the authenticity of this picture," she said. "We should like you to examine it carefully before you commit yourself."

Mr. Fringley Pole suspected nothing. He had merely been gazing complacently at his new possession. He resented any attempt to spoil it for him.

"My dear lady, it speaks for itself. And here," he pointed, "we have the well-known signature. What a fine, large, painterly hand!"

"But you know, a signature isn't always enough to go on," said Hester diffidently.

Mr. Fringley Pole smiled. "Oh, I think we may accept this one. I fancy I know Van Huysum's hand."

"Have you seen many Van Huysums?"

"I specialize in flower pieces," Mr. Fringley Pole reminded her reproachfully. "Van Huysum, De Heem, Breughels—they are all old friends. I picked up one not so long ago that bears a resemblance to this. But I was forgetting, of course you know it. It is very like this indeed, probably a companion piece, and certainly by the same hand. Your daughter, Miss Barbara, was anxious to secure it for herself."

From the way he looked at her, Hester wondered if he thought she had some ulterior motive, and was trying perhaps to make him withdraw his offer so that she could buy the picture cheaper for Barbara. Her heart hardened towards Mr. Fringley Pole, and she had a good mind to let him have his own way, if he was so opinionated about his judgment. But her conscience still stuck at taking his hundred and fifty guineas, and she persevered.

"Are you quite sure, Mr. Fringley Pole, that the other picture is genuine?"

Mr. Fringley Pole drew himself up. "My dear Madam, really—need we carry this to the point of absurdity?"

Hester viewed him with exasperation. He professed to care about pictures, and still could not see anything wrong with the cooked-up canvas in front of him! It was his find, so it had to be a masterpiece. He deserved to be robbed, and she would take his check without any compunction.

Unfortunately she had said too much already. In spite of his hauteur, Mr. Fringley Pole was shaken. In the act of fishing out his checkbook from his inside coat pocket he stopped and said, "Well, after all, to ease our minds about it, we might perhaps seek another opinion. There is our mutual friend, Mr. Silke. Shall we ask him to pronounce judgment?"

"He's a very sound opinion on all such matters," said Hester. She reflected that it was more to the point that he was a friend of Fergus. Whatever he might think, he would refrain from asking awkward questions at this juncture if she gave him a hint. It was a lucky choice, though natural enough in the circumstances. She agreed to ring the dealer up.

Mr. Fringley Pole was still on the look out for a catch. He said, "I have your sister-in-law's acceptance of my offer in writing. Whatever Silke thinks of the picture, the price stands, so long as the offer is not withdrawn."

"Certainly," said Hester coldly, and turned her back on him.

She found Arnold Silke, as usual, both capable and obliging. A messenger was to have been sent from the Galleries that afternoon to collect the pictures Nell had sent up for Fergus' exhibition. Mr. Silke said he would drive out himself, if Hester did not mind keeping Mr. Fringley Pole there another twenty minutes.

Hester ordered tea, and she and Mr. Fringley Pole made stilted conversation with many pauses, during which Mr. Fringley Pole blew his nose. Arnold Silke's arrival could not often have been more welcome.

The dealer's competent manner and well-tailored clothes always inspired confidence. At ease in all company, he favored the seller of church furniture with a casual nod, but bowed over Hester's hand like a member of the *Corps Diplomatique*. He beamed indulgently on them both. Then his eye fell on the picture, and he immediately became the man of business, stepping forward with responsible tread. He bent seriously over the canvas. The handy little magnifying glass came into play.

Hester watched him with amusement. She felt certain he had summed up the fake at the first glance, and that all the rest was window-dressing. She was curious to hear in what precise words he would tactfully break the truth. She looked forward to seeing Mr. Fringley Pole receive a shock to his self-esteem.

But the shock, when it came, was for Hester.

"Really," said Mr. Silke, "one never cares to be too dogmatic—"

"Your opinion is good enough for me," said Mr. Fringley Pole.

"That's very kind of you," said Mr. Silke, "and since you like this picture, I should say, have no misgivings. A delightful thing, a little gem in its way. I compliment you on your acquisition."

"Thank you," said Mr. Fringley Pole. "It's satisfactory to have one's own opinion confirmed." He gave Hester a glance which somehow implied a sweeping judgment on the entire female sex.

Hester looked wildly from one man to the other and again at the picture. "But Mr. Silke, the date—and those are dahlias—impossible so early in the century—"

"Dahlias?" said Mr. Silke, bringing out his magnifying glass again. "Those dahlias? Oh no, you are mistaken. They could not be dahlias in 1737. I take them for some kind of striped ranunculus. An old florist variety, such as we don't see nowadays."

Hester felt like the character in the fairy tales against whom everyone conspires to make him doubt the evidence of his senses. She gave it up. It was ridiculous to have to apologize to Mr. Fringley Pole for having wasted his time in trying to prove to him that a picture which she wanted to sell, and which he was anxious to buy, was not worth the money he wished to pay for it. Let him write his check. She opened the flap of her Sheraton writing bureau and gave him every facility.

Mr. Silke helped to pack up the picture. He was handy at the job from early training.

They put it in Mr. Silke's car together with the other pictures, the more legitimate offspring of Fergus' genius, and Mr. Silke gave Mr. Fringley Pole a lift back to town.

Hester put the cheque in an envelope for Nell. She muttered to herself, "Ranunculus my foot!" It seemed to her that Arnold Silke must be a greater friend of Fergus than she had previously imagined.

CHAPTER 20

WHEN for the third time Superintendent Lancey called a full conference of everyone working on the Gandon case, he had at last a fact for them to chew on. There was no doubt any more about the method by which the poison had been administered to the victim. Several of the paints in Gandon's water color box had been found mixed with a sulphide of arsenic, and this corresponded with the analysts' various reports.

The fact that it was sulphide of arsenic, and not the oxide, the commonest form used in commerce or for poisoning people, had given somebody at the technical bureau an idea, which might at last lead to a material clue.

The case now came up for discussion on the highest levels. Lancey was ready to report to the deputy commissioner for crime. If he approved, the only remaining step was to consult a state solicitor as to whether the evidence was strong enough to make a conviction likely, and would justify them in proceeding to an arrest.

The conference met in the deputy commissioner's own room, where the ashtrays were enormous and there was a real fire in the grate. Austerity ruled in other respects. Maps, wall charts, and bundles of statistical leaflets showed how all human crime and folly can be reduced to the simplicity of an equation.

The deputy commissioner was sitting in an armchair, talking to his next in command, the superintendent of the special section for murder, when Lancey came in, ten minutes before the conference was due to begin. They were soon joined by the metropolitan divisional superintendent and the superintendent of the technical bureau (who had cleared up a simple blunt instrument murder since we saw them last). The VIPs offered each other cigarettes and talked shop, all letting on to each other how overworked they were, while Lancey's assistants dealt round stenciled reports on which the clerical staff had done overtime and sorted out the files. By degrees they were joined by Inspector Devlin (who had been spared with difficulty from an enquiry into the sale of nylons), by a superintendent and a sergeant from the barracks nearest where the Purtills lived, which conveniently was also the district where the Fennellys lived; by the local sergeant, who had been before to testify about the Fennellys; by Chief Superintendent Healy and Sergeant Nolan, who had risen at six that morning in order to drive up in time from Clogh; by Inspector Grace, covered with glory for finding the second paintbox, and by Detective Officer Lemon, covered with shame for getting hold of the wrong one and wasting valuable time.

Detective work is judged by results. When a detective officer is sent to fetch a certain object necessary to an investigation, there is no excuse for bringing something else instead. Where there is a risk of duplication, as in the case of mass-manufactured objects like paintboxes, a detective officer must make sure he gets the right one. Every article borrowed by the police in the course of an enquiry must be identified by a responsible person, and a receipt given for it with full particulars of ownership and description, on the appropriate form. As to who is a responsible person, a detective officer must use his judgment. If the owner's sister and the owner's sister's cook turn out afterwards to have been completely irresponsible, that is the detective officer's own funeral. All this had been rubbed into Mick Lemon till his neck felt permanently red. Everybody had heard about the mistake; nobody remembered that it was his brilliant intuition which first brought paintboxes up at all. Thus he learned that ideas are as dangerous as bacilli, that junior officers should be immunized against them if possible, and that if you do catch one you should never pass it on.

The deputy commissioner took the chair. The other VIPs chucked their cigarette ends into the fire, lit fresh cigarettes, and distributed themselves round the table. The rank and file filled in the gaps. There was a general shuffling of pages of reports; the report from the analysts, the report from the search party who went through the Dower House, the report of Sergeant Nolan on the interview with Lord Kilskour; and Inspector Grace's account of the discovery of the second paintbox and a subsequent interview with Gandon.

One of Lancey's assistants read aloud a summary of the proceedings at the last conference, the accuracy of which passed unchallenged. Lancey himself then reported on developments since that date, as follows:

No arsenic, nor anything of a compromising nature, had been found at the Dower House, unless any significance attached to a spare key to Gandon's studio at the bottom of a cracked vase in the pantry. None of the household admitted to any knowledge of this. Letters from Lord Kilskour to Mrs. Gandon had been found, but their purport was harmless.

Lord Kilskour had spent one night only at the castle, where he had been interviewed as related in Sergeant Nolan's report. Before leaving, he had stopped at the Dower House to say good-bye but had not got out of the car. Mrs. Gandon and the children had come out and seen him off in the presence of Guard Eugene Roche. None of the detectives on duty at the castle had anything suspicious to report. Mrs. Gandon and Mosney both seemed fully occupied about the house. Inspired by the search party, Mrs. Gandon was spring cleaning.

On his return to Dublin, Lord Kilskour had visited his solicitor. Also two personal friends who were senators, one member of the Dail, and an aunt of his who knew the deputy commissioner's wife. All these persons had since made representations to the police why the charge against Lord Kilskour of falsifying the Poisons Register should not be brought against him in court.

Lord Kilskour had crossed back to England the previous night. Scotland Yard had been requested to watch his movements, on a form marked "Discreetly."

The officer commanding investigation then turned to deal with the Dublin end of the case; to the paintbox and the analysts' report, and in reference to that, to a personal visit he had received from Mr. Arnold Silke. Mr.. Silke was oppressed with a sense of his own responsibility for the sale of paints to the public. He thought that he had a right to early information if there was evidence of the paints having been contaminated, and that it would be his duty to get in touch with the manufacturers. At the time of his visit Lancey had not yet had the analysts' report on the second box and so had no information to give. Mr. Silke could not understand the delay, as Lancey did not tell him that there were two boxes in question. He went away expressing himself as very dissatisfied.

"That was unfortunate," said the deputy commissioner, with a slight frown on his august brow. "You might have said enough to set his mind at rest. There's nothing accidental about this business, and whoever has to worry it shouldn't be the retailers or the manufacturers."

But Superintendent Lancey had principles of his own for the conduct of an investigation, and a leading one was that outsiders had no right to information. He argued respectfully but firmly that the less said the better.

"In my opinion, sir, it's time enough to set his mind at rest when the case is finished. You never know what may turn up. You don't think it was an accident, I don't think it was an accident, but counsel for the defense might dig something up to prove it was. Suppose, now, I'd told Mr. Silke the first box was all right, then, when we found the second one, I'd have had to go back on that. Well, and how do we know there mightn't be some other box as well?"

"Heaven forbid!" said the deputy commissioner, stopping the tide of Lancey's eloquence with an upraised hand. "Have it your own way, man. Tell nothing to nobody. I spoke in haste."

The conference blinked at this triumph for Superintendent Lancey, and the superintendent's normally watchful and pessimistic expression eased into a slight smirk.

The preliminaries having thus been got out of the way, the conference settled down to the central problem: Who mixed sulphide of arsenic with Fergus Gandon's paints?

Lancey went on doing the talking, expounding facts in his precise voice with the flat Dublin accent. Some of those present knew already what he was leading up to, and the rest soon got his drift. They all knew that he would not have requested the deputy commissioner's attendance until he was able to present a case in proper style.

Lancey remarked that at first sight the new discovery seemed to widen the field of suspicion. The trap could have been laid at any time, and the poisoner be miles away before the first effects were felt. But closer examination of the circumstances and a further interview with Fergus Gandon had revealed that there were limiting factors.

First, the attempting murderer must have been someone who knew of Gandon's habit of sucking his brush. This would include all members of his household, his sister, possibly Lord Kilskour, and his guest and pupil, Paddy Purtill.

Second, the poisoner must have had access to the paintbox itself. This enabled them to eliminate several possible suspects. By good luck, the box had been a new one. Silkes' had supplied it free to Gandon the previous April, in consideration of his undertaking a commission to illustrate a book on the technique of watercolor. The firm were to get some allowance for stating that all the illustrations had been carried out in paints of this particular manufacture. The box had been posted direct to Gandon at the Dower House, so that all his Dublin relations and their servants could be taken as cleared.

Even at Kilskour, the paintbox was not open to interference from every passerby. Gandon was jealous of the tools of his trade. His studio was kept locked, and the paintbox, when not in use, hung in a satchel of materials for watercolor sketching from a peg on the studio wall. The entrance by a trap door from the garage was bolted and the bolt secured with a padlock, and there was a padlock also on the outer door of the garage. The same key fitted both locks. Inspector Grace had been inclined to wonder at all these precautions, but Gandon explained that he did not want the children to get in and make the place untidy—at which Sergeant Nolan and Inspector Devlin exchanged a grin. Another reason was that the murals in the garage had to be protected from Lord Kilskour, who had threatened to have the place whitewashed.

"So Lord Kilskour himself could not get in," said Chief Superintendent Healy. He wanted to do what he could for the man, so made sure the point was noted.

Inspector Grace said that Gandon himself kept the key on a ring in his pocket and only took it off to give it to Mrs. Gandon when he went up to Dublin. Mrs. Gandon left it with Mosney, with her other keys, when she came up to Dublin too, after Gandon was taken ill.

"One moment now," said the deputy commissioner from the chair. "Wasn't there a second key in existence?"

Lancey admitted that there was, but he did not think it had been used. It had been found in a cracked vase on a top shelf out of the children's reach, underneath some miscellaneous rubbish and some crumpled bills dated four years back. Lancey was too conscientious to wish that the search party had been less thorough, but he felt this key was a nuisance and he wished it need not have been mentioned. His case against one suspect would have been clearer without it.

He regarded his third point as much more important. This arose out of a suggestion which emanated from the technical bureau, as mentioned above. The suggestion was that sulphide of arsenic might be an ingredient of artists' pigments, and might have been purchased in this form, possibly from a foreign manufacturer.

The superintendent of the technical bureau had brought with him the member of his staff who had raised the point and who had since been looking it up. He had found that bisulphide and trisulphide of arsenic had been colors used by the Old Masters. The first was a red called realgar. The second and commoner in use was orpiment, otherwise auripigmentum, also called King's yellow. One would have done to mix with Gandon's light red and vermilion, the other might have been incorporated with yellows, light browns or made greens. Their presence would tend to blacken the colors in the course of years, but the poisoner would have counted on Gandon absorbing the few grains out of each paint before he or anybody else noticed anything the matter.

Orpiment and realgar are now out of date, being deadly poisonous and found to deteriorate with age. It would not be very easy to obtain them in their old and genuine form. Some English manufacturers retain the old names but produce the same shade out of different chemical constituents. "King's yellow" in watercolors is made from cadmium and Chinese white. But there are still firms who preserve old recipes and specialize in supplying colors in their original form to painters with antiquarian tastes. It may not be possible to obtain everything of which the Old Masters availed themselves. Painters working in the dawn of chemistry inclined to muck and mysteries of their own; their choice ingredients were dragon's blood and powdered Egyptian mummy. Bisulphide and trisulphide of arsenic, however, are not beyond the resources of the twentieth century.

The colors would have to be dry, in cake or powder form, but the kind of faddist for whom such pigments were manufactured would be quite likely to want to grind them for his own use instead of buying them ready ground in some oil of which Cennino Cennini, fifteenth-century writer on the subject, might not have approved.

Here Sergeant Nolan and Inspector Devlin broke in together to say that Gandon himself ground his colors. They had seen a grinding stone in his studio. But Inspector Grace had asked him whether he ever used orpiment or realgar, and he said that though he knew the names he had never dreamed of buying any of either. There seemed quite a chance that the paints might have been ground on his stone; another job for the analysts, to find traces of arsenic in the studio dust.

What it all came to was that the poisoner must have had recondite knowledge of artists' materials and where to obtain them, and he must have been at Kilskour Castle since April, when the paintbox arrived, and have had access to the studio.

As Chief Superintendent Healy put it, out of the list of suspects—Mrs. Gandon, Lord Kilskour, Mosney, Paddy Purtill—it was Purtill that Lancey napped.

Purtill had worked with Gandon and must have known that he sucked his brushes, though he had affected ignorance when questioned.

Purtill had the run of the studio, and he had a duplicate of Gandon's paintbox. He could have doctored the paints in his own box and substituted them for Gandon's.

The dates of his visits coincided with Gandon's attacks.

The motive would be to prevent Gandon from damaging his sales and his reputation.

Detective Officer Lemon would have liked to add that it looked very bad for Purtill the way he had contrived to have his own paintbox substituted for Gandon's box to throw dust in the eyes of the police, but Detective Officer

Lemon had taken a resolution never again to open his mouth at a conference.

Such was the theory of the Gandon case that Superintendent Lancey laid before the deputy commissioner. Now it had to come under fire.

Before proceeding to an arrest, an investigating officer must submit the evidence to every possible criticism and test. For the worst that can possibly happen is a case against the police for wrongful arrest. This fear, unknown in continental countries, haunts the mind of the British or Irish policeman. It is bad enough to arrest the right man and have the lawyers get him off the just penalty for his crimes. But to put the wrong man in the dock means shame, disgrace, and an action for damages. Better far to let a murderer go free. He will probably murder someone else before long, and you will get him all right in the end.

The deputy commissioner asked for comments, and two men spoke at once. The metropolitan divisional superintendent asked where was the evidence that Purtill had any orpiment in his possession. The superintendent of the special section for murder said that he supposed they knew defense counsel would get his teeth into that second key to the garage.

The superintendent of the technical bureau asked if anybody had asked Mrs. Gandon what she knew about orpiment. She might be just as familiar with artists' materials as if she painted pictures herself.

Sergeant Nolan said that that fellow Mosney might or might not have had any orpiment, but he knew how to pick a lock.

The man from the staff of the technical bureau said that he did not think Lord Kilskour could be entirely dismissed. Surely the nature of a substance like orpiment might be presumed familiar to every educated man?

The chairman asked if Superintendent Lancey wished to apply for a warrant to search Purtill's studio for orpiment?

This was just what Lancey was longing to do, but he had given the matter a lot of thought and decided not to search yet. It would put Purtill on his guard. Moreover it might be useless, for a small supply of arsenic in the form of a cake of yellow pigment could not have been difficult to dispose of. Purtill might have thrown it out of the train window anywhere between Dublin and Clogh.

He thought he might be able to get evidence of the purchase of the poison. His theory was that, since nothing of the kind was on sale here, and no other mention of arsenic sulfides had turned up in the check on Poisons Books, it must have been obtained abroad.

Purtill's travels had not been extensive. Inspector Grace had been able to find out all about them from the Gandons. He had stayed six weeks in Paris, and a fortnight each in Rouen and Arles.

Foreigners are lax, and it is admittedly easier to buy yourself some arsenic in France than in Ireland. Chemists only sell it on a doctor's prescription, but you can buy weedkiller or insecticide or anything of that kind in an ordinary shop without signing a Poisons Book. Nevertheless the shops stocking such commodities are all registered with the mayor of their *Communauté*, and caution is enjoined on them. Add to this that the French are curious by nature, that orpiment is a color not likely to be much in demand, and that an Irish visitor would to them be a foreigner and therefore suspect. Lancey thought there was a very good chance of some employee of an artists' colorman remembering that he had sold a cake of orpiment to an Irish artist and being able to identify him from a photograph.

The only drawback was the delay. The Gandon case had caused talk in some quarters, and a prompt arrest would make a good impression, if the deputy commissioner considered that the existing evidence justified such action.

But the deputy commissioner shook his head. So did the superintendent of the special section for murder. The superintendent of the technical bureau pursed his lips. The metropolitan divisional superintendent pulled his ear. Chief District Superintendent Healy rubbed his nose and muttered that many a favorite was beaten at the post.

The deputy commissioner for crime recognized by these signs that they were all in agreement. He glanced at his watch, and saw he had time to make a little speech. He remarked that the first virtue in police work was patience, patience all the way from the man on the beat to the man in the witness box. There were times when the least delay might be harmful, and there were times when it was best to hasten slowly. This was one of the second kind. Where was the harm in waiting a little? Nothing more was likely to happen to Mr. Gandon. The police had uncovered the source of danger to him, and there they were entitled to congratulate themselves. It was something on the credit side that Mr. Gandon might now leave hospital whenever he liked and go his own way in safety. But as for arresting anybody, or even bringing a name before the state solicitor, such action would be premature. They still had four suspects, or three suspects if they felt they could eliminate the man Mosney. They still, if they saw it the way he did, needed to be satisfied that neither Mrs. Gandon nor Lord Kilskour would have thought of orpiment, and that neither Mrs. Gandon nor Lord Kilskour could have tampered with the paintbox. Let them all three, and Purtill, be kept under observation. Further evidence might turn up, in the course of Superintendent Lancey's enquiries abroad, or otherwise, which would make it possible to bring a case against one or the other of them. Those engaged in the investigation had all done some hard work and hard thinking already.

There was yet more to be done before they could invite the state solicitor to meet them in that room and weigh the evidence for and against the person whom they would ultimately be in a position to indicate as most likely to have committed the crime.

With this Lancey had to be content. Indeed it was the sort of speech he often made himself. But he felt confident of securing that extra evidence, and even while listening with half an ear to the deputy commissioner's peroration, he had been jotting down the points for a letter to be translated into French.

As the conference broke up, Chief Superintendent Healy was heard to murmur: "Six to four Purtill. Ten to one the field."

CHAPTER 21

FERGUS GANDON'S one-man show of experiments in oils and watercolors was to open the same week as the Annual Exhibition of the Royal Hibernian Academy of Arts and would look like a challenge to academic standards. There would be plenty of art patrons in town and an atmosphere of artistic controversy in which people would be apt to talk themselves into buying pictures, or shamed into doing so in order to prove their own *bona fides.*

It did not seem worthwhile for Fergus to return to the country for the intervening few weeks. Hester felt better qualified to nurse him back to health than Nell and Mosney, so when he left hospital he went back to the Fennellys'. His reappearance had a sobering effect on local gossip. The neighbors could now watch him dressing and undressing in the spare bedroom with the blind up and the light on, and could see that the story of his having been murdered was exaggerated. They only talked now about the ridiculous way people had talked. Life for the Fennellys returned to normal, and Hester even succeeded in engaging a new houseparlormaid.

After the discovery about Fergus' paintbox it seemed as if the case was concluded. The guard on the house was withdrawn, and it was agreed that there was no point in further police protection. The Detective Branch were understood to be still following a line of enquiry, but somehow that sounded more like a face-saving formula than a promise of future developments.

Inspector Grace had paid Fergus one last visit and warned him in the strictest confidence that the police considered he ought to be on his guard against Paddy Purtill. The inspector cautioned Fergus not to mention this to any person whatever. Fergus told Hester and Hester told Paul, but it was some days before it reached the ears of Barbara.

Barbara's first intimation of it was in her mother's expression of face when an invitation arrived from Mr. Purtill to the opening of the RHA.

The portrait was now finished, but still a secret. Mr. Purtill had asked Barbara's permission to send it to the exhibition, and Barbara had consented willingly, for not only did it mean social and artistic prestige, but it would make a much more exciting surprise for her parents if, instead of tamely producing her present on a birthday, she could lead them up to it as it hung before the eyes of the admiring public and tell them it was theirs. It might even be the Picture of the Year.

It was important to make sure that Paul and Hester would attend the opening. Mr. Purtill obliged with an invitation card for Miss Fennelly and party.

When Barbara showed this with pride to her mother, it gave Hester a shock she could not conceal.

For all Hester knew, Mr. Purtill had only met Barbara once. Young men do sometimes invite pretty girls out on short acquaintance, without causing parents to ask if their intentions are honorable. But in this case Hester feared the intentions might be worse than dishonorable: sinister. She shuddered to think what ulterior motive might inspire the man whom Fergus Gandon had wronged to cultivate Fergus Gandon's niece.

Like any Victorian mama, Hester forbade Barbara to have anything to do with That Man. Barbara, not being a Victorian miss, insisted on being told why not.

Then she became indignant.

"It's silly to pay any attention to Uncle Fergus suspecting people. Why, Mummy, you know what Uncle Fergus is! It's just like him to say such things about his best friend."

"I should hardly call Mr. Purtill that," said Hester.

"Well anyway, he isn't at all the sort of person—"

"My dear, how do you know? From what your uncle tells me, he might quite well be the sort of young man to develop a complex, or whatever the jargon for it is. Poverty, lack of recognition, a stunted emotional life—"

"Did Uncle Fergus say he had a stunted emotional life?"

"Oh, not in so many words," Hester admitted, "but he did say he was poor, and had a mother and sister who didn't understand him, and thought he was wasting his time and ought to get a job in business and earn more money. And then, you see, he hasn't been able to marry—"

"Perhaps he's never wanted to."

"That's what I mean. He hasn't had a normal development."

"He looks perfectly normal to me."

"Yes, but darling, believe me, the more normal artists look the more repressed they usually are. It's better if it comes out in harmless eccentricities, like with Fergus."

"I don't believe a word of it," said Barbara, almost crying, and she ran out of the room.

Hester's interpretation of this behavior was that her impressionable daughter had been flattered at receiving an attention from an artist whom she admired and irritated with her mother for rubbing the bloom off the compliment. It never entered her head that there was any fear of Barbara telling Mr. Purtill the position of affairs.

This was exactly what Barbara now set out to do, without giving herself a moment to think. She pulled her fur cap on the back of her head, clenched her fists in the deep pockets of her tweed coat, and went hurrying down the long lines of suburban railings that led with few breaks, down a gradual decline into dinginess, from her neighborhood to his.

She never glanced nowadays at the stone eagle or the stucco garlands or the sooty gardens pricked out with crocuses. The eagle likewise ignored her. A car by the curb, a shining elliptical monster that had no affinity with its surroundings, checked her only for a moment before she resolutely climbed the steps to the Purtills' front door.

Mrs. Purtill opened the door with a duster in her hand and a cigarette in her mouth. She said that Paddy was busy painting.

"I've got to talk to him about a serious matter," said Barbara.

"He has a sitter with him," said Mrs. Purtill, with a glance at the large car.

"Will he be long?"

"I've no idea. Would you care to come in and wait?"

"Yes, please," said Barbara. "I must see him, Mrs. Purtill. It's important in his own interests."

Mrs. Purtill gave Barbara a penetrating look. Once or twice before, young women had come asking for Paddy in a great state of emotion. She did not think Paddy was to blame; it was his being an artist that affected their romantic imaginations. She never interfered in Paddy's affairs, but all mothers of sons know there are times when they need protection. This looked to Mrs. Purtill like such an occasion.

"Come down and have some tea," she invited Barbara. "I was just going to make some for myself."

She led the way down to the basement kitchen. It was down a flight of stairs but on ground level, looking out on the front garden. It was less depressing than the sitting room but still vaguely squalid. It did not smell of cooking but of cats and cigarettes. On the shelves were packets and tins and bottles of synthetic foods which Barbara knew only from advertisements.

Mrs. Purtill moved a pile of women's magazines from a chair for Barbara to sit down and lit the gas under a kettle which came to the boil almost at once. "Couldn't get through the morning without a cup of tea," she said. "But then I never eat my breakfast. Doesn't seem to agree with me. Cigarette? You don't mind me smoking, do you? Now, what's the trouble between you and Paddy?"

She handed Barbara a cup which had a smear of lipstick at the rim. Barbara turned it round, hoping her hostess would think she was left-handed, but there was a mark on the other side too.

"I suppose you think it's no business of mine," said Mrs. Purtill, "but I'm his mother, aren't I? I've a right to ask. And anyhow, I mean, we're both women, aren't we?"

Barbara suddenly realized that there was room for misunderstanding, and felt herself redden.

"You needn't be afraid I'll take his side," said Mrs. Purtill. "I'll talk to him for you, if he's done anything wrong."

"No, no, Mrs. Purtill, he hasn't," cried poor Barbara. "At least I mean, I'm sure he couldn't have, whatever people say. It's nothing to do with me, at least only indirectly. It's my uncle, you know, Fergus Gandon."

Mrs. Purtill's expression relaxed and her tone altered. "Oh, him," she said. "I was glad to hear he didn't die after all."

"No, no. He's almost well again."

"And they still don't know who did it?"

"That's what I've come about, Mrs. Purtill."

Mrs. Purtill was quick in the uptake. Barbara had hardly begun to explain before she sized up the situation. She made the child tell her everything she knew, which was not much, and sat drinking tea and smoking, and nodding from time to time, in a grim calm, as if trouble was only what she expected out of life.

"Paddy never did it," she said. "I haven't a doubt about that. Not because I'm his mother, but because it wouldn't be like him. Poison's a sneaky, underhand way of putting anybody out, and this business with the paintbox I call downright disgusting. I'm quite sure Paddy never thought of such a thing. But, oh my God, he'll be raging if I tell him. I don't know whether to tell him or not. There might be murder done in good earnest if Paddy knew."

As she spoke, steps and voices on the upper levels told them that Paddy was showing his sitter out. They heard the front door open. The kitchen window was beside the front steps, and when the painter and client came out into the little front garden they were in full view. Barbara took in a sleek, immaculate blonde head, a pair of high heels attached to the foot by the slenderest of straps, and a fur coat that had cost a lot more than fifty pounds.

Then Mr. Purtill, hovering behind, obscured her view. He opened the gate and the car door, and when a hand was extended to him from within the car Barbara almost thought he was going to kiss it.

"American," said Mrs. Purtill briefly. "Pots of money."

Barbara watched the car glide soundlessly off, watched Mr. Purtill watch it disappear, and turned away from the window to find Mrs. Purtill watching her. Barbara put her cup down and stood up.

"I'm sorry I've taken up so much of your morning, Mrs. Purtill," she said. "Will you tell him or not, just as you think ? Of course I don't know him well enough to judge."

"Right you are," said Mrs. Purtill

After they had heard Paddy shut the front door again behind him and go upstairs, she let Barbara out by the back door under the steps.

If Barbara imagined she was never going to see Paddy Purtill again, she was mistaken. He came round to the Fennellys' that afternoon and demanded Fergus.

Fergus was in the study writing out envelopes for the invitations to his private view. He made heavy weather of it, as he hardly knew any of the addresses, and some could not be found in the telephone book. Hester and Barbara were helping him to hunt people down through lists of members and subscribers with which the Fennellys were amply supplied by charitable and cultural organizations. It was an occupation agreeably conducive to gossip, and they were all quite enjoying it, though Barbara was a little pensive, and Hester felt she was wasting a fine afternoon and looked wistfully out at the garden every now and then.

Spring had really come. The daffodils and hyacinths in Barbara's indoor bowls had burst into flower, as often happened, only a week earlier than those outside. The last of the late pears had vanished from the desk. Some had been eaten, but some—alas!—had gone bad because everyone had been too busy to keep an eye on them.

Mr. Purtill was not allowed to burst in without warning; the new housemaid knew better than that. She showed the visitor into the drawing room, switched on an electric fire for him, and came to ascertain if Mr. Gandon was at home.

On hearing the name, Fergus and Hester consulted each other with mute enquiring glances. Neither of them happened to look at Barbara.

"Better not, I think," said Hester.

"Pity," said Fergus. "He'd be just the person to help with these addresses."

A thought struck Hester. "Perhaps he's come for his paintbox. He must think it strange that we never returned it. We'll have to get him another, Fergus. But how are we to explain?"

"Oh, we'll have him in and tell him something," said Fergus. "Don't worry, Hester. It'll come to me."

Hester did not like it, but could not think of any objection she could raise in front of the maid. So a minute later an angry young man stalked into their midst.

Mr. Purtill's chin stuck out belligerently above a high-necked pullover. His hands clenched themselves at his sides. But his temper was not completely out of control; he was able to wait until the maid had shut the door behind her before he spoke to Fergus.

Then he said, towering over Fergus' armchair:

"If you think I've come to bring you grapes and magazines, you're wrong. I want to know what lies you've been telling about me now."

"Easy now, Paddy, I'm a sick man," said Fergus, looking as pathetic as possible, with his head resting limply on the back of his chair.

"Your own conscience ought to be enough to sicken you if nothing else ailed you," said Mr. Purtill sternly. "Sickness is the time for repentance, so come on now, answer me Did you or did you not tell the Guards it was I tried to poison you? Speak up, man! Deny it if you dare!"

"Do please sit down, Mr. Purtill," pleaded Hester. "Can't we talk this over quietly? Fergus ought not to be excited."

"I'm not doing anything to excite him, Mrs. Fennelly. I'm only asking for a simple answer to a simple question," replied the young man, resisting all her attempts to persuade him to sit down. His eye fell on the heap of invitation cards and appeared to strike sparks from them. "So you're having a show at Silkes', are you?" he growled.

"There's one there for yourself, Paddy," said Fergus sweetly. "Written with my own fair hand."

"Rot and burn your own fair hand," said Mr. Purtill. "Do you think I don't know why my booking there was canceled?"

"Well now, Paddy, didn't I warn you what would happen?"

"It was you damn well made it happen," retorted Purtill. "I don't know what spell you put on Arnold Silke to boycott my work. I shouldn't be surprised if it hurt him more than it hurt me. I don't need Silke to put business in my way."

"Well then, Paddy, you've no complaint," said Fergus.

"No complaint? That's not what I'm complaining of. You heard me, Fergus Gandon. I'm not going to stand for you taking away my moral character as well as my professional reputation. Let me remind you, I know things about you that would land you in clink. I've only to open my mouth." It clamped shut like the jaws of a trap.

"Ah no, Paddy," said Fergus with calm conviction. "It wouldn't be like you to do a dirty mean thing like that."

"I would, too, you old slootherer."

"Oh do stop being childish," said Hester desperately. "Mr. Purtill, please! We don't know what story you may have got hold of—"

"The story you spread yourselves," said Mr. Purtill. "That I poisoned your brother here, Mrs. Fennelly."

"Mr. Purtill, if you were in our shoes you would suspect everybody. We live under this horrible shadow, and we don't know what to think or whom to trust. If we've injured you in our thoughts, you should pity rather than blame us. I give you my word your name has never been mentioned outside the family. Whatever story you heard did not originate with us."

In contradiction of this assertion there came a tearful sniff from the far side of the desk, which for the first time reminded Fergus and Hester that Barbara was also present. Mr. Purtill also looked in her direction. "Did you not know?" he said to Hester. "She told my mother the whole of it this morning."

"It only seemed fair," sobbed Barbara.

Hester gazed at her. "But why should she? What made her think of it? Does Barbara know your mother?"

"They've met at the house when she came round to me," said Mr. Purtill, in a matter-of-fact voice.

"Barbara came to see you!" said Hester incredulously.

"Now, what have you been up to?" said Fergus.

"Oh shut up, Fergus," said Mr. Purtill rather more amiably. "I wish to God you were well enough for me to kill you the way you deserve. She only came to sit to me, Mrs. Fennelly. It was a secret, but I forgot. Miss Barbara, please forgive me."

So it all came out about the portrait and the fifty pounds, and the surprise was spoiled, but Hester's maternal mind was relieved of its chief anxiety. At last she knew the reason for Barbara's mysterious absences. There was a tender scene between mother and daughter by which even the hardened Fergus and the injured Mr. Purtill could not but be affected. Hester wanted to cry and Barbara did cry, and Fergus lay back in his chair and laughed himself nearly sick. When Mr. Purtill could get a word in he said he had better go.

"Do forgive us," said Hester with compunction.

"Hester, this girl of yours is the most divine goose," said Fergus.

"She's the only decent one among the lot of you," said Mr. Purtill, which was rude to Hester, but left Barbara feeling not quite without reward. She smiled at him through her tears.

"By the way, Paddy, before you go," said Fergus. "Are we to understand from all this that it wasn't you at all?"

"Understand what you like," said Mr. Purtill, in a goaded groan. "I can't prove I didn't, but I defy anyone to prove I did. It doesn't matter much what people think. I'm going abroad, if your Civic Guard friends don't stop me." He grinned at Barbara. "You can get a long way on fifty pounds."

He walked out of the room, and when they all followed him to the hall door he was already wheeling his old bicycle out on to the gravel. Suspect number one mounted the saddle and bicycled out of the case.

CHAPTER 22

PAUL FENNELLY, with a lifetime's experience of management in various connections, on numerous committees and boards, could not understand how the simple business of presenting twenty or thirty pictures to the public could take up the whole time and energy of several educated adults. Even Nell came up to town to help, bringing all three children with her. Only she and the baby Faustine came to the Fennellys'. Hester hardly felt any surprise on learning that Grania and Colm were to stay at the Purtills. She was merely relieved that she was not expected to find room for them all.

Arnold Silke had congratulated Fergus warmly on his recovery, but Hester could not help thinking that if his client could have remained incapable of attending to business just a little longer, till the exhibition opened, the art dealer could have borne up very well. Fergus now devoted himself to harrying the Gallery staff. He also wanted to suppress half the pictures at the last minute, including all those Nell had sent up when he was in hospital, and to compensate for this by marking the others up to double the prices that Silke thought they might fetch. The iniquities of dealers, slowness of printers, expensiveness of framers, and ignorance of customers provided so much fodder for abuse, that the minor nuisance of an unknown poisoner in the background almost escaped notice.

Then, three days before Fergus' own show should have opened, there came round that annual landmark in Dublin social life: the opening day of the RHA.

This function takes place in the middle of April and everybody goes to it. As a newspaper report once put it: "Not only members of the diplomatic corps, ministers and clergy, but people with only a slight interest in art come along." It is the first chance for women to wear new spring clothes. Hats are what matter most; the crowd is so dense that little else of one's *ensemble* can be seen, but one may crown oneself with anything from a cornucopia to a cockatoo in the happy confidence that it will not be wasted.

The weather, always inimical to Irish finery, often spoils things. An icy blast down Kildare Street, just when everybody is going in, tips over the cornucopias and sends the cockatoos flying away, But on this occasion no such misfortune befell. The day was a foretaste of summer, and more people came than ever before.

It was fortunate for once that Mrs. Purtill was allergic to art. She nobly took the Gandon children to the zoo, leaving their parents free.

Barbara Fennelly drove her mother, aunt and uncle to the gates, where Paul stood waiting for them. Barbara was in green, with the year's first straw hat, a saucerful of spring flowers, looking as if Primavera had been taken in hand by *Vogue.* Hester wore a slenderizing black coat and skirt with pink ostrich feathers which she had preserved for years, and entrusted to milliners periodically whenever they were said to be "in." Nell, in her red tweed suit, miraculously contrived, with matching lipstick and a lapel ornament, an air of chic which surpassed them both. Fergus wore a new suit of gray-green homespun tweeds and a yellow tie. Paul was in navy blue, with touches of white at the neck and wrists. All the press cameras clicked as the party ran the gauntlet between the pillars of the National Library and the iron defenses of Leinster House, for anyone could see that Fergus was a celebrity and that Barbara was the kind of girl who gets her portrait painted.

Hester and Barbara were simmering with suppressed excitement over Barbara's portrait, for both of them were to have the fun of springing it on Paul. They had managed to keep Fergus from telling him, and half the surprise was still intact.

At the art schools' door they attached themselves to the tail of the queue crawling up the stairs, realized what they were in for, and told each other that this academy was going to be just as crowded as all the others they had ever attended. At the upper door an attendant for a moment dammed the stream. They parted with their invitation card and found themselves for a moment in a clear space alone with the president. The Fennellys greeted the president respectfully, and Fergus cut him ostentatiously because he disapproved of all he stood for, but nobody noticed, least of all the president, already drooping under his red silk robes of office. Then they were engulfed in a larger crowd.

Paul secured catalogues, wishing to be fully documented, but when he stood still and tried to read one he caused a stoppage of circulation in the crowd. Hester urged him on, and Paul, still reading, stumbled painfully on a block of carved Connemara marble, and stopped again to lecture Hester on the stupidity of leaving such things about in the way. Indeed the sculpture exhibits at the academy, though useful if you wish to dodge an acquaintance, do rather impede progress.

The main direction of the traffic was clockwise, down the left-hand wall and back the other side, in two streams separated by a row of flower arrangements, like the hedge in the middle of an *autobahn*. At this early stage in the afternoon a narrow corridor was still kept open between the crowd and the walls hung with pictures, at which some new arrivals still wanted to look. To dodge along this savored of cheating, but was the only way to get on.

Fergus did not mind cheating, so he reached Barbara's portrait first. It had been hung well, in the next best place to a politician and two church dignitaries, between an opulent bunch of chrysanthemums and a landscape with conical blue hill. People were pausing as they drifted by, and said either "That's a nice portrait; who's it by?" or "There's a pretty girl; who is she?" according as their interests were more artistic or human.

Fergus stood in front of the picture and stared at it with his lips pursed, and nobody could have traced any family resemblance between this supercilious bearded critic and the gray-eyed girl who sat looking out over the crowd with a shy smile. Mr. Purtill had not grudged the portrait a handsome frame of gray wood, with a little gilt scroll work at the corners to pick up the gilding of the armchair and the gold lights in the girl's hair. But the eye was chiefly led to linger on the face, and not, as in the politician's portrait, to travel quickly down to the watch chain, or as with the ecclesiastics, to dwell on the robes and ignore the faces altogether.

Fergus pursed his lips more, and when the Fennellys struggled up to him he was whistling a popular tune:

" Every little girl would *like* to be
The fairy on the Christmas tree . . ."

People looked round and laughed.

"Nobody expected you to like it, Uncle Fergus," said Barbara, piqued.

Hester and Paul stood transfixed. Paul looked at the picture, hastily consulted his catalogue, and said in a stunned voice

"Good heavens, it's Barbara!"

"Darling, it's lovely," said Hester quickly. "Most successful; I couldn't like it more. What a clever young man he is, after all!"

Paul stood as stone still as the sculpture exhibits. He knew he was expected to say something, and was too flabbergasted to think what. Such goings on behind a father's back! And who, he wondered, was paying for it? However, Hester seemed to know all about it, so he hoped it was all right. He produced what he felt was an intelligent comment

"It's not a bad likeness, but her mouth doesn't look quite right to me."

Not having been brought up to art, Paul did not know that a portrait is, by definition among the elect, a picture in which there is something a little wrong about the mouth. So he did not see what there was to make Fergus wink at Hester. Hester properly disregarded it.

"Well dear, you've got your money's worth," said Fergus. "Has it left you on the rocks? Never mind, so was the Mona Lisa. I might find a subject in that, by gor."

"By gor, you won't," said Hester. "I'm not going to have my lovely daughter sitting to you, Fergus."

"I could make a nice streamlined Madonna out of her," murmured Fergus. "Always a sale for an elegant Virgin in this country."

Meanwhile Nell, jammed in the crowd, heard her Christian name spoken just over her head, and screwed her neck round to see, of all people, Lord Kilskour.

He had come up from Kilskour that day. His coming to stay there again had been, though Nell did not say much about it, the main reason why she herself had come up to town. It may have been a slight attack of conventionalism caused by contact with Hester Fennelly that had caused her to feel slightly embarrassed at the thought of being down there unchaperoned with a man who was not yet completely cleared of the suspicion of trying to poison her husband. But in the safety of a crowd she did not mind giving him a cordial greeting.

Lord Kilskour was in good spirits, for his aunt, who knew the deputy commissioner's wife, had assured him that morning that the police did not mean to press the charge about the falsification of the Poisons Book. The aunt took great credit to herself for this and would see that he requited her by doing a great many tiresome errands in London, but on the whole he felt pleased with life.

"Thought I might run into you here," he said. "Fergus too, I hope? I've a bit of news to interest you both. Made a remarkable find down at home, only yesterday."

"A find? " said Nell. "A clue, do you mean?"

"Good God, no!" said Lord Kilskour. "I leave all that to our friends the Guards. It's not for me to cast into the other fellow's water. I'm speaking of something entirely different. It was pouring wet yesterday, down at home. Nothing doing out of doors. I started mooching round the old house, thought I'd have a look at what was in the attics. Found one of them was full of pictures—old pictures I mean. Dutch school and all that. Some of them rather took my fancy. Names on some of them too. Van Der Ast, Kessel, Van Goyen— I seem to have heard of them. I mean to say, clean them up and some of them might turn out to be worth something. I'd be interested to have your good husband's opinion."

Nell said, "Oh Alban, how marvelous! I must tell Fergus."

She glanced round wildly and located Fergus on the other side of the room talking to Mr. Fringley Pole. She led Lord Kilskour in the opposite direction. She did not feel this was the moment to introduce them.

Mr. Fringley Pole was saying to Fergus: "Great art is always serene, is it not? This contemporary cult of ugliness and monstrosity is merely a phase, a passing manifestation, related to the unrest of our times. It may impress a few sensation mongers and cranks, but never anyone who truly understands. 'Beauty is truth,' " said Mr. Fringley Pole, breathing deeply. "That is what modern artists fail to grasp."

The room was now packed with people all talking hard.

The RHA is an annual revelation of how hard Irish people can talk, even though no refreshments are supplied.

Very few of those present were now looking at the pictures. Indeed, to do so amounted to an admission of social failure, since everyone who had any acquaintance in Dublin must have found someone to talk to by now. A few red tabs had appeared on the corners of certain works early in the afternoon, when all the obvious investments and bargains had been snapped up. Cautious buyers now hung fire. A lady whose hat and handbag had cost ten guineas each was heard to complain that the prices of paintings were far too high. Barbara Fennelly asked Mr. Arnold Silke if he thought so.

Mr. Silke smiled. "They aren't too high for the people who buy pictures to show they can afford to."

"Oh, but those people ought not to be let buy them," said Barbara.

"Why not? They pay."

"But they don't care a bit about art."

"So much the better; they're not above taking advice. People who care, as you say, about art, fall in with every crazy fashion and generally waste their money. So genius is neglected and mediocrity subsidized."

Barbara felt depressed. She had already discovered that she and Mr. Silke felt differently about pictures. She did not care for any of those he recommended her to buy. Formerly she had supposed that among the beneficent functions of art was the bringing together of minds in a higher plane of understanding than could be attained by means of words. You were drawn to people when you found they shared your taste in pictures. But how often they did not, and then what a gulf opened between you! Gulfs had been opening on every side of her today. Her father's taste seemed to her childish; her mother's old-fashioned; her uncle's perverse. But artists themselves, as she had learned from Mr. Purtill, were little interested in any art but their own.

Mr. Silke, who knew everybody, turned away to talk to someone else, but that was not why Barbara was oppressed by a sense of isolation. She stood listening to the clamor of talk, from which snatches of conversation detached themselves

"They hang far too many." "Why isn't so-and-so here?" "I know for a fact it was refused through jealousy." "Dublin has no standards." "Painting equal to the best in Europe." "Bottom's fallen out of the art market." "Americans are coming over to buy." "Do you think a Gandon will ever fetch the price of a Yeats?" "I can't understand either of them." "Lady X's portrait, so like!" "Yes indeed, quite malicious." "Have I seen that hat before, darling?" "Darling, you have, but you aren't meant to recognize it." "I don't know anything about art and I daren't say what I like."

There was very little air left in the room, especially where Barbara stood, at the far end from the door. She felt half suffocated and desolate.

She was startled suddenly out of her dismal meditations. Her Uncle Fergus, breaking out of the clutches of Mr. Fringley Pole, had leapt suddenly on a chair.

Fergus clapped his hands for silence, and actually got it. It is unusual for anyone to leap on chairs at the RHA. Conversations were interrupted and attention drawn to the phenomenon. Most people expected some official announcement, concluding that this informality was characteristic of artistic circles.

Fergus' first words showed that the announcement was quite unofficial.

"Ladies and gentlemen, it makes me laugh to look at the crowd of you in here and wonder how many of you ever go to the National Gallery. I know damn well that most of you don't take the slightest interest in art, but the few of you who do make a big mistake in coming here at all. This stuff," he swept his arm round contemptuously, "isn't art, it's imitation. The pictures are all very carefully painted to look like pictures. If there hadn't been thousands like them exhibited already and no harm come of it, they wouldn't have been let in. 'Beauty is truth,' somebody's just been dinning into my ear. Yeah, and so is truth beauty, as Keats knew better than you. Do you suppose the selection committee of any academy could bear the blast of furious truth? Academies are like churches; they daren't let anyone blow the gaff. None of you know any better because you never look at anything with your own eyes, and you never dip into your own minds. All your views on life are predigested and secondhand. That's why it's easier to palm off an imitation on you than a genuine work, as I know from my own experience. I'll prove it to you—"

General amazement paralyzed any interference with the beginning of this speech. The secretary and other officials all happened to be near the door, separated from the speaker by a solid wedge of the general public. Those who stood nearer, all well brought up persons in their best clothes, called, "Hush!" and "Get down!" but shrank from direct action. The protests of the well-behaved were countered by slight cheering from an art student element and by calls for silence from those who wanted to hear what this apparent lunatic would say next. A reporter who had come looking for nothing more interesting than a list of names whipped out his notebook and gleefully got Fergus' remarks down in shorthand.

Nell Gandon began to laugh. The Fennellys, father, mother and daughter, managed to come together in a corner and contemplated flight.

"I'll prove it to you," cried Fergus. "There are pictures hanging on the walls of this city, bought and sold for anywhere round five hundred pounds each. Do you think the man who painted them could get his work hung in the academy? Not he! Now why did those pictures sell? Because every one of them was labeled with the name of some Old Master. They weren't Old Masters—they were the work of a contemporary artist who'd have starved before any academician gave him a hand."

Somebody called out "Name?" But there was now a stir in the audience. An avenue was cleft through the crowd by a determined figure which launched itself at the orator. Fergus, clutched round the legs, wavered precariously for a split second, then crashed to the ground in the arms of his assailant, whom his numerous clients had time incredulously to recognize Mr. Arnold Silke.

There was a sudden hasty retreat on all sides in which hats, combs and catalogues were scattered and painful injuries inflicted by fashionable high heels. Women screamed. One fainted and was carried out, but most of them resisted all attempts by their male escorts to remove them from the arena. The reporter rushed off to telephone to his paper and the secretary rushed off to stop him. The two men on the floor, locked in a wrestler's hold, were thrashing about in a manner which discouraged anyone in their best clothes from coming near them, though tentative grabs were made at their coats and hair. A red-faced lady from the country, who had experience in separating fighting dogs, seized the largest flower arrangement and, casting out the vegetation, turned the vase upside down over the heads of the combatants. Unfortunately, owing to the heat of the room and the quantity of flowers, there was only the merest trickle of water left.

Nell Gandon cried that Fergus would be killed. Paul Fennelly, who thought so too, had just managed to get near enough to seize him by the collar, when help came in the shape of the Civic Guard. Two huge constables who had been tamely employed in keeping guard over the entrance to the Dail in Leinster House next door came marching to the rescue, easily frayed themselves a passage through flimsier human material, and, politely intercepting Paul, yanked up a wrestler each.

Fergus immediately went limp in the arms of the law; he had not been convalescent long enough to indulge in such antics. Arnold Silke too, had hardly been training for such a bout. Once they were separated they offered no resistance. One Guard took them both outside, while the other started taking names and addresses of witnesses, which seemed likely to occupy him the rest of the afternoon.

Nell followed Fergus. So did the Fennellys. They might have deserted him when he was merely making an exhibition of himself, but they could not abandon him under the ignominy of arrest.

More Civic Guards arrived. They fetched taxis. The whole party was conveyed in installments to College Street Police Station.

CHAPTER 23

AT the police station there was a long, long wait. All the waiting any of them had ever endured, in queues, at railway junctions, at the customs, or in doctors' waiting rooms, if it had been arranged consecutively, would not have seemed so long.

As a matter of fact it was about three quarters of an hour, the time it took for a teleprinter message to reach Superintendent Lancey at the Detective Branch, for him to get in touch with Inspector Grace, and for Inspector Grace and Detective Officer Lemon to walk down Dame Street from Dublin Castle to College Street.

When first the prisoners were brought in, it was an open question whether Arnold Silke should be charged with assaulting Fergus Gandon, or Fergus Gandon with disturbing the peace. If it had just been a matter of a couple of drunks in a public house the Guards might have been glad enough to patch up the quarrel and send them home with a warning, but not when the whole fabric of society was threatened. You cannot allow a roughhouse in a place like the RHA without bringing somebody to book.

As soon as the name "Gandon" came before the station superintendent he knew he had heard it before. It was not in the pages of *Fogra Tora,* the Irish Criminal Record (issued weekly, Part I: Wanted, Part II: Released). But when it came back to him he thankfully passed this case to another department.

When Superintendent Lancey received the message, he was conning over a letter he had received about the Gandon enquiry from the Paris *Police Judiciaire.*

The *Police Judiciaire* had made a thorough check on sales by manufacturers of pigments all over France. There were only three whose catalogues still contained orpiment and realgar. Only one of these had been asked to supply any quantity of either of these two out of the way colors to any customer since the war. This firm had a record of a small consignment despatched to Ireland along with some other paints. The name of their Irish customer was a surprise to Lancey. It was not Purtill.

Lancey had been informed of Purtill's intention to go abroad. He decided that he need raise no objection.

He sent for Inspector Grace and gave him his instructions.

As Inspector Grace and Detective Officer Lemon walked down Dame Street, Mick Lemon asked, "What was that Mr. Gandon said about the goose that laid the golden eggs?"

"Maybe the fella thought the goose might peck him," said Inspector Grace.

The Guard on point duty in College Green recognized them. Traffic stopped for them with shrieking brakes. They marched across, shoulder to shoulder.

They marched into College Street Police Station and arrested Arnold Silke for the attempted murder by poison of Fergus Gandon.

The art dealer had occupied the time of waiting in brushing himself down, re-tying his tie, and combing his hair with a comb borrowed from one of the station staff. He had recovered his habitual poise. When he was arrested, Inspector Grace warned him in the usual form that anything he said might be used in evidence. The dealer nodded, gave Mick Lemon time to get his pencil ready, and said, in his clearest articulation, to Fergus Gandon:

"Now, you dirty little forger and blackmailer, everything's going to come out."

Fergus had collapsed with exhaustion after the fight and had almost had to be carried into the police station. He was sitting up now, but still looking shaken. He blinked at Silke in a puzzled way.

"I don't mind if you don't," he said.

"You wait," Silke spat the two words out like a venomous snake. Inspector Grace touched him on the shoulder. He turned his back on Fergus and let them take him out.

"Well, if you must know," said Fergus Gandon afterwards, "I once did a copy for him which he sold as an original Jacob Octerveldt for three thousand pounds. I found out, and it seemed to me rather a good joke. There happened to be a run on flower pieces at the time, all the old ones were bought up, and the dealers were running round in circles to supply the demand. It would have been sheer waste not to take advantage of it. I did quite a number for Arnold, and he paid me for them, outside my ordinary contract. I don't know why he should call me a blackmailer. I never asked more than a fair percentage on what pictures fetched. It was an ordinary business arrangement. And on top of that, I gave him the exclusive right to handle my own signed work, and my advice was of the utmost value to him in running his business. The trouble with Arnold is, he doesn't really know his own job. I don't know how often I've had to browbeat him for his own good, just to get him to make some necessary change of policy."

Paul Fennelly, on hearing the inner story of Fergus' relations with his dealer, told Hester that his sympathies were entirely with Arnold Silke. He must have led a dog's life, with Fergus continually butting in on business matters, and it must have seemed to him that if he was not ruined by blackmail he would be by interference.

At the Detective Branch it was remarkable how many people had known beforehand how the case was bound to end.

Chief Superintendent Healy had known all along that it was ridiculous to imagine Lord Kilskour being implicated.

Sergeant Nolan had known all along that there was no real harm in Mr.

Gandon. It was not likely that large scale black-marketing or any kind of racket could be carried on so near Clogh, under the noses of the Civic Guards.

Inspector Devlin had known all along that there was something funny about those pictures. It wasn't for him to take it up. He was sent to investigate black-marketing, and when there was none to investigate he was taken off the case and sent somewhere else, but he did think somebody would have followed the picture lineup after he had specially mentioned it in his report.

Inspector Grace said that to anyone who looked into this art business it was obvious that a thing like the cancellation of Mr. Purtill's exhibition cut both ways. The dealer, as well as the artist, was injured, and from what he heard, Mr. Purtill was well able to sell his own pictures nowadays without assistance, and what Mr. Silke stood to lose was a steady income from commissions that he hardly had to work for at all. Silke's interest was to keep in with Purtill, but he canceled Purtill's show for the sole reason that Gandon told him to. That showed Gandon had some hold over Silke.

Superintendent Lancey said he was always suspicious of anybody who tried to be extra helpful to the police. It wasn't natural. First Mr. Silke had tried to distract their attention from the paintbox by telling them the poisoned brush theory wouldn't work. Then when he heard they were going into it and getting the paints analyzed, he invented a wonderful suggestion about how arsenic might have got into them by accident. He kept on trying to pump the police for information, and the Deputy Commissioner himself—Lancey liked to remind everyone—had said they ought to tell the poor man enough to set his mind at rest. He, Lancey, had known better, and the moral, which he never tired of pointing out to everyone from the deputy commissioner downwards, was : never give away more than you can help.

Among the many forms in use at the Detective Branch is one headed GOOD POLICE DUTY REWARD. On this form a member of the Civic Guard who has done any extra-bright work in the course of an investigation may set forth the particulars, and if his application is approved by higher authorities, he may look to receive a small bonus on his pay.

We leave Mick Lemon filling one in. After all, it was he who first pointed out the dangers of sucking one's brush.

Incidentally, the file of these forms contains some of the best detective stories ever written.

EPILOGUE

ONE afternoon some weeks later, just before the exhibition was due to close, Hester and Barbara Fennelly revisited the RHA. The rooms were now deserted by rank and fashion and not much frequented even by the rank and file.

They offered a peaceful refuge from the stress of contemporary life.

Life had certainly been hard on the Fennellys for a time. Hester's premonition of trouble, when first the idea of Fergus' visit was mooted, had been amply fulfilled. Her long-standing fear of bringing scandal on the family had been only too well justified by events, and everything had turned out worse than the worst she had imagined. Yet things were better than they might have been.

Fergus had fully expected to be sent to prison on charges of blackmail, forgery, and obtaining money by false pretenses. He had consulted Mosney on how to make himself comfortable under prison conditions and the finer points of behavior for convicts, and was almost looking forward to trying out his instructions. But an expensive lawyer had succeeded in convincing the court that his client had incurred no penalty beyond a fine.

From what the lawyer said, the idea of blackmail had arisen only in the warped mental processes of Arnold Silke. It was not the fact of being blackmailed, it was the mere fact of being in a vulnerable position, that had operated so disastrously on the art dealer's mind. Arnold Silke had obtained money by false pretenses, but Fergus Gandon had merely sold his pictures to Silke for what they actually were. The prosecution could not prove that he had ever stated in so many words that any one of them was the work of an Old Master. Mr. Fringley Pole, who had been so honorably warned, gave evidence for the defense. As for the charge of forgery, it has been held at law that a picture is not a document, and therefore that "to fraudulently write the name of a painter on a picture is not a forgery," i.e. it is not a felony, though it may be a common law cheat.

Readers may imagine that this excellent lawyer's fee, and Fergus' fine, came out of Paul Fennelly's pocket. But not at all. Fergus was making his fortune. His one-man show had perforce been abandoned, but the publicity had worked magic, and at last Fergus had arrived. The simple argument that anyone whose work had been mistaken for that of an Old Master must be as good as an Old Master encouraged buyers, and people were rushing to get in before the rush.

Not only had all the signed work on Fergus' hands been disposed of, but Lord Kilskour had bought the entire collection of Old Masters at the castle for two hundred pounds down. This was after Nell had made a clean breast to him of the whole story. Instead of grumbling at the way his house had been used and making extra difficulties for Fergus, his lordship had, with true nobility, conspired to keep that part of the story dark. The pictures were all hung in the drawing room again, and they had the chimney swept.

Besides doing so well out of the sale of his works, Fergus had offers of employment for the future. One was the post of art adviser to a film company about to produce an educational film called "Lives of the Medic" (sic). The other was from a millionaire collector who was much pestered to lend his treasures to public exhibitions, and who approached Fergus confidentially to provide him with a set of replicas which could be used for this purpose.

So the future was by no means dark for the Gandons, and as for the Fennellys, Hester was relieved to find that so far not one client had deserted Paul by reason of the public exposure involving his brother-in-law.

It was not, therefore, primarily for refuge that Hester and Barbara revisited the RHA. Every year, whether or not they had attended the opening, they would drop in at a quieter time to look at the pictures in peace. This year, Hester had a particular desire to go back and have another look at Barbara's portrait.

Who should be standing in front of it but Dr. Brian Caraway? He confessed that he had come for the sole purpose of seeing it. Never before had he been to the academy, and he felt quite out of his element.

"What do you think of it?" Hester asked.

"I prefer the original," said Dr. Caraway.

He said, when pressed, that it was a fair likeness but not half pretty enough. "Mind you," he added, "I don't know anything about art."

"Neither do I," said Barbara with a sigh.

Hester went to arrange with the secretary for the removal of the picture on the closing day, while Barbara did the honors of the exhibition for the young doctor. When she rejoined them, they were deep in conversation, and Hester heard Caraway say emphatically,

"It's far and away the best picture in town."

She wondered what he meant. It turned out to be the film at the Metropole.

"Brian thinks we all ought to see it," said Barbara, with a twinkling smile.

"Yes, do come, Mrs. Fennelly," said Dr. Caraway politely.

"Not if it means missing my tea," said Hester. "You two go. I'll just have another look round here and then get back to Paul."

"Second house starts in ten minutes," said Dr. Caraway, briskly consulting his watch. "Come on, Barbara, let's go."

They hurried gaily out, turning their backs on art. Hester was left alone with the portrait. She put on her glasses to look at it. The girl in the portrait smiled shyly out at her, looking, it seemed to Hester, a little puzzled and very young.

Hester took off her glasses and wiped them. She said to herself, "Whatever happens, I shall have this one to keep."

THE END

About The Rue Morgue Press

The Rue Morgue vintage mystery line is designed to bring back into print those books that were favorites of readers between the turn of the century and the 1960s. The editors welcome suggests for reprints. To receive our catalog or make suggestions, write The Rue Morgue Press, P.O. Box 4119, Boulder, Colorado (1-800-669-6214). The Rue Morgue Press tries to keep all of its titles in print, though some books may go temporarily out of print for up to six months.

Catalog of Rue Morgue Press titles July 2002

Titles are listed by author. All books are quality trade paperbacks measuring 9 by 6 inches, usually with full-color covers and printed on paper designed not to yellow or deteriorate. These are permanent books.

Joanna Cannan. The books by this English writer are among our most popular titles. Modern reviewers favorably compared our two Cannan reprints with the best books of the Golden Age of detective fiction. "Worthy of being discussed in the same breath with an Agatha Christie or a Josephine Tey."—Sally Fellows, Mystery News. "First-rate Golden Age detection with a likeable detective, a complex and believable murderer, and a level of style and craft that bears comparison with Sayers, Allingham, and Marsh."—Jon L. Breen, *Ellery Queen's Mystery Magazine.* Set in the late 1930s in a village that was a fictionalized version of Oxfordshire, both titles feature young Scotland Yard inspector Guy Northeast. *They Rang Up the Police* (0-915230-27-5, 156 pages, $14.00) and *Death at The Dog* (0-915230-23-2, 156 pages, $14.00).

Glyn Carr. The author is really Showell Styles, one of the foremost English mountain climbers of his era as well as one of that sport's most celebrated historians. Carr turned to crime fiction when he realized that mountains provided a ideal setting for committing murders. The 15 books featuring Shakespearean actor Abercrombie "Filthy" Lewker are set on peaks scattered around the globe, although the author returned again and again to his favorite climbs in Wales, where his first mystery, published in 1951, *Death on Mile-stone Buttress* (0-915230-29-1, 187 pages, $14.00), is set. Lewker is a marvelous Falstaffian character whose exploits have been praised by such discerning critics as Jacques Barzun and Wendell Hertig Taylor in *A Catalogue of Crime.* Other critics have been just as kind: "You'll get a taste of the Welsh countryside, will encounter names replete with conso-nants, will be exposed to numerous snippets from Shakespeare and will find Carr's novel a worthy representative of the cozies of two generations ago."—*I Love a Mystery.*

Clyde B. Clason. Clason has been praised not only for his elaborate plots and skill-ful use of the locked room gambit but also for his scholarship. He may be one of the few mystery authors—and no doubt the first—to provide a full bibliography of his sources. *The Man from Tibet* (0-915230-17-8, 220 pages, $14.00) is one of his best (selected in 2001 in *The History of Mystery* as one of the 25 great amateur detective novels of all time) and highly recommended by the dean of locked room mystery scholars, Robert Adey, as "highly original." It's also one of the first popular novels to make use of Tibetan culture. Locked inside the Tibetan room of his Chicago apartment, the rich antiquarian was overheard repeating a forbidden occult chant under the watchful eyes of Buddhist gods. When the doors were opened, it appeared that he had succumbed to a heart attack. But the elderly Roman historian and some-time amateur sleuth Theocritus Lucius Westborough is convinced that Adam Merriweather's death was anything but natural and that the weapon was an eight century Tibetan manuscript.

Joan Coggin. *Who Killed the Curate?* Meet Lady Lupin Lorrimer Hastings, the young, lovely, scatterbrained and kindhearted newlywed wife to the vicar of St. Marks Parish in Glanville, Sussex. When it comes to matters clerical, she literally doesn't know Jews from Jesuits and she's hopelessly at sea at the meetings of the Mothers' Union, Girl Guides, or Temperance Society but she's determined to make husband Andrew proud of her—or, at least, not to embarass him too badly. So when Andrew's curate is poisoned, Lady Lupin enlists the help of her old society pals, Duds and Tommy Lethbridge, as well as Andrew's nephew, a British secret service agent, to get at the truth. Lupin refuses to believe Diane Lloyd, the 38-year-old author of children's and detective stories could have done the deed, and casts her net out over the other parishioners. All the suspects seem so nice, much more so than the victim, and Lupin announces she'll help the killer escape if only he or she confesses. Imagine Billie Burke, Gracie Allen of Burns and Allen or Pauline Collins of *No, Honestly* as a sleuth and you might get a tiny idea of what Lupin is like. Set at Christmas 1937 and first published in England in 1944, this is the first American appearance of *Who Killed the Curate?* "Coggin writes in the spirit of Nancy Mitford and E.M. Delafield. But the books are mysteries, so that makes them perfect."— Katherine Hall Page. "Marvelous."—*Deadly Pleasures* (0-915230-44-5, $14.00).

Manning Coles. The two English writers who collaborated as Coles are best known for those witty spy novels featuring Tommy Hambledon, but they also wrote four delight-ful—and funny—ghost novels. *The Far Traveller* (0-915230-35-6, 154 pages, $14.00) is a stand-alone novel in which a film company unknowingly hires the ghost of a long-dead German graf to play himself in a movie. "I laughed until I hurt. I liked it so much, I went back to page 1 and read it a second time."—Peggy Itzen, *Cozies, Capers & Crimes*. The other three books feature two cousins, one English, one American, and their spectral pet monkey who got a little drunk and tried to stop—futilely and fatally—a German advance outside a small French village during the 1870 Franco-Prussian War. Flash forward to the 1950s where this comic trio of friendly ghosts rematerialize to aid relatives in danger in *Brief Candles* (0-915230-24-0, 156 pages, $14.00), *Happy Returns* (0-915230-31-3, 156 pages, $14.00) and *Come and Go* (0-915230-34-8, 155 pages, $14.00).

Norbert Davis. There have been a lot of dogs in mystery fiction, from Baynard Kendrick's guide dog to Virginia Lanier's bloodhounds, but there's never been one quite like Carstairs. Doan, a short, chubby Los Angeles private eye, won Carstairs in a crap game, but there never is any question as to who the boss is in this relationship. Carstairs isn't just any Great Dane. He is so big that Doan figures he really ought to be considered another species. He scorns baby talk and belly rubs—unless administered by a pretty girl—and growls whenever Doan has a drink. His full name is Dougal's Laird Carstairs and as a sleuth he rarely barks up the wrong tree. He's down in Mexico with Doan, ostensibly to convince a missing fugitive that he would do well to stay put, in *The Mouse in the Moun-tain* (0-915230-41-0, 151 pages, $14.00), first published in 1943 and followed by two other Doan and Carstairs novels. *Staff pick* at The Sleuth of Baker Street in Toronto, Murder by the Book in Houston and The Poisoned Pen in Scotsdale. Four star review in *Romantic Times*. "A laugh a minute romp…hilarious dialogue and descriptions…utterly engaging, downright fun read…fetch this one! Highly recommended."—Michele A. Reed, *I Love a Mystery*. "Deft, charming…unique…one of my top ten all time favorite nov-els."—Ed Gorman, *Mystery Scene*. The second book, *Sally's in the Alley* (0-915230-46-1, $14.00), was equally well-received. *Publishers Weekly*: "Norbert Davis committed suicide in 1949, but his incomparable crime-fighting duo, Doan, the tippling private eye, and Carstairs, the huge and preternaturally clever Great Dane, march on in a re-release of the 1943 *Sally's in the Alley*, the second book in the dog-detective trilogy. Doan's on a government-sponsored mission to find an ore deposit in the Mojave Desert, but he's got to manage an odd (and oddly named) bunch of characters—Dust-Mouth Haggerty knows where the mine is but isn't telling; Doc Gravelmeyer's learning how undertaking can be a 'growth industry;' and film star Susan Sally's days are numbered—in an old-fashioned romp that matches its bloody crimes with belly laughs." The editor of *Mystery Scene* chimed in: "If you write fiction, or are thinking of writing fiction, or know someone who is writing fiction or is at least thinking of writing fiction, Davis is worth studying. John D. MacDonald always put him up, even admitted to imitating him upon occasion. I love Craig Rice. Davis is her equal."

Elizabeth Dean. Dean wrote only three mysteries, but in Emma Marsh she created one of the first independent female sleuths in the genre. Written in the screwball style of the 1930s, *Murder is a Collector's Item* (0-915230-19-4, $14.00) is described in a review in *Deadly Pleasures* by award-winning mystery writer Sujata Massey as a story that "froths over with the same effervescent humor as the best Hepburn-Grant films." Like the second book in the trilogy, *Murder is a Serious Business* (0-915230-28-3, 254 pages, $14.95), it's set in a Boston antique store just as the Great Depression is drawing to a close. *Murder a Mile High* (0-915230-39-9, 188 pages, $14.00), moves to the Central City Opera House in the Colorado mountains, where Emma has been summoned by am old chum, the opera's reigning diva. Emma not only has to find a murderer, she may also have to catch a Nazi spy. A reviewer for a Central City area newspaper warmly greeted this reprint: "An endearing glimpse of Central City and Denver during World War II. . . . the dialogue twists and turns. . . . reads like a Nick and Nora movie. . . . charming."—*The Mountain-Ear*. "Fascinating."—*Romantic Times*.

Constance & Gwenyth Little. These two Australian-born sisters from New Jersey have developed almost a cult following among mystery readers. Critic Diane Plumley, writing in *Dastardly Deeds*, called their 21 mysteries "celluloid comedy written on paper." Each book, published between 1938 and 1953, was a stand-alone, but there was no mistaking a Little heroine. She hated housework, wasn't averse to a little gold-digging (so long as she called the shots), and couldn't help antagonizing cops and potential beaux. The Rue Morgue Press intends to reprint all of their books. Currently available: *The Black Coat* (0-915230-40-2, 155 pages, $14.00), *Black Corridors* (0-915230-33-X, 155 pages, $14.00), *The Black Gloves* (0-915230-20-8, 185 pages, $14.00), *Black-Headed Pins* (0-915230-25-9, 155 pages, $14.00), *The Black Honeymoon* (0-915230-21-6, 187 pages, $14.00), *The Black Paw* (0-915230-37-2, 156 pages, $14.00), *The Black Stocking* (0-915230-30-5, 154 pages, $14.00), *Great Black Kanba* (0-915230-22-4, 156 pages, $14.00), and *The Grey Mist Murders* (0-915230-26-7, 153 pages, $14.00), and *The Black Eye* (0-915230-45-3, 154 pages, $14.00).

Marlys Millhiser. Our only non-vintage mystery, *The Mirror* (0-915230-15-1, 303 pages, $17.95) is our all-time bestselling book, now in a sixth printing. How could you not be intrigued by a novel in which "you find the main character marrying her own grandfather and giving birth to her own mother," as one reviewer put it of this supernatural, time-travel (sort-of) piece of wonderful make-believe set both in the mountains above Boulder, Colorado, at the turn of the century and in the city itself in 1978. Internet book services list scores of rave reviews from readers who often call it the "best book I've ever read."

James Norman. The marvelously titled *Murder, Chop Chop* (0-915230-16-X, 189 pages,

$13.00) is a wonderful example of the eccentric detective novel. "The book has the butter-wouldn't-melt-in-his-mouth cool of Rick in *Casablanca*."—*The Rocky Mountain News*. "Amuses the reader no end."—*Mystery News*. "This long out-of-print masterpiece is intricately plotted, full of eccentric characters and very humorous indeed. Highly recommended."—*Mysteries by Mail*. Meet Gimiendo Hernandez Quinto, a gigantic Mexican who once rode with Pancho Villa and who now trains *guerrilleros* for the Nationalist Chinese government when he isn't solving murders. At his side is a beautiful Eurasian known as Mountain of Virtue, a woman as dangerous to men as she is irresistible. Together they look into the murder of Abe Harrow, an ambulance driver who appears to have died at three different times. First published in 1942.

Sheila Pim. *Ellery Queen's Mystery Magazine* said of these wonderful Irish village mysteries that Pim "depicts with style and humor everyday life." *Booklist* said they were in "the best tradition of Agatha Christie." *Common or Garden Crime* (0-915230-36-4, 157 pages, $14.00) is set in neutral Ireland during World War II when Lucy Bex must use her knowledge of gardening to keep the wrong person from going to the gallows. Beekeeper Edward Gildea uses his knowledge of bees and plants to do the same thing in *A Hive of Suspects* (0-915230-38-0, 155 pages, $14.00). *Creeping Venom* (0-915230-42-9, 155 pages, $14.00) mixes politics and religion into a deadly mixture.

Charlotte Murray Russell. Spinster sleuth Jane Amanda Edwards tangles with a murderer and Nazi spies in *The Message of the Mute Dog* (0-915230-43-7, 156 pages, $14.00), a culinary cozy set just before Pearl Harbor. Our earlier title, *Cook Up a Crime*, is currently out of print.

Juanita Sheridan. Sheridan was one of the most colorful figures in the history of detective fiction, as you can see from Tom and Enid Schantz's introduction to *The Chinese Chop* (0-915230-32-1, 155 pages, $14.00). Her books are equally colorful, as well as showing how mysteries with female protagonists began changing after World War II. The postwar housing crunch finds Janice Cameron, newly arrived in New York City from Hawaii, without a place to live until she answers an ad for a roommate. It turns out the advertiser is an acquaintance from Hawaii, Lily Wu, whom critic Anthony Boucher (for whom Bouchercon, the World Mystery Convention, is named) described as an "exquisitely blended product of Eastern and Western cultures" and the only female sleuth that he "was devotedly in love with," citing "that odd mixture of respect for her professional skills and delight in her personal charms." First published in 1949, this ground-breaking book was the first of four to feature Lily and be told by her Watson, Janice, a first-time novelist. No sooner do Lily and Janice move into a rooming house in Washington Square than a corpse is found in the basement. In Lily Wu, Sheridan created one of the most believable—and memorable—female sleuths of her day. "Highly recommended."—*I Love a Mystery*. "This well-written. . .enjoyable variant of the boarding house whodunit and a vivid portrait of the post WWII New York City housing shortage, puts to lie the common misconception that strong, self-reliant, non-spinster-or-comic sleuths didn't appear on the scene until the 1970s. Chinese-American Lily Wu and her novelist Watson, Janice Cameron, are young and feminine but not dependent on men."—*Ellery Queen's Mystery Magazine*. The first book in the series to be set in Hawaii is *The Kahuna Killer* (0-915230-47-X, 154 pages, $14.00). A hulu dancer is murdered near squatters who have reestablished a native village.